MADELINE BAKER

**Winner of the 1988 *Romantic Times*
Reviewers' Choice Award for Best Indian Series!**

"Lovers of Indian Romance have a special place
on their bookshelves for Madeline Baker!"

—Romantic Times

SAVAGE DESIRE

"How long are you going to blame me for what happened to your father?" he asked brusquely. "How long will you go on hating me because I'm an Indian, and hating yourself because you married me?"

"Rafe. . . ."

"I'm not a savage, Caitlyn. I've never murdered anyone, red or white. I'm not a savage," he repeated, his ebony eyes hot on her face. "If I were, you'd be a woman now, and, oh, hell," he muttered, "maybe I am a savage."

His mouth covered hers in a kiss that was almost brutal in its intensity, his lips grinding into hers, his tongue sliding over her lower lip, demanding entrance to the honeyed sweetness within.

MADELINE BAKER

FORBIDDEN FIRES

LEISURE BOOKS   NEW YORK CITY

To my aunts,

Stella
Claire
Leona, and
Alice

with love and hugs,

and

To

Sharon Day, and
Donna Bartels
They know why!

A LEISURE BOOK ®

September 1990

Published by

Dorchester Publishing Co., Inc.
276 Fifth Avenue
New York, NY 10001

Printed in the United States of America.

CHAPTER ONE

HE HAD NOT CRIED SINCE HE WAS A SMALL child, and he did not weep now. Stone-faced, he stood before the council elders while they decided his fate. Stone-faced, he accepted their decision. Banishment.

It had been inevitable and it was final.

Wordlessly, he left the council lodge and returned to his father's tipi. The eyes of the People followed him as he walked through the village. Their faces were sympathetic but they did not speak to him. Banishment was like death, and the dead were to be avoided.

The words of the council elders echoed in his head as he made his way to his father's lodge: *"The warrior known as Stalking Wolf is no longer of the blood, no longer of the blood. . . ."*

His little sister, Yellow Flower, wept softly as he told of the council's decision. His stepmother, Tall Grass Woman, stood mute, the sorrow on her face more eloquent than words, more expressive than tears.

Too soon, it was time to go. He would be allowed to take nothing with him save the clothes on his back. No horse to make his journey easier, no food to sustain him, no weapons for protection against enemies.

He embraced his stepmother, hugged his little sister one last time, and stepped outside. Overhead, the sky was blue and breathtakingly clear. The vast Lakota horse herd grazed in the distance, a riot of grays, blacks, and browns against a sea of lush green buffalo grass.

He stood beside his father's lodge for a long moment, his dark eyes sweeping over the village. Each lodge stood in its appointed place in the camp circle, their doorways all facing east. Wooden drying racks stood in the sun, weighed down with long strips of buffalo and venison. The familiar smells of roasting meat, sage, and tobacco filled his nostrils; the shrieks and laughter of carefree children at play reached his ears.

He waited a moment more, wondering at his father's absence. Was Killian Gallegher so ashamed of his only son that he would not even come forward to say farewell?

His face impassive, Stalking Wolf squared his shoulders and walked swiftly toward the forest that rose beyond the rear of the village. He could feel the eyes of the People on his back and he lengthened his stride, anxious to reach the cover of the woods.

He had known, somehow, that Summer Wind would be there, though he wondered how she dared face him. She stood in the shadow of the giant pine tree where they had so often met in the past. She was a vision of loveliness in an ivory doeskin tunic and beaded moccasins. Her shiny black hair fell over her shoulders in two long braids. There were tears in her voice as she called his name.

Stalking Wolf came to an abrupt halt, his placid expression masking his turbulent emotions.

They faced each other, the events of the past two days rising like an invisible barrier between them.

"Do you hate me now?" Summer Wind asked.

"No."

"Where will you go?"

Stalking Wolf shrugged. Where *would* he go?

"I am sorry, Stalking Wolf," she murmured contritely. "I did not think it would end this way."

"Didn't you?" His anger shattered his cool facade, and Summer Wind took a step backward, frightened by the rage glittering in his deep-set black eyes.

"I *am* sorry," she repeated. "Please forgive me."

"Tell Hump Back Bear of your sorrow," Stalking Wolf retorted coldly. "When he hears you, I will hear you."

Shame flooded Summer Wind's cheeks with color. Bowing her head to hide her tears, she hurried back toward the village.

Stalking Wolf stared after her for several minutes. He had loved her, he thought bitterly, and it had cost him dearly. Hump Back Bear was dead because Summer Wind had played them both false, and now his home and family were lost to him. Never, he vowed, never again would he trust a woman.

Heavy-hearted, he followed the narrow deer trail that cut through the heart of the forest and emerged on the vast grassy plains that stretched westward as far as the eye could see.

He had gone about two miles when a deep male voice called out to him.

Stalking Wolf whirled around, his heart lifting as he saw Killian riding toward him. He felt a surge of pride as his father drew near, reining his big black mare to a rearing halt. Killian Gallegher was a handsome man, still strong and fit despite his fifty-odd years. Tall and broad, with wavy brown hair and dark brown eyes, his skin was a deep bronze, the result of spending the last six years living under the harsh Dakota sun.

Killian smiled as he saw the relief in his son's eyes. "You didna think I would let ye go without saying good-bye?" he chided gently.

"I wouldn't have blamed you," Stalking Wolf replied. "I have shamed our family."

"Ye've not shamed me, nor Tall Grass Woman," Killian protested as he slid from the back of his horse. "'Tis proud of ye I've always been, and ye've done naught to change me mind."

Stalking Wolf nodded, touched by his father's words.

The two men stood quietly close for several moments, knowing these few minutes were the last they would share.

"Where will ye go, laddie?" Killian asked after a while.

"I don't know. West, perhaps."

"Aye. Maybe ye'll be the one who strikes it rich in the California gold fields."

Stalking Wolf shook his head. "It was the father who dreamed of riches, not the son."

"'Tis true," Killian admitted with a wry grin, "but a little hard cash is nothing to be turning your nose up at, and don't you be forgetting it."

"I'll remember, as I've remembered everything you ever taught me."

Killian smiled his winning grin. "I'm not so sure I ever taught ye anything an honest man should be knowin'."

"You mean cheating at cards, sleeping late, and a fondness for fine Kentucky bourbon are not the pursuits of a fine gentleman?"

Killian punched his son on the arm affectionately. "'Tis exactly what I mean, laddie, although the first may come in handy if ye have trouble finding a respectable job." Killian's expression grew serious and the merriment left his eyes. "I'll miss ye, laddie." He stared past his son, his dark eyes thoughtful. "I never gave much thought to what life would be like for ye when I married your ma. Perhaps I shouldna wed her and got her with child, but I loved her, laddie, more than ye can imagine. She was such a gentle thing, so bonny and soft spoken. And when she looked at me, I saw the whole world in her eyes."

Stalking Wolf said nothing. He had never known his mother. She had died of a fever a few months after his birth. Following her death, Killian had hired a woman to care for Stalking Wolf while Killian drank himself into oblivion each night, trying to forget the beautiful young Cherokee girl who had run away from her family to marry a poor Irishman, only to die before she had ever really lived.

Stalking Wolf's first memory of his father was of finding him lying dead drunk on the doorstep. He had been frightened of his father then, frightened and ashamed. He remembered how lonely he had been as a child. Other children weren't allowed to play with him because he was a half-breed and his father was a drunkard. He had not learned what a half-breed was until later.

It wasn't until the housekeeper quit and Killian found himself in full charge of his son that the two got to know each other. Killian sobered up when he realized how much his son needed him. He sold their house in Georgia and moved to New Orleans where he returned to the trade he knew best: gambling.

As Stalking Wolf grew older, Killian taught his son the things his own father had taught him: how to play poker and monte and faro—and how to cheat at poker and monte and faro. He also taught Stalking Wolf how to detect the signals that meant someone else was cheating at cards, and, most importantly, how to defend himself with his bare fists or a knife. Killian instilled in his son a love of fine whiskey, a taste for expensive, imported cigars, and an appreciation for beautiful women, be they ladies of unblemished virtue or back-street tarts.

When Stalking Wolf was almost twenty, they had to leave New Orleans because Killian had killed a man over a card game. Fleeing with only the clothes on their backs, they headed for California where it was rumored that pure gold lined the streets and nuggets the size of a man's fist waited in the rivers.

Along the way, they had encountered a trader who sold Indian women to any man who could pay the price. Killian had taken one look at Tall Grass Woman and been smitten. Not having the money to buy her, he made off with her in the dead of night and then, to appease her tears, he had offered to return her to her people. Her father, over-joyed at the return of his only daughter, had given a feast in honor of the two white men who had rescued his daughter and, in the course of the evening, Killian and Stalking Wolf had been adopted into the tribe. They were given their own lodge and encouraged to spend the coming winter with the tribe.

Killian and Stalking Wolf had been fasci-nated by the Indians and they had readily embraced the Lakota lifestyle. Before that first year was out, Killian married Tall Grass Woman. Yellow Flower had been born the following summer, and Stalking Wolf had become a Lakota warrior.

It hadn't been easy. Stalking Wolf had had to learn to hunt and fight, Sioux-style, to use a bow and arrow, and to throw a lance. He learned to read the signs of the seasons, to track a man, or a buffalo. He gave up trousers for fringed buckskin leggings, discarded his boots for moccasins, and let his hair grow long. He felt at home among the Lakota. The ancient warrior songs stirred his blood, whispering to him of old battles, old victories. He went to war against the Pawnee and the Crow, and hunted the deer and the elk. And in the autumn of his twenty-sixth year, he fell in love with a beautiful young maiden whose smile was as soft as dandelion down —Summer Wind. . . .

Killian chuckled softly, bringing Stalking Wolf back to the present. "I seem to have a weakness for Indian women," he mused. "First your mother, and now Tall Grass Woman." Killian sighed heavily. "It willna be easy for ye, out there among the whites."

Stalking Wolf laughed a soft, bitter laugh. It had never been easy.

"Take care of yourself, laddie. There's many a man, and many a woman, too, who'll shun ye because of your mixed blood." Killian laid a hand on his son's arm and gave it a squeeze. "May all the gods, red and white, go with ye."

"And with you," Stalking Wolf replied. "Take good care of my stepmother and my sister."

"Ye can count on it."

The two men stood together, reluctant to part, then Killian wrapped his arms around his son and hugged him, hard. "I love ye, laddie. Never forget that."

Stalking Wolf nodded, unable to speak past the lump in his throat.

When they parted, there were tears glistening in the older man's eyes. "Here," he said, thrusting his horse's reins into his son's hands. "Take the mare. She'll see ye safely on your journey."

"You shouldn't help me," Stalking Wolf said quietly.

"Not help me own son! Are ye daft? Go on, take her."

The two men embraced one last time, and then Stalking Wolf vaulted onto the mare's back. Black Wind was taller than any of the Lakota ponies. She had a long muscular neck, a deep chest, and wide-set intelligent eyes. And she was fast. Unbelievably fast. She was not a mustang, but a Thoroughbred mare Killian had captured in a raid against a white settlement the year before.

"My thanks, Father," Stalking Wolf murmured.

"My prayers go with ye, laddie." Killian drew a long-bladed knife from his belt and pressed it into his son's hand. "Good journey, my son."

"Long life to you, my father," Stalking Wolf replied. He gazed down at Killian, for another moment, then touched his heels to the mare's flanks. Head high, he rode west, toward the land of the setting sun.

He did not look back.

CHAPTER TWO

BLACK WIND CARRIED HIM EFFORTLESSLY across the miles as he rode westward, always westward, looking for a place to call home. He had never really had a home of his own. As a child, he had lived with his father. As a young man, in New Orleans, he had lived in hotels or rented rooms. During the last six years, he had shared a Lakota lodge with his father and Tall Grass Woman. He had never realized until now, when he was alone with nowhere to go, just how deeply he had yearned for a place to call his own.

Day after day he rode toward the setting sun, the hours passing in serene sameness as he sought graze and water for his mount, and food and shelter for himself. He explored the country, lingering now and then in some verdant valley to rest himself and the mare, pausing to study the lay of the land, to contemplate the granite spires that rose in the distance.

He passed sharp ridges and blood-red buttes that looked like mythical castles as he crossed a corner of the *Mako Sica*, the Badlands. The Indians called it the place of the crying wind. It was a vast stretch of ground made up of steep ridges and high-walled canyons, gullies and pyramids, colorful sandstone spires, pinnacles, and deep gorges. He heard the wind whining through the canyons, wailing like a bereaved child, and felt the short hair prickle along the back of his neck as the sound crept into his soul. High overhead, he saw a pair of turkey vultures riding the updrafts in a constant search for prey, and he urged Black Wind into a lope, eager to leave the Badlands behind. He breathed a sheepish sigh of relief when the prairie spread before him once again.

He had been traveling for almost a month when he came to the huge upthrust rock the Kiowas called *Mateo Tepee*, Grizzly Bear Lodge. Though he had never seen it before, he recognized it instantly, for there could be no other rock so solitary or so large. He sat the mare a long time, studying the gigantic rock tower, remembering the Kiowa legend he had heard back in the Dakotas.

According to Kiowa mythology, seven sisters had been playing a distance from their village when they were chased by bears. The girls ran toward home and when the bears were about to catch them, they jumped onto a low rock. One of the girls began to pray to the rock, "Rock, take pity on us. Rock, save us." The rock heard them and began to rise upward, pushing the children higher and higher until they were out of the bears' reach. The bears scratched the rock, breaking their claws, and fell to the ground, while the seven little girls were born into the sky and became the stars of the Big Dipper.

Stalking Wolf pondered the legend as he rode onward, fascinated by the rich folklore of the Indians. Each tribe had its own mythical heroes, its own version of how the earth came into being, of the creation of man.

His father had told him some of the Cherokee legends and history so that he would have a feel for his mother's people, and an appreciation for his heritage.

He recalled his pride when he'd heard the story of Sequoya, who was the son of a Cherokee mother and an Englishman. Believing that literacy was the source of the white man's power, and having no formal education, Sequoya had singlehandedly created a written language for his tribe.

For days, Stalking Wolf continued to ride westward, looking for a home.

Nights were the worst time. It was then he missed the companionship of his friends and family, the community dances, the tribal feasts, and celebrations. It was then that Summer Wind haunted his dreams. He could keep her memory at bay during the day, but he could not keep her image out of his dreams. Once again, he courted her, his arms around her shoulders as they stood close under a large red courting blanket, his heart hammering in his chest as she whispered secret words of love and fidelity.

He lay on his back beneath a star-studded April night, his hands clasped behind his head, his eyes staring at a bright yellow moon. Sweet words, he mused bitterly. Sweet lying words. . . .

A muffled sound disturbed the quiet of the night, and he rolled nimbly to his feet, his hand reaching for the knife at his belt.

Silent as the stalking wolf for which he had been named, he made his way toward the sound. He paused in mid-stride as he neared the shallow stream where he had hobbled his horse. Black Wind stood silouetted against the darkness, her dainty ears pricked forward, her nostrils flared as a big blood bay stallion pranced toward her.

Stalking Wolf let out a sigh of admiration as the bay paused to sniff the air. The stallion was a magnificent animal, big-boned, sleek, with a heavy black mane and a long flowing tail.

The stud let out a trumpeting call as he closed in on Black Wind. Nose to nose, they sniffed each other, exchanging breath for breath, then the stallion sidled up to her, nuzzling her neck, nipping her shoulder, obviously excited by her musky scent and the inviting lift of her tail.

Stalking Wolf watched as the stallion circled the black mare, snuffling softly. Then, rearing up on his hind legs, the huge bay mounted Black Wind, his powerful forelegs gripping her flanks.

Quietly, Stalking Wolf moved downwind of the horses, determined to capture the bay. As he drew closer, he noticed the stallion was wearing a halter and a slow grin moved across his face. The horse had obviously been caught before, which would make it so much easier this time.

At that moment, the wind changed and the stallion caught the scent of a man. Startled, the bay withdrew from Black Wind and backed up, its nostrils flaring as it sniffed the night air.

Stalking Wolf remained still as the bay stud drank in his scent.

"*Hohahe*," Stalking Wolf murmured. "Welcome."

The horse snorted and shook its head at the sound of the man's voice.

"Easy, boy," Stalking Wolf said in the same quiet voice, "easy, now."

The stallion blew softly as Stalking Wolf walked slowly toward it, one hand outstretched, palm up.

The bay's ears were forward, its head lifted, as it focused on the man moving toward it.

"Easy, boy," Stalking Wolf murmured. "Easy, now. There's nothing to be afraid of."

The stallion was no stranger to men, and its curiosity and the presence of the black mare kept it from bolting as Stalking Wolf reached for the halter.

The bay snorted and tossed its head when it realized it had been caught, but Stalking Wolf stroked its neck, murmuring to the horse, and the stallion soon calmed down.

He tethered the stallion to a sturdy oak, checked the mare's hobbles, and went back to bed to dream of the fine long-legged fillies and colts that would be sired by the big blood bay with Black Wind.

* * *

Just before dawn rough hands jerked Stalking Wolf to his feet. Instantly coming awake, he instinctively lashed out at his attackers, but grunted with pain as knotted fists and booted feet drove into his back, ribcage, and groin. A sharp uppercut bloodied his nose and mouth, and a second blow connected with his left eye.

The three men worked him over expertly, relentlessly. When they finally tired of their sport and released him, Stalking Wolf fell to the ground, curling into a tight ball to protect himself from further harm. He felt a sharp pain explode in his right side as one of the men kicked him again, cracking a rib. Through a red haze of pain he heard a voice call, "Wylie, that's enough!"

"Luther's right." Paulie Norton was quick to agree. He did not like violence of any kind and ganging up on a man, even an Indian, did not sit well with him. He had been ready to call it quits before they got started.

"Let's string him up and be done with it then," Abner Wylie muttered, running his left hand over the bruised knuckles on his right hand. A small smile played over his thin lips as he looked down at the Indian, pleased with the damage he had done. With Luther Hicks's help, Abner hauled the Indian to his feet and dragged him toward the horse

Paulie had positioned beneath a low-hanging branch.

They were going to hang him. The realization hit Stalking Wolf like a physical blow and he began to struggle violently as the three men bound his hands behind his back, then wrestled him onto the back of the horse. Abner Wylie was grinning with anticipation as he dropped a noose over the Indian's head and snugged the noose tight.

Stalking Wolf sat rock still, the rough hemp cutting into his throat, his heart pounding like a Lakota war drum. The horse stirred restlessly beneath him and he felt his muscles tense in awful anticipation of what was to come.

The quick tattoo of approaching hoofbeats halted the men. Glancing over their heads, Stalking Wolf saw two mounted figures reining in their horses a short distance away. The rider nearest Stalking Wolf was a burly man dressed in denim work clothes and a broad-brimmed black Stetson. The second rider was similarly dressed, but even with his left eye swollen shut, Stalking Wolf could see it was a girl.

"Go on home, Caitlyn," the man said gruffly. "There's no need for you to see this."

Caitlyn Carmichael shook her head. She had no desire to see a hanging, but she'd never run from a disagreeable task before and she wasn't about to start now. "I've come this far, Pa," she said, a slight quiver in her voice. "I'll stay and see it to the end."

"Suit yourself," Brenden Carmichael muttered. "Wylie, are you sure he's the one?" When Abner Wylie nodded curtly at his boss, Carmichael replied, "Then let's get on with it."

Stalking Wolf felt his blood go cold as Abner Wylie moved behind the horse. Hanging was a bad way to die. The Lakota believed that a man's spirit left his body with his dying breath, but when a man was hanged, his spirit was forever trapped in his corpse. Though he knew his father did not believe in such nonsense, the Lakotas' beliefs were strongly embedded in Stalking Wolf, especially now, when death was near.

But his pride made him lift his head, and he stared at the eastern horizon where a brilliant sunrise was paying homage to a new day. The sky grew brighter, changing from pale gray to bright gold, then exploding in a spectacular display of fiery reds and oranges as the sun crested the skyline.

Wakan Tanka, give me strength and courage. The silent prayer rose in Stalking Wolf's heart as Wylie took a firm grip on the loose end of the rope while the man known as Luther reached for the horse's reins. The brassy taste of fear was strong in Stalking Wolf's mouth as he imagined the horse moving out from under him, and the quick sensation of falling. If he was lucky, death would come quickly. If not, he would slowly strangle.

Caitlyn's mouth went dry as she tried to imagine what the Indian was feeling. What would it be like to know death was only a heartbeat away? To know you had no hope of a reprieve? She gazed at the Indian's face, set in impassive lines, and the sympathy she'd been feeling vanished. Her brothers had been killed by marauding savages; perhaps this very man had been responsible for their deaths.

Brenden Carmichael, owner of the Circle C ranch, felt a grudging admiration for the Indian who, though facing certain death, glared at him with bold defiance. Although he harbored no love for Indians, it suddenly seemed unfair to hang a man without giving him a last chance to speak and to confess his guilt before he went to meet his Maker.

"Wait." Carmichael's voice cut across the heavy stillness as he rode toward the Indian. He drew his horse to a halt, facing the condemned man. "You speak English?"

Stalking Wolf nodded. The girl had followed the man and though he knew these two held the power of life and death over him, he focused his gaze on the fading streaks of vermillion that still stained the sky. The color reminded him of blood and death. His blood. His death.

"Why did you steal my daughter's horse?" the man demanded.

Stalking Wolf licked the blood from his lips. Drawing his gaze from the horizon, he focused on the girl and found himself staring into a pair of deep green eyes fringed with long, golden lashes. The fact that she was quite beautiful despite her rough garb registered somewhere in the back of his mind.

"I did not steal the horse." He spoke through swollen lips, grimacing from the effort, and knowing that they would not believe him.

"He's lying, Mr. Carmichael," Abner said with a sneer. "Let's hang him and be done with it."

Surprised that he had directed his answer to her and not to her father, Caitlyn studied the Indian. His eyes were dark; the left one was badly swollen and discolored. His nose and mouth were bloody, and a shallow line cut across his left cheek. His clothing, a loose-fitting buckskin shirt, fringed leggings, clout, and moccasins, were covered with trail dust and splattered with blood. He looked wild, untamed, and completely savage, but she had to admire the way he faced her, with his head high and his shoulders back. She knew he was afraid. He *had* to be afraid, but it didn't show on his face.

"What if he's telling the truth, Pa?"

Abner snorted disdainfully. "They're all liars, Mr. Carmichael. Everybody knows you can't trust a redskin any farther than you can throw one. Especially one that's got a noose around his neck."

Caitlyn gazed steadily at the Indian as Abner accused him of being a thief and a liar. She felt a cold shiver in the pit of her stomach as she saw a flash of anger flicker in the Indian's eyes, and then his expression became impassive once again.

"I believe him," she decided, surprising everyone, including herself. She glanced at Luther Hicks, hoping he would agree with her, but even Luther looked skeptical.

Abner snorted in disbelief. "When did you get to be an Injun lover?"

"I don't have any love for Indians and you know it," Caitlyn retorted, her cheeks flushed with anger. "But I don't intend to stand by and watch you hang an innocent man, either."

Her outburst was met by astonished stares from Abner and her father. No one on the

Circle C had any love for Indians, and Caitlyn had always been the most outspoken, the most unforgiving. Yet now she was defending one.

Caitlyn did not understand her feelings any better than anyone else. She only knew that, though she had been determined to see the Indian hang, she was now just as determined to see that he didn't.

Dismounting, she walked over to where the black mare stood grazing placidly on the lush prairie grass.

"This mare's in season," Caitlyn announced. "Red must have caught her scent last night. It isn't the first time he's run off after a mare."

Stalking Wolf held his breath, knowing his whole future would be decided in the next few minutes.

Brenden rode to where his daughter stood beside the black horse. For a moment he forgot all about the Indian as he openly admired the mare. She was as fine a piece of horseflesh as he had ever seen, with a coat like black velvet and near-perfect conformation. A sudden need to own the fine animal took hold of him, and his mind whirled with the realization that the mare would be his once the Indian was disposed of.

"Pa?"

Caitlyn's voice brought him back to the matter at hand. "The mare's in heat," Brenden agreed. "Hang the Indian and let's go home."

Caitlyn stared at her father. "You can't be serious."

Brenden glanced at the brand on the mare's left hip. "She's wearing a Texas brand, a double *D*," he pointed out, "and I've never heard of any Indians, from Texas or anywhere else, branding their stock. It's obvious he stole the mare, and he'll steal our horses, too, if he gets the chance."

Stalking Wolf felt his last hope drain out of him at the old man's words. Black Wind *had* been stolen, and Killian had been the culprit. Stalking Wolf would have laughed at the irony of it if the situation wasn't so serious.

"Get on with it," Brenden said. "Luther, bring the mare." He glanced briefly at the Indian. "Leave the body. Maybe it'll discourage any other redskins in the area."

"Pa, I won't let you do this," Caitlyn said, grabbing her father by the arm. "You can't hang a man because you *think* he's a horse thief. And even if he did steal the mare, he didn't steal it from us. You have no right to act as judge, jury, and executioner."

"Dammit, Caitlyn, the West would be a better place if every last Indian was dead and buried and you know it."

She heartily agreed, but she could not let her father hang the Indian. She could not explain why she felt so strongly that he was innocent, or why she found the thought of his death so unbearable.

"Hanging this Indian won't bring Arlo and Morgan back," she said quietly.

At the mention of his sons, all the fight went out of Brenden. Hanging the Indian wouldn't bring his sons back, or heal the raw ache in his heart. He gazed at Caitlyn. She was all he had left, and he loved her dearly. He couldn't bear to have her think badly of him. He'd always been her hero. How could he bear it if her admiration turned to disgust?

"Very well, turn the Indian loose," Brenden said gruffly. "But bring the mare along. I'll send a wire to the marshal in San Antonio and see if he's heard of anyone missing a black mare."

Brenden bit back a smile. The chances of finding the mare's owner were slim, but in the meantime, he'd treat the animal like one of his own.

He was about to rein his horse for home when Caitlyn's voice stopped him.

"He's hurt, Pa," she said, her huge green eyes dark with concern. "We can't take his horse and leave him out here on foot."

Brenden swore under his breath. The redskin was more trouble than he was worth, but since he had the black mare, he could afford to be generous. "Bring him along," he said curtly. "Never let it be said I didn't do my Christian duty."

CHAPTER THREE

Stalking Wolf didn't argue as the man called Paulie cut his hands free, lifted the noose from his neck, and then took up the reins of his horse. It was all he could do to remain in the saddle and he sat stiffly erect, one hand grasping the horn, his other arm wrapped protectively around his broken rib. Each step the horse took sent jolting shafts of pain through his side. His head throbbed, and there was a dull ache in his groin where Wylie had kicked him.

They rode across flat grassland for almost an hour and then the land dipped slightly and Stalking Wolf saw the Carmichael ranch.

Made of native stone and sun-bleached

wood, the house was long and low with a shingled roof, a red brick chimney and a covered porch that ran the length of the house. Several clay pots held a variety of flowers. Stalking Wolf recognized roses and daisies but the others, in colors of bright pink and lavender, did not look familiar. A rectangular building to the left of the house appeared to be the bunkhouse, and a large red barn with a sloping roof and several well-built corrals were to the right. Tall pines grew in scattered clumps behind the house and on a distant ridge. There were no shrubs close to the house that might provide a hiding place for Indians or other intruders.

A slow-moving river gurgled merrily on its way some twenty-five yards from the front door, running straight as an arrow from one end of the shallow valley to the other until it disappeared from sight behind a stand of timber.

As they neared the house, Stalking Wolf saw a dozen Rhode Islands Reds scratching in the dirt. A large yellow hound thumped its tail as Brenden Carmichael swung out of the saddle.

"Paulie, look after the horses. Wylie, take the Indian inside. Luther, you get busy and add another rail to that corral. Wylie will give you a hand. That damned stud's run off for the last time."

Caitlyn grinned at her father as he issued the last of his curt commands. "And what are my orders, Captain?"

"Hell's fire, girl, you know you'll do whatever suits you."

"Now, Pa, that's not so."

Brenden snorted. "You'd best keep an eye on that Injun. I don't think he's in any shape to cause trouble, but I want to know just where he is until we decide what to do with him. Wylie'd just as soon cut his throat as look at him, you know." A dark shadow passed over Brenden's face. "Can't say as I blame him, at that."

"I'll watch him, Pa," Caitlyn said, her voice tinged with resentment. She hadn't realized she'd be saddled with being the Indian's keeper when she insisted he was innocent.

"I know you will. I'll be out cutting timber if you need me. Send Paulie out when he's finished feeding the stock."

Stalking Wolf refused Wylie's help. His teeth set, he slid to the ground unaided, then stood leaning against the horse's flank, gathering his strength.

"I'll look after him, Abner," Caitlyn said, her voice carrying a note of dismissal. "You go on and help Luther."

"Whatever you say, Miss Carmichael," Abner replied. "But you'd best watch yourself around that buck."

Stalking Wolf's eyes narrowed ominously at the derogatory tone of the man's voice. Had he not been in such pain, he would have taught him a little respect, but not now, when just drawing a breath was an effort.

Caitlyn saw the fury in the Indian's eyes and hoped she would be on hand when Abner got his comeuppance from the Indian. She had never liked Abner Wylie. He reminded her of a weasel, always skulking around, his narrow, close-set pale blue eyes forever lingering on her figure with a look that bordered somewhere between insolence and lust. But he was a top hand, which was why her father had hired him, and why he still had a job.

"Thanks for the warning," Caitlyn said dryly, "but I don't think the man's in any condition to do me harm."

Abner turned away, muttering under his breath, and Caitlyn reached for the Indian's arm. "Come on, I'll help you inside."

"I can manage."

"Suit yourself," Caitlyn said with a shrug, opening the front door, and waiting for him to enter the house.

Stalking Wolf moved away from the horse, his arm wrapped protectively around his ribcage. His jaw set with determination, he crossed the yard to the house and followed the girl inside.

The parlor was large, furnished with a faded blue sofa and two overstuffed leather chairs. A fireplace took up most of one wall and a Navajo rug was spread before the hearth.

"Take off your shirt," Caitlyn said brusquely. It was her duty to see to their prisoner's injuries, she supposed. "I'll get some water and bandages."

Stalking Wolf sat on the edge of the raised hearth and removed his shirt, every movement sending a painful jolt through his right side. After tossing his shirt on the floor, he looked around the room again. There was a Winchester rifle resting on a pair of pegs over the front door, and a painting of a pinto horse galloping across a yellow prairie hung on the far wall. A pair of blue-and-white figurines, a blue china plate, and a pair of silver candlesticks were arranged on the mantle.

He looked up as Caitlyn emerged from the doorway that he assumed led to the kitchen. She was carrying a tray laden with a bowl of water, a pair of scissors, a dark green bottle with no label, and a roll of white cloth.

He had never seen a woman in pants before and he tilted his head to one side, watching her as she walked toward him, captivated by the sway of her hips, and by the way the faded denim clung to her long coltish legs.

Caitlyn knelt at the Indian's side and placed the tray on the floor. In a swift movement, she removed her hat and tossed it onto one of the chairs.

Stalking Wolf felt his breath catch in his throat as a wealth of honey-gold hair fell in luxurious waves about her face and shoulders. After having spent six years with the Lakota, it was a rare treat to see a woman with hair that was not as black as midnight, or as straight as a string. But, more than that, she was beautiful. Her golden hair emphasized her peaches-and-cream complexion and accentuated her eyes, which were as deep and green as a high mountain stream beneath a warm summer sun. He noticed that her nose was small and straight, that her brows were slightly arched, and that her lashes were incredibly long and dark. Her mouth was full and pink and perfect.

Caitlyn flushed self-consciously under the Indian's scrutiny, but she was all business as she tended to him. She was accustomed to treating any number of injuries that occurred on the ranch; only in dire emergencies did they summon the doctor from town.

When she had washed the blood from his face, she placed a cold cloth over his black eye, wondering if she had done the right thing when she insisted her father spare the Indian's life. Maybe he *had* stolen Red, and the black mare, too. Maybe he'd murder them all in their beds, and scalp them as well.

Lost in thought, her hands were less than gentle as she probed his ribs.

"Damn!" The oath exploded from Stalking Wolf's lips as the girl's slim fingers pressed against his side.

"I'm sorry," Caitlyn said quickly.

"Look, I don't want to be here, and I'm sure you'd all be happier if I just rode on."

"Not until Pa decides what to do with you. Maybe he'll turn you over to the sheriff," Caitlyn said in a voice that left no room for argument.

As gently as possible, she examined his side again, ascertaining that at least one rib was broken, perhaps two. His entire right side was bruised and discolored, and she silently cursed Abner. The man seemed to take great pleasure in inflicting pain.

After carefully washing the Indian's midsection, Caitlyn bound it with several layers of cloth to stabilize the break. He would be in considerable pain for several weeks, but broken ribs eventually mended on their own and until they did, he would have to move carefully.

"Are you hungry?" Caitlyn asked.

Stalking Wolf shook his head.

"Thirsty? There's coffee warming on the stove."

"Got any whiskey?"

Caitlyn's right eyebrow lifted. "I thought Indians and whiskey didn't mix."

"Maybe not, but I'm half Irish, and I'd like a drink."

"Irish!" Caitlyn exclaimed. "You're joking."

Stalking Wolf shook his head. "My father came here from Ireland thirty years ago."

"Well, you look more Indian than Irish to me." Caitlyn spoke the words over her shoulder as she went into the kitchen. Standing on tiptoe, she opened the cupboard and reached for a bottle of sourmash that her father kept on hand for medicinal purposes. Taking a glass from the bottom shelf, she poured a quarter of an inch of liquid into it and carried it to the Indian.

He sniffed it, wrinkled his nose, and tossed it off in a single swallow. It was the cheapest kind of whiskey, likely homemade, but it quickly spread a warm glow throughout his body, easing the pain in his side.

"Thanks." He handed her the empty glass, his fingers lightly brushing against hers.

The heat from his touch spread from her fingertips to her arm, making her heart lurch queerly. Startled by the sensation, she took a step backward, wondering if he had felt it, too.

"My name's Caitlyn," she said, flustered and hoping to cover it with casual conversation.

Stalking Wolf nodded. It was a pretty name, and it suited her. "I'm . . ." He started to introduce himself as Stalking Wolf, and then thought better of it. "Gallegher," he said, trying out the name he had not used in over six years. "Raiford Gallegher. But I answer to Rafe."

"Irish, indeed," Caitlyn murmured.

He nodded again, suddenly overcome with weariness as the beating, the long ride, and the shot of whiskey taken on an empty stomach began to take their toll.

"You're tired," Caitlyn observed. "I guess Pa won't mind if I put you in the spare room."

"Thanks." He stood up, swaying, and Caitlyn stepped forward and placed her arm around his waist to steady him, then helped him down the narrow hall that led to the bedrooms. His thigh brushed against hers and she felt a quick flutter in the pit of her stomach. What *was* the matter with her? She'd been around men her whole life and none of them had ever affected her so strangely.

Rafe's pulse quickened at her touch and he cursed under his breath. He had been aware of the almost instantaneous attraction between them, but he was determined that nothing would come of it. She was a woman, a pretty, desirable woman, and he had vowed never to trust a woman again.

Caitlyn opened the last door on the left, revealing a small whitewashed room furnished with a big brass bed and a three-drawer oak dresser. A colorful rag rug brightened the stark decor.

"Why don't you get some rest?" Caitlyn suggested.

Rafe nodded. "Thanks again."

"I'll bring your dinner in so you won't have to get up," Caitlyn offered, and left the room, closing the door behind her.

Rafe grimaced as he sank down on the bed, his hand straying to his side as he silently cursed the man who had kicked him while he was down. He'd make Abner Wylie pay for that kick, he vowed as he carefully lowered himself to the bed. Yes, indeed, he'd make the bastard pay. . . .

Caitlyn was frowning when she went into the kitchen to help the ranch house cook, Consuelo, prepare lunch. Life was so unfair, she mused as she sliced a loaf of freshly baked bread. For the first time in her life she had met a man who excited her, who was tall, dark, and sinfully handsome, a man she felt drawn to, and he was an Indian.

It just wasn't fair, she thought glumly, but then, no one had ever said life was fair.

CHAPTER
FOUR

CAITLYN BENT OVER THE WASHTUB, SCRUB-
bing one of her father's heavy cotton work
shirts. The day was warm, and perspiration
dotted her forehead and slid down between
her breasts. Straightening, she rinsed the
shirt and tossed it into the laundry basket at
her feet.

Pausing for a moment, she pressed a hand
to her back and glanced toward the side of
the house where the Indian sat cross-legged
in the shade of a tall tree. She smiled self-
consciously when she saw that he was watching her.

Rafe had been at the ranch for over a week
now. His broken rib pained him a great deal,

she knew, but he never complained. He spent most of his time confined to the spare room, though he spent a part of each day with the big black mare, grooming the Thoroughbred's coat until it glistened like wet ebony.

Caitlyn had caught her father in the barn several times covetously gazing at the beautiful animal, but Caitlyn could hardly blame him. The black was exquisite, her conformation near perfect, her bloodlines, though unknown, obviously of the highest caliber. With wide, intelligent eyes, long legs, a deep chest, and a long muscular neck, she would be a perfect mate for Red.

Caitlyn bent over the tub again, all too aware of Rafe's eyes studying her every move. They had not spoken much to each other so she knew nothing about him other than that he was a half-breed—*what a vile term*, she thought absently—and that he was quite the most fascinating man she had ever met.

As to the men's feelings about Rafe, there was no doubt.

Luther had accepted the Indian's presence without a qualm, but then, Luther was probably the kindest, most tolerant man Caitlyn had ever known. Tall and wiry, with dark gray hair and twinkling blue eyes, Caitlyn thought he must be at least sixty, though he might have been older or younger. It was hard to tell with men who had spent their whole life in the sun. Luther's skin was the color and texture of aged saddle leather, but he moved with the speed and agility of a young man.

Abner despised Rafe simply because he was half Indian. Abner had no use for Indians, Mexicans, or Negroes, or for most anyone else, for that matter. He refused to speak to Rafe except when absolutely necessary.

Paulie Norton came and went as always, a man apart from everyone else. He was a strange one, Paulie was, preferring the company of animals to people. He had never been to school; he was slow of speech and economical of movement. But he could perform miracles. He was only eighteen or nineteen, but he possessed a power to heal that was nothing short of remarkable. Caitlyn had seen him stitch cuts that healed without a scar, set broken bones, cure fevers, and lance boils. Mostly, he used his curative powers on the stock; once she had seen him nurse one of the saddlehorses through a bad case of sand colic. Paulie was not a handsome young man. His hair was light brown and lanky, his eyes were set close together, his nose as long and thin, but he had a warm smile and a friendly nature, and he accepted Gallegher without reservation.

Caitlyn's own reactions to Rafe however were mixed. She had vowed to hate all Indians until the day she died because they had been responsible for her brothers' deaths. Fearing them and praying for their destruction, she had rejoiced when she heard that John Chivington had massacred a Cheyenne village at Sand Creek. The Indians had been at peace under a white flag, but the thought stirred no compassion within her breast. Her family had been at peace, too, wanting only to cross the plains to start a new life, when the Indians attacked. Was it any wonder she had vowed to hate them? And yet, to her chargin, she was having a great deal of difficulty maintaining that hatred where Rafe Gallegher was concerned. She was physically attracted to him and, though she hated to admit it, intrigued by him as well. Who was he, really? Half Irish, indeed! And yet, it was obvious now that he was not a full-blooded Indian. He spoke English too well, he was familiar with American customs and traditions, and his table manners were passable if not impeccable.

If only he weren't so devilishly handsome. If only her blood didn't heat each time his eyes met hers. If only she could stop wondering what it would be like to stand in the circle of his arms, to feel his mouth on hers.

He's Indian, she told herself, repeating

again and again, *Indian. Indian. Indian*! But even that talisman failed her. In any other man, the suspicion that he was part Indian would have been enough to repulse her, but Rafe's mixed blood only served to make him more fascinating.

He was watching her now. She could feel his eyes on her back, as tangible as though he had touched her. It brought a quick flush to her cheeks, and sent a warm tingling sensation skittering down her spine.

"Indian," she muttered. She had the uneasy feeling that Rafe knew she was attracted to him; worst of all, she felt he was amused by it.

Heaving a sigh, she dropped the last of the wet wash into the basket, stretched, and then picked up the basket and carried it to the clothesline, glad that it was around the corner of the house and out of Rafe Gallegher's line of vision.

Brenden studied the black mare with a practiced eye and found no fault in her. He was addicted to fine horseflesh, he admitted, just as some men were hopelessly addicted to whiskey. After his wife Elizabeth's death, he was determined to fulfill a lifelong dream to breed Thoroughbred horses. To that end, he had sold his business, packed up Caitlyn and her brothers, and headed West. But bad luck had plagued them from the beginning. The weather had been unseasonably hot, and then it had rained for weeks. They had been attacked by Indians twice, his sons killed in the second attack. Caitlyn had been his strength then, comforting him, giving him a reason to go on. He had pushed steadily onward, drowning his grief in hard work. They had found a good piece of land, built a snug house, planted their crops, bought several hundred head of cattle to sustain them until they could turn a profit on the horses he hoped to raise. And then, when it seemed all was going well, disaster struck. His best brood mare had been attacked by a mountain lion. She had aborted her foal; two days later, she died of her injuries. A week later, his second brood mare disappeared, apparently stolen by Indians.

All these things darted through Brenden's mind as he admired the big black mare. He had sent a wire to the marshal in San Antonio the day after they found the Indian. The reply had come only the day before, informing him that the Double D Ranch had been burned to the ground the year before and the owners killed.

Brenden let out a long sigh. He had more than enough work to keep him busy. The bank loan was due in a year and a half and there was no money to pay it. He had a damned half-breed prisoner in his house, and a headstrong daughter, yet here he stood, admiring a horse. But what a horse. After his own mares had been lost, he had spent several months visiting the nearby ranches, looking for a couple of horses as good as those he had lost, but his search had been in vain. Most of his neighbors rode mustangs caught off the range, a few rode top quality quarter horses, and one rode a fine Arabian mare. But no one had a Thoroughbred of the caliber he wanted, and he had almost decided he would have to make the long trip back East to find one when the Indian appeared with the big black mare. She was perfect, and he was determined to own her at any cost.

It was with that in mind that he went in search of the half-breed. It galled him to think he would have to do business with a man he had come close to hanging, a man he still thought of as a thief, but there was no help for it. And the sooner he got it over with, the better.

Rafe felt a sense of unease as he watched Brenden Carmichael striding purposefully toward him. He wondered if the man had finally made up his mind about what to do with him. He was fully aware of the fact that he was little more than a prisoner in this place.

He looked up, shading his eyes against the sun, as Carmichael came to a halt a few feet from where he sat. Caitlyn's father was a striking figure, his hair as white as wool, his eyes the same vibrant shade of green as his daughter's. He was not tall, but he was solid and well built.

"Mornin'," Carmichael said gruffly.

"Mornin'."

Carmichael cleared his throat. "I've decided to let you go. But I want that black mare. I'll give you two hundred dollars for her."

Rafe shook his head. "Black Wind's not for sale."

"Three hundred."

Again, Rafe shook his head.

"Five hundred and my buckskin gelding."

"She's not for sale," Rafe repeated. "Not at any price."

"Everything has a price!" Carmichael snapped. "I'll give you eight hundred and not a penny more."

Caitlyn frowned as she came up behind her father. Eight hundred dollars for one horse? Had her father lost his mind?

Brenden glared at Gallegher. Damn stubborn redskin. What did he want?

"Why won't you sell Black Wind, Mr. Gallegher?" Caitlyn asked, her curiosity getting the best of her.

"I like her."

"Eight hundred dollars is a generous offer," Caitlyn remarked.

"Probably more than she's worth," Rafe replied. "But she's still not for sale."

"Dammit, that mare might be in foal by my stud!" Carmichael exclaimed.

"He came looking for us," Rafe said with a wry grin. "We didn't come to you."

"That's your story. I could still turn you over to the sheriff. . . ."

Brenden's face was livid.

Before he could say another word, Caitlyn placed her hand on his arm. "Pa, perhaps we can work something out."

"Like what?"

Caitlyn looked at Rafe. He was still sitting in the shade, his face a blank, while her father looked about ready to burst.

"Well?" Brenden said impatiently.

"Perhaps we could buy the foal," Caitlyn suggested.

"I want the mare *and* the foal," Brenden said, practically shouting.

"Well, you can't have the mare," Caitlyn replied calmly.

"I should have let Wylie string him up," Brenden muttered under his breath, and then he fixed Rafe Gallegher with a hard stare. "Well, how about it? Will you sell me the foal?"

"It'll be eleven months before Black Wind drops that foal, if she's *in* foal. And another six months or so until it's weaned. What am I supposed to do until then?"

"You can stay here until the foal's born," Brenden said.

"As a prisoner?"

"No, we'll forget about all that," Carmichael replied. He was calmer, more rational, now that he was about to get at least a part of what he wanted. And he'd make certain the mare conceived. He'd breed her to Red until she settled, no matter how long it took. "I'll pay you a decent wage, and give you two hundred dollars for the foal."

"What if Black Wind aborts, or the foal's born dead?"

"That's a chance you'll have to take. In the meantime, you'll have a job and three meals a day. What do you say?"

The offer was more than fair, Rafe allowed. If he accepted Carmichael's terms, he would have a place to live, a chance to save some money for a place of his own. He studied Carmichael's face, wondering if he could trust the man, and then he glanced at Caitlyn. He had vowed never to love again, but he didn't intend to live like a eunuch, either. Caitlyn Carmichael was the prettiest thing he had ever seen, and it occurred to him that spending the next eighteen months or so on her father's ranch might not be so bad after all.

He rose slowly to his feet and stuck out his hand. "It's a deal."

Rafe had been on the ranch ten days when the seven cowhands who had been out on the range returned to the Circle C. To a man, they were appalled to learn that the boss had hired a half-breed in their absence.

Luther assured them that the situation was only temporary, and that Gallegher would be gone as soon as the black mare foaled and the foal was weaned. Luther was the ranch foreman, and Caitlyn knew it was only because the men admired and respected Luther that they agreed to stay on, but they grumbled about working alongside a half-breed just the same.

It took several weeks for Rafe's ribs to heal. In that time, he did little more than rest in the shade. He was unfailingly polite to Caitlyn and her father, though he spoke little unless spoken to.

Mealtimes were filled with tension. Seated at the far end of the table opposite her father, Caitlyn was ever aware of the animosity that stretched like an invisible wire between Rafe and Abner. It was evident that Rafe had not forgotten Abner's eagerness to string him up, nor had he forgotten Abner's derogatory remarks, or the fact that Abner had kicked him while he was down.

Abner was outspoken, blunt to the point of rudeness. The first night he sat at the table and learned that Rafe would be joining them, he had made several nasty remarks about heathen Indians, and it was only when Brenden had told Abner in words direct and to the point that Gallegher was riding for the brand that Abner curbed his tongue. Brenden also remarked that anyone who wasn't happy with the seating arrangements could take their meals outside.

Later, Caitlyn had told her father that she feared there would be trouble between the two men if Abner didn't learn to keep his mouth shut in Rafe's presence.

Brenden had laughed heartily. "You can bet your bottom dollar there's going to be trouble," he had agreed. "It's only a matter of time."

Caitlyn was pondering her father's words several days later when Rafe entered the kitchen where she was crimping the edge of a pie crust.

Caitlyn nodded in his direction. "Mr. Gallegher."

"Miss Carmichael."

"Was there something you wanted?"

"Coffee, if you've got it."

Caitlyn smiled as she wiped her hands on

her apron. "Ranch kitchens always have a pot of coffee warming on the back burner," she told him as she took a cup from the shelf.

Rafe nodded as he swung a leg over a chair, his eyes watching her every move. He smiled his thanks as she handed him a cup filled with hot black coffee.

There was an awkward silence as Rafe took a sip. Caitlyn turned back to the counter, aware that her hands were trembling. Rafe's presence seemed to fill the kitchen.

"We're having apple pie for dessert," she said, breaking the silence between them. "I hope you like it."

"I do," Rafe replied, "though I haven't had any in quite awhile."

Caitlyn laughed softly. "I guess the Indians don't make pie, do they?"

"No."

"Did you like living with the Indians, Mr. Gallegher?"

"Why don't you call me Rafe?"

"All right. Rafe." She liked the way his name sounded when she said it. Picking up a knife, she began to peel a large green apple. "You didn't answer my question."

"I liked it."

His reply was curt, almost rude, and Caitlyn slid a glance in his direction, wondering if she were bringing up a subject he didn't wish to discuss. Her intuition told her to change the subject. Her curiosity wouldn't let her.

"How long did you live with them?"

"Six years."

Caitlyn's eyes widened at that bit of information. Somehow, she hadn't expected that it had been such a long time. "Why did you leave?"

Rafe shrugged, and his eyes grew dark. "Things happen," he answered succinctly.

"And you'd rather not talk about it?"

"Right."

He drained the last of the coffee from the cup, his eyes cool and assessing as he watched her deftly peel one apple after another.

Caitlyn worked quickly, conscious of his steady gaze. She felt her cheeks bloom with color and in her haste to finish her task, she grew careless. She yelped as the knife sliced through the apple and into her finger. A huge drop of blood splattered on the counter top.

Rafe was on his feet instantly. Taking the knife from her hand, he reached for the towel draped over the back of a chair and wrapped one corner of the cloth around her finger.

"I'm all right," Caitlyn said, feeling foolish because she had been so clumsy. "It's nothing."

"Let me look."

He was standing so close she could see the fine lines that fanned out from the corners of his eyes, smell his musky male scent. Her heart began to pound wildly as he removed the towel and studied the injury.

"Have you got something to use for a bandage?"

"Yes, I'll get it."

"Better get some disinfectant, too."

Caitlyn nodded and Rafe stepped away from her. She continued to stare up at him, flustered by his nearness. His eyes, intent upon her face, trapped her gaze. The heat from his eyes warmed her to her toes, and she found herself staring at his mouth, wondering, always wondering, what it would be like if he kissed her.

Rafe felt his pulse quicken at Caitlyn's nearness. Her eyes were as green as spring grass, wide and innocent—and scared. Definitely scared of him, of the attraction she felt toward him and tried so hard to hide. He wondered if she had admitted to herself how she felt, or if she denied her feelings for him because he was an Indian, a man to be hated, not desired.

There was a faint smudge of flour on her cheek and he was sorely tempted to slide his tongue across the faint white smear, to press his mouth to hers and watch her eyes grow cloudy with passion.

Muttering an oath, he drew his gaze from hers. "You'd best get that bandage before you bleed all over the floor," he suggested, his voice strangely thick and uneven.

"What? Oh, yes," Caitlyn agreed absently, the shallow cut in her finger all but forgotten. With an effort, she pulled her gaze from his face and left the room.

Rafe was gone when she returned to the kitchen a few minutes later.

CHAPTER FIVE

ABNER WAS VISIBLY EXCITED WHEN HE ENtered the main house for dinner the following night. Tossing his hat on the rack in the corner, he straddled his chair, his face flushed and his pale blue eyes bright.

"I saw the herd," he told Brenden, his words coming in a rush. "They're grazing in Big Sully Meadow."

Brenden grinned. "The men and I will leave at first light," he told Luther.

"I'm going this time," Caitlyn said, her green eyes glowing with excitement.

"No," Brenden said firmly. "It's too dangerous. You stay here with Luther and Paulie."

Brenden turned an appraising eye on Rafe Gallegher. "You feel up to chasing a herd of mustangs?"

Rafe nodded. He'd been sitting idle too long.

"Good," Brenden remarked. "I've got a contract to furnish remounts to the Army. If this herd's as big as Wylie says, it'll just fill the bill."

Caitlyn slammed her fork down beside her plate. "I said I'm going, Pa."

Brenden sighed wearily. "We've had this argument before, Caitlyn. I said no then, and I'm saying no now."

Caitlyn's mouth thinned in an angry line. Her father rarely denied her anything, but on this one subject he was adamant.

Rafe's gaze shifted from Brenden Carmichael to Caitlyn. Her color was high and her eyes fairly snapped with fury. The mood suited her, he mused, for she had never looked more vibrant, or more desirable. A glance in Wylie's direction told him the head wrangler was thinking the same thing.

A muscle worked in Rafe's jaw as an unwanted surge of jealousy tightened his gut. So, Wylie was sweet on the boss man's daughter. The thought left a bad taste in his mouth. Grim-faced, he turned his attention to the juicy steak on his plate. Whatever went on between Abner Wylie and Caitlyn Carmichael was their business, not his.

Caitlyn finished the meal in silence, and her sullen mood stifled the normal flow of conversation at the dinner table. Wylie and the other cowhands excused themselves as soon as they finished eating, except for Luther, who sat back in his chair and rolled a smoke. He had known Caitlyn for most of her life and he knew her anger never lasted long. She'd had a lot to be angry about on the long trip West—Indian attacks, bad weather, onery mules, water shortages. But her anger had rarely lasted more than a few minutes, and then she was right there, pitching in to do what she could, encouraging others to cheer up, assuring them that the future would be better. He'd never seen her discouraged for long, except when her brothers had been killed. That had taken its toll, sure enough.

Luther looked across the table at the half-breed, his eyes thoughtful. "You ever done any bronc bustin'?"

"A time or two."

Luther nodded. "We lost our best wrangler last season. Wylie's pretty good, but he's kinda rough. Heavy hands, if you know what I mean."

Rafe nodded.

"We could use a good bronc rider," Luther said, directing his remark to Brenden.

Brenden shrugged. "You want the job, Gallegher?"

"Sure, it beats chasing cattle."

Luther chuckled. Any man worth his salt would rather work horses than cattle. "It's settled then. When we get that herd rounded up, you'll have enough work to keep you busy till fall."

"Suits me," Rafe replied, glancing at Caitlyn. She was sitting straight in her chair, her eyes focused on the cup in her hand. The angry color had faded from her cheeks, but her eyes were still turbulent.

A few minutes later Brenden excused himself from the table. Rafe left the room a short time later, leaving Luther and Caitlyn alone.

"He doesn't say much," Luther remarked. "The half-breed, I mean."

Caitlyn shrugged. "Maybe he doesn't have anything to say."

"Maybe, maybe not."

"I've never known you to hire on a man without asking him for references, or watching him work."

"I know, but I've got a gut feeling about Gallegher. I've seen the way he handles that black mare. He knows horses inside and out, or I miss my guess."

Caitlyn nodded, and then she let out an irritated sigh. "Luther, why won't my father let me go after the mustangs? I can ride as well as any of the men."

"Sure you can," Luther agreed. "Didn't I teach you myself? But the trail's no place for a girl. Now, now," he said, holding up his hands to quiet her objections. "It isn't that you can't ride or hold up your end. It's just that the men don't want to have to watch their manners or their language while they're trailing a bunch of broomtails, and they'd have to mind both if you went along. Not only that, but it's hard, dirty work, and dangerous to boot. You'll be better off at home here with me and Paulie, and your pa won't have to worry about you."

Caitlyn's shoulders slumped in defeat. If Luther was against her going, too, she didn't have a chance.

"They'll be leaving early," Luther said as he stood up and reached for his hat. "Tell Consuelo for me, will you?"

Caitlyn nodded. "Good night, Luther."

Caitlyn stood on the front porch, watching as the men rode out of the yard. It wasn't fair, she thought irritably. They got to go off and have a good time while she had to stay at home and keep house. She remembered listening to Luther talk about the excitement of seeing a wild herd on the move, the thrill of chasing them across the prairie. It was an unforgettable sight, he had said. The mares and foals lined out in a dead run, manes and tails flying like flags in the wind, the stallion running alongside, nipping at the flanks of the mares who lagged behind.

Caitlyn glanced toward the barn. The big herds were disappearing as more and more settlers pushed their way westward. Wild horses were being driven from their grazing lands as farmers moved in, fencing the land. Many of the younger animals were being caught and domesticated; the old ones were being culled from the herd and destroyed. The Indians accounted for a fair number, as well, using them for transportation in good times and for food when game was scarce and times were hard.

Caitlyn frowned. For all she knew, this might be the last wild herd in the territory. If she didn't see it now, she might never get another chance.

With a toss of her head, Caitlyn went into the house and changed into a pair of faded denim pants and a long-sleeved wool shirt. She threw an extra shirt, a jacket, a comb and a brush into her saddlebag, then ran down to the barn to saddle her horse.

Paulie frowned as she tied her saddlebags in place behind her saddle. "Where're you goin', Miss Carmichael?"

"With Pa."

"Miss Carmichael, wait!" Paulie called as

she rode out of the yard at a gallop. "Dammit, girl, your pa will have my hide for this!"

Rafe rode a fair distance behind Brenden Carmichael and the other cowhands. It was all too evident that his presence was not welcome. Despite Carmichael's insistence that he tag along, and Luther's guarantee that Rafe's presence was only temporary at Circle C, the other men refused to accept him. He didn't really mind. He enjoyed riding alone, out of the dust stirred by those ahead.

His thoughts strayed toward Summer Wind as he rode. He had first noticed her the night her father had announced that his daughter had become a woman. During the four-day celebration that followed, Rafe had watched her with new interest, noticing for the first time the way her eyes followed him, the way she smiled, shy yet inviting, the lilting sound of her laughter.

He had trailed after her when she went to the river for water, waiting for an opportune moment to catch her alone. At first they had only smiled at each other from a distance. Later, they talked of mutual friends, of village gossip, of dances, and games. And still later they had talked about themselves, gradually exchanging more personal information and ideas as they became better acquainted.

They had courted for over four years. He had become a proven warrior by then, able to support a wife, and she had grown more beautiful, more desirable.

Rafe's eyes grew hard as he remembered the fateful day when he had gone to Summer Wind's lodge to ask for her hand in marriage. But Summer Wind was not there. She had gone to look for wood, her mother said with a knowing smile. He had been whistling softly when he started down the path Summer Wind usually followed. His heart had been light, his pulse racing with anticipation. He had waited over four years for this day.

He had walked deep into the heart of the forest before he found her, and when he finally saw her standing beneath a sun-dappled oak, she had not been alone. Hump Back Bear had been with her, his brawny arm curled around her slender waist. They had been laughing softly, but the laughter died in Summer Wind's throat when she saw Rafe standing there.

Hump Back Bear had whirled around, his face growing dark with fury. There had been angry words between the men. Summer Wind had tried to explain, had begged Rafe to understand, to forgive her. Her tears had infuriated Hump Back Bear and he had pulled his knife, vowing he would kill Rafe rather than live without Summer Wind.

Rafe had backed away, unwilling to fight over a woman who had deceived him. But Hump Back Bear, who was beyond reason, would not be denied. With a furious growl, he had charged Rafe, his knife slashing wildly. Rafe had drawn his own weapon, but he had fought defensively, making no effort to attack the other man, until Hump Back Bear drew blood. Pain and the desire to live drove all else from Rafe's mind. He fought for his life then, using all the tricks his father had taught him in the back streets of New Orleans. It had saved his life, but it had cost him his place in the tribe.

He shook the memories from his mind, surprised to find he had fallen far behind the others. He was about to urge his horse into a trot when he heard the muffled sound of hoofbeats coming from behind. Reining his horse to a halt, he turned in the saddle, frowning when he saw Caitlyn round a bend in the trail.

Caitlyn gave a sharp tug on the reins when she saw Rafe. Then, realizing she had been seen, she lifted her chin defiantly and gigged her horse forward.

"Aren't you supposed to be waiting at home?" Rafe inquired with a wry grin.

Caitlyn shrugged. He knew the answer to that as well as she did.

"You don't mind very well, do you?"

"What business is that of yours?"

"None," Rafe admitted easily. "None at all. He rubbed a hand over his jaw as he glanced down the trail, and then returned his gaze to Caitlyn. "I don't think your pa will be too happy to see you."

"Probably not, but I intend to stay out of his way until tomorrow afternoon. By then it'll be too late to send me back."

"How are you gonna keep your presence here a secret until then?" Rafe asked curiously.

"I was hoping you'd mind your own business and keep your mouth shut," Caitlyn retorted, "although I guess that's asking too much."

"I won't say a word if that's the way you want it."

"Well, good," Caitlyn said, unable to believe her good fortune.

"Just one thing. What are you gonna do about dinner? And where were you planning to spend the night?"

"I've missed meals before," Caitlyn replied, regretting that she had forgotten to pack a lunch. "And I'll just bed down under a tree."

Rafe nodded. She had spunk. He had to give her credit for that, even if she didn't have much sense. Apparently little things like wild animals, cold nights, and the fact that she was unarmed hadn't occurred to her.

"Well, guess I'll see you tomorrow," Rafe remarked. "I hope chasing a bunch of mustangs turns out to be everything you hoped for."

Me, too, Caitlyn thought to herself as she watched Rafe put his horse into a lope, *because my father is going to be madder than a wet hen when he finds out I'm here.*

Brenden stayed on the trail until dusk, and then he and the cowhands made camp in a sheltered draw out of the rising wind. They would reach Big Sully Meadow just before dawn tomorrow when the herd came to drink. Wylie couldn't have found the herd at a better time, Brenden mused as he poured himself a cup of coffee. If they were lucky, the herd would bring enough to pay off that bank loan with some left over for needed repairs on the ranch. Yessir, maybe his luck had finally changed.

Rafe kept to himself, spreading his bedroll away from the other men. After a quick meal of bacon, red beans, and sourdough bisquits, he rolled into his blankets, his arms crossed behind his head, and gazed up at the sky, his thoughts on other nights when he had slept beside a cosy fire under a blanket of stars. He could hear Carmichael's men talking around the campfire, reminiscing about other roundups and other herds, laughing as they recounted the exploits of top hands they had known in the past.

The Indians had liked to reminisce, too. They had discussed old battles and old friends. Sometimes they had told stories of how the earth was created. As a young boy, he had been fascinated by the Indians belief that bears had once been men, but because they were too lazy to endure the rigors of human life, they had chosen to be transformed into animals. The scariest tale his father had told him had been of *Uktena*, who was the incarnation of evil and had the attributes of the snake, the deer, and the bird. *Uktena* was a great snake, his father had told him, as big around as a tree trunk, with horns on its head, and a bright blazing crest on its forehead. It had scales that glittered like sparks of fire. It was believed that just seeing *Uktena* could bring misfortune; smelling its breath meant certain death.

Gradually, the talk around the campfire died down as the men sought their blankets and a good night's sleep.

Rafe remained awake long after the fire was out and the other men were snoring. Every time he closed his eyes, he pictured Caitlyn huddled under a tree somewhere down the trail, hungry, cold, and alone. He thought of *Uktena*, and wondered if a similar monster lurked in the tales her father had told her.

Time and again, he told himself she was none of his concern. He'd had his fill of women and he had no intention of getting involved with the boss's headstrong daughter. Nevertheless, it wasn't long before he found himself walking quietly through the dark night, a blanket draped over his shoulder, a couple of cold sourdough bisquits wrapped in a kerchief he had slipped from the neck of a soundly sleeping Brenden Carmichael.

He'd gone about a mile and a half when he heard the soft whinny of a horse. Pausing in mid-stride, his eyes searched the darkness until he saw the silhouette of a horse outlined against the night sky.

Caitlyn shivered as a gust of wind swept over her. Though she had donned her extra shirt and jacket and wrapped the saddle blanket around her shoulders, she was still cold—and frightened. More frightened than she had ever been; more frightened than she dared admit. She had slept outdoors before, of course, but always with her father nearby. The friendly darkness of those times did not seem so friendly now, when she was alone. Cold and hungry and alone.

She jumped a little as the lonely wail of a wolf cut across the stillness, felt her heart go cold in her breast as a tall, dark shape materialized out of the blackness of the night. Her mouth went dry as the creature came closer, closer. Her eyes were wide with fright and she opened her mouth to scream, only to find that her throat was too tight to make a sound.

She was certain she was about to meet some dreadful fate when she recognized Rafe Gallegher. Relief washed through her like water through a sieve and a deep sigh escaped her lips. But anger came hard on the heels of relief. "What are you doing prowling around out here in the dead of night?" she hissed. "You scared the daylights out of me."

"I'm glad to see you, too," Rafe muttered, tossing the blanket in her lap, then handing her the bisquits.

Caitlyn tucked the blanket around her, then quickly gobbled down one of the bisquits. No matter that it was cold and a little stale, she was famished.

She flushed with shame when she remembered her less than polite welcome. Rafe had brought her warmth and nourishment and she had behaved like a shrew.

"I'm sorry I snapped at you like that," she said contritely.

"Forget it." He hunkered down on his heels beside her, noting the way the moonlight caressed her cheek, the way the saddle blanket fell over her shoulders not quite concealing the swell of her breasts.

"You must be cold," Caitlyn remarked.

Rafe shrugged, as if it were of no consequence. In truth, just looking at her made him warm all over.

"Would you like to share the blanket?" Caitlyn asked, not meeting his gaze. "After all, you brought it."

Rafe hesitated. He was wearing a sheepskin jacket he had borrowed from Luther before they left the ranch so he wasn't really cold, but the thought of sharing Caitlyn's blanket was tempting, even though every nerve and fiber of his being warned him that she was trouble of the worst kind.

"Thanks," he said gruffly, and dropped down beside her. He knew immediately that it had been a mistake. The curve of her breast brushed against his arm as she made room for him under the blanket. His nostrils flared as he inhaled the sweet womanly scent of her, and his left thigh, barely touching her right thigh, tingled at her nearness. His eyes moved over her face and delighted in what they saw. He clenched his hands into tight fists to keep from reaching out to explore the delicate curve of her ear and the slender column of her throat.

Caitlyn stared straight ahead, all too aware of the man sitting beside her. The night surrounded them, hiding them in a cocoon of darkness. She did not have to look at Rafe to know the shape of his jaw, the color of his eyes. In the past few weeks she had memorized the lines and planes of his face, the color and texture of his skin. She was fascinated by his ruggedly handsome features, even as she was repelled by his Indian blood.

Once the bruises and swelling had disappeared, she saw that he was far more handsome than she had ever imagined. His eyes were dark, so dark she could not decide if they were black or dark dark brown. His brows were the color of ink and quite straight, his lashes short and thick. His nose was slightly crooked and she surmised that it had once been broken. His jaw was strong and square, his mouth full and wide. His skin was a dark reddish brown, clearly proclaiming his Indian ancestry. She wished that the fact that he was a half-breed didn't bother her so much, but it did.

Rafe slanted a look in Caitlyn's direction. She was staring straight ahead, her back straight, her body rigid, and he wondered if she was afraid of him.

"Do you want me to go?" he asked abruptly, prepared to leave her if she said yes.

"No, please," Caitlyn said quickly. She turned her head and found herself gazing into Rafe's eyes, those dark dark eyes that held secrets she yearned to know. "You were right," she admitted ruefully. "I should have come better prepared."

"Do you want me to take you home?"

"No." If she left now, she'd be admitting defeat and giving up her chance to see what might be the last wild herd in this part of the territory.

"I'll spend the night here if it will make you feel better," Rafe offered.

Caitlyn stared at him, shocked by his bold suggestion. No decent woman would spend a night alone with a man, especially when that man was not a relative, or even a close friend, but a stranger. And a half-breed as well. But then, it was a little late to worry about her reputation. He was already there and they were quite alone.

"Stay," Caitlyn murmured. "Please."

Rafe shifted his weight to a more comfortable position. "Why don't you get some sleep?" he suggested.

Caitlyn nodded, and resting her head against the tree trunk, she closed her eyes.

"That doesn't look very comfortable," Rafe remarked. Pulling the saddle blanket from her shoulders, he spread it on the ground next to him. "Lie down," he said. "You'll sleep easier."

Caitlyn did as he suggested, and Rafe tucked the other blanket around her.

"What about you?" Caitlyn asked.

"I'm fine."

"But . . ."

"Go to sleep," he urged. "It'll be morning soon."

Caitlyn nodded, obediently closing her eyes. She heard a rustle in the underbrush as some night creature went about its business, heard the far-off call of a coyote, but the sounds of the night no longer filled her with trepidation. Rafe was here and he would protect her.

In minutes, she was asleep, a faint smile touching her lips as a dark-skinned stranger with fathomless black eyes rode into her dreams and into her heart.

Rafe rested his head against the tree, all too conscious of the girl sleeping peacefully beside him. He was grateful for the breeze that fanned his heated flesh. Perhaps it would also cool his desire.

He watched the shadows play over her face, saw her lips curve into a faint smile. What was she dreaming about that made her smile with such pleasure?

As the night grew colder, she snuggled against him and it seemed like the most natural thing in the world when she rested her head in his lap. Of its own volition, his hand moved to her hair, his fingers threading through the heavy blond strands, while his other hand rested protectively on her shoulder.

Caitlyn slept peacefully, totally unaware of the riot of emotions her presence aroused in the man beside her.

CHAPTER
SIX

CAITLYN OPENED HER EYES SLOWLY, COAXED into wakefullness by a bright shaft of sunlight that had found its way through the leafy canopy above. Sitting up, she spread her arms wide and stretched, her muscles feeling stiff after spending the night on the hard ground.

A quick glance around revealed that she was alone and she felt a momentary sense of loss at Rafe's absence. His presence had been comforting when she woke during the night.

Rising, she saddled her horse. She was hungry and would have welcomed some of Web's sourdough biscuits and hot black coffee, but there was no point in fretting about that now. Big Sully Meadow and the wild horses were only a few miles away.

Swinging into the saddle, she put her horse into a trot, eagerly looking forward to the day ahead.

"Here they come," Wylie called softly, and Brenden, Nate Jackson, Hal Tyler, and Josh Turner, turned to look in the direction Wylie indicated. Sure enough, moving across the meadow toward the lake came a large herd of mustangs, lead by a big, rawboned chestnut mare.

Brenden smiled. All was going according to plan. Scott and four of the other cowhands, Wishful Potter, Rusty Jordan, Riata Jones, and Marty Davis, were positioned behind the incoming herd, downwind, ready to cut them off should they turn back the way they had come.

Rafe shaded his eyes as he watched the horses approach the lake. Most of the animals were mustangs, but scattered through the herd were a number of mares and foals that carried Arabian blood, as well as a couple of long-legged animals that bore the unmistakable stamp of a Thoroughbred. Rafe knew these animals were strays— horses that had wandered away from wagon trains headed westward—that others had been stolen by Indians and then had been lost or their riders killed in battle.

One animal in particular caught his eye. It was a sleek gray mare with dainty fox-like ears and the dished face peculiar to Arabians. She had a deep chest, good withers, a beautifully arched neck, and a magnificent head. He would have her for his own, he decided, no matter what the cost.

The last mustang to reach the lake was the stallion. He came prancing across the meadow, head high, tail swishing arrogantly, nostrils flared as he sniffed the wind.

"Now!" Brenden called, and the men broke from cover, shouting and swinging their lariats over their heads as they closed in on the herd.

The mustangs lined out in a dead run, heading away from the pursuing cowhands and down the winding, tree-lined trail that led back to the ranch.

Brenden grinned as he brought up the rear, pleased by the size of the herd, and the ease with which they had found it. The money he made from the sale of the mustangs would just about pay off the bank loan.

Rafe was riding at the front of the herd when they rounded a narrow bend in the trail. He felt his heart slam against his chest as he saw Caitlyn a short distance ahead. She was hunkered down beside her horse, apparently trying to dislodge a stone from the mare's hoof.

Rafe glanced over his shoulder, his insides going cold as he imagined Caitlyn being crushed by the oncoming herd.

Caitlyn's head jerked up as she heard the thunder of hoofbeats, felt the earth vibrate beneath her. She glanced over her shoulder to see Rafe bearing down on her, the wild herd close on his heels.

She reached for her mare's reins, but the animal reared up, its eyes showing white as the mustangs galloped toward them.

With an oath, Rafe slammed his heels into his mount's flanks and the game little cow pony shot forward. Leaning from the saddle, Rafe swept Caitlyn off the ground and rode hell for leather down the narrow path.

Bile rose in Caitlyn's throat as she looked over Rafe's shoulder and saw her horse stumble and go down beneath the stampeding herd. But for Gallegher's swift intervention, she, too, would have been crushed under hundreds of pounding hooves. Shuddering at the thought, she buried her face in Rafe's neck, clinging to him for all she was worth.

Dust filled her nostrils and the sound of drumming hoofbeats and the snorts and whinnies of the mustangs echoed in her ears, louder than the hammering of her own heart. She felt the heat of Rafe's arm around her waist, heard him mutter a vile oath as he urged his horse onward.

She gasped as she felt the horse stumble. Rafe gave a sharp tug on the reins, pulling the horse's head up, and the cow pony bunched its muscles and stretched out, belly to the ground.

Rafe held Caitlyn tight against him. He could feel her trembling in his arms and he asked his weary horse for another burst of speed, wanting to put some distance between himself and the herd.

They had gone about two miles when the trail widened and he saw a break in the trees. He reined his horse to the left, waving his hat in the face of the mustang that tried to follow him. In minutes, the herd had passed by.

Caitlyn was sobbing with relief when Rafe drew his horse to a halt beneath a towering oak. She felt his arm drop from her waist, but she didn't pull away. It felt good to be near him, to rest her head against his chest. After a moment, she felt his hand move in her hair.

As her sobs subsided, Caitlyn became aware of the rough texture of his buckskin shirt beneath her cheek, of the smell of dust and sweat that clung to him, the hard-muscled arm that had found its way back to her waist. But, most of all, she was aware of the way his thighs cradled her buttocks, the heat of him against her hips.

Embarrassed by the intimacy of their position, she drew away, reluctant to meet his eyes. After a few moments, she risked a glance at his face, felt her indignation rise when she saw he was smiling impudently, obviously aware of, and enjoying, her discomfort.

"I think you can put me down now," she snapped.

"Whatever you want," he replied obligingly, and grasping her forearm in his large brown hand, he lowered her to the ground.

It was then that Brenden rode up. "What the hell's going on here?" he demanded angrily. "Caitlyn, I thought I told you to stay home."

"I know, Pa, but . . ."

"Your foolishness cost us a damn fine horse, young lady," Brenden went on, his voice rising to match the color in his cheeks. "Perhaps you'd like to ride back and have a look at what's left?"

"No, Pa."

"You be quiet, miss!" Brenden yelled. His hard green gaze swung to Rafe. "What the hell happened?"

"Why ask me?"

"Because I've got a better chance of getting the truth from you than from that daughter of mine. Now, what the hell happened?"

"I saw Miss Carmichael coming on the trail as I rounded that last bend. Her horse panicked and I figured you'd rather have your daughter than the horse, so I grabbed Miss Carmichael and left the horse behind."

Brenden's lips twitched as he bit back a grin. "I guess you made the right decision."

"Pa!"

"I'll deal with you when I get home, miss," Brenden said curtly. "Gallegher, I'd appreciate it if you'd see my daughter safely home. Don't let her out of your sight. I reckon you'll make better time going home than we will, so tell Luther we're behind you and for Paulie to have the corral gates wide open. And tell Consuelo to have plenty of hot coffee ready."

Rafe nodded once to show he understood, and Brenden rode off down the trail after bestowing one last furious glance at his daughter.

There was going to be hell to pay when her father got home, Caitlyn mused bleakly, and she had no one to blame but herself.

"You ready to go?" Rafe asked.

Caitlyn nodded, and Rafe reached down and lifted her into the saddle in front of him. "We can take a shortcut through the trees," she said, pointing to a narrow deer trail off to their right.

Rafe grunted softly as he reined his horse toward the trail. It was much too narrow to allow for the passage of more than one horse at a time, but it was a pretty little path, lined on both sides with oaks and pines whose leafy branches formed a canopy overhead.

They rode without speaking, Caitlyn feeling horribly humiliated because her father had scolded her as if she were a naughty child and in front of Rafe Gallegher, of all people.

Some of her anger evaporated as she thought of Rafe. She was, she knew, spending far too much time and energy thinking of him, but she couldn't seem to stop. There was something about him that appealed to her, though she could neither understand nor define it. But one thing was clear: Whatever the attraction was, strong as it was, it had to stop. He was a half-breed, a man she knew nothing about other than his name. And in a little over a year, he would be gone.

They reached the ranch late in the afternoon. Paulie's face was stern when Caitlyn told him what had happened to her horse. She felt a twinge of guilt as she left the barn, knowing that Paulie was going to catch hell, too.

"Is your pa far behind?" Paulie called, following after her.

"They'll be in late," Rafe said, answering

for Caitlyn. "Be sure to tell Luther and have the corral gates open."

Paulie nodded. He was not looking forward to Carmichael's return, or the tongue-lashing that was sure to come. He'd already been chewed out good by Luther, who had upbraided him more than once for not going after Caitlyn and bringing her back home.

"I guess you'll catch hell," Rafe mused, staring after Caitlyn.

Paulie shrugged. What was done, was done.

Caitlyn hurried toward the house. All she wanted now was a hot bath and a few hours' sleep in her own bed.

Consuelo scolded Caitlyn as they dragged the big iron tub into the kitchen, reprimanding the girl in English and Spanish for disobeying her father, for continually wearing pants when nice girls wore dresses, for riding astride, for not behaving like a lady.

Caitlyn had heard it all before and she sighed with relief when Consuelo finally left the room. Slipping out of her dusty trail garb, she stepped into the tub, smiling with pleasure as the hot water closed around her, its heat drawing the soreness from her muscles, relieving the tension of the past twenty-four hours.

Alone in the kitchen, Caitlyn closed her eyes and put everything from her mind. She knew her father would be angry when he returned home, and that he had every right to feel that way, but she refused to dwell on it now.

The hot water and the silence in the house relaxed her completely. She was almost asleep when she heard the back door open.

"Hand me a towel, will you?" Caitlyn requested, thinking it was Consuelo.

"Sure," came the reply.

Caitlyn's eyelids flew open at the sound of his voice. She flushed scarlet from head to toe when she saw Rafe Gallegher standing beside the tub, his teeth flashing in an amused grin. He was holding a towel in his brown-skinned hand, just out of reach.

"What are you doing here?" Caitlyn demanded, her voice shrill.

"I came in for a cup of coffee."

Caitlyn gazed up at him, her eyes imploring him to go away, her whole body tingling under his amused regard.

The smile faded from Rafe's face as he met Caitlyn's dismayed gaze. Her eyes were as green as new grass, her skin flushed. Her hair was pinned atop her head save for a few wayward strands that curled around her face.

He swallowed hard, sorely tempted to lift her from the tub and into his arms. He clearly remembered how good it had felt to hold her as they rode home. Her breasts had warmed his chest, and his body had responded to her nearness.

Caitlyn was trying not to remember what it had been like in Rafe's arms, but she could not forget the easy strength that had allowed him to pluck her from the ground, the strong arms that had held her, the broad chest where she had pillowed her head on the long way home.

For a long moment their eyes met and held. Caitlyn's breath was trapped in her throat, her pulse racing wildly as she waited, hoping and afraid.

Rafe kept his gaze on Caitlyn's face, knowing if he caught so much as a glimpse of bare flesh beneath the frothy bubbles he would do something they would both regret.

Expelling a ragged breath, he thrust the towel into her hand and left the house.

Caitlyn was sitting at the kitchen table later that night, her right hand curled around a cup of coffee gone cold, when she heard the sound of thundering hooves and the shouts of the men as they drove the mustangs into the corrals.

Rising, she went into the parlor and looked out the front window. Clouds of dust swirled under the horses feet as they were driven into the corrals. Foals whinnied for their dams, mares whickered to their young. The shrill scream of an enraged stallion cut across the din, combining with the hoots and calls of the cowhands as they chased the last of the horses into the holding pens and closed the gates. Paulie had strung several lanterns around the yard and Caitlyn saw Rafe leaning against a tree, his arms folded across his chest, a cigarette dangling from the corner of his mouth as he watched the excitement. Who was he, really? she wondered, and then she saw her father striding purposefully toward the house and she forgot all about Rafe Gallegher.

"Caitlyn!"

"Yes, Pa."

Brenden whirled around, his green eyes hard. "Am I wrong, or did I distinctly tell you to stay here?"

"You told me."

"Then would you mind explaining just what you were doing out on the trail? Do you realize you might have been killed? Dammit, Caitlyn, when I tell you to do something, I expect you to do it!"

She had no argument, and so she stood mute, guilty, defenseless, and ashamed.

Brenden's expression softened, and his voice lost its edge. "Dammit, Caitlyn, you're all I've got left in the world. I don't want to lose you, too."

"I know, Pa. I'm sorry."

He held out his arms and Caitlyn went to him, dropping her head on his shoulder as her eyes filled with tears.

Brenden patted Caitlyn's back, his hand heavy and awkward. If only Elizabeth had lived. He was constantly at a loss where Caitlyn was concerned. Consuelo did the best she could, but she was not Caitlyn's mother, only a hired housekeeper and cook. The real responsibility for his daughter's welfare rested solely with him, and he feared he was not doing a very good job. If only Caitlyn would marry Abner Wylie, settle down, have kids, at least then he'd feel as though his troubles were over. But Caitlyn had refused Wylie's proposal of marriage not once, but three times.

Brenden sighed. There was going to be a Fourth of July picnic and dance in town next week. Perhaps Caitlyn would finally meet a young man to her liking. Much as he loved his daughter, he was ready to turn her over to a younger man.

CHAPTER SEVEN

Rafe, Wylie, and Luther began culling the horse herd the following morning. Caitlyn paused in her chores to watch them from time to time, her eyes forever straying toward Rafe. As the morning wore on, he removed his shirt and her stomach did funny little flip flops every time she saw his sweat-sheened back and chest.

They had turned the stallion loose. He had been wild too long for them to tame now. The older mares had also been released with the stud. A few of the mustangs, those who were lame or sick, were destroyed. Caitlyn knew it was the merciful thing to do. If they were turned loose, they would likely die during the winter, pulled down by wolves. Still, it was hard for her to accept.

At the end of the day, only prime stock remained in the corrals. The mature horses would be broken to ride, and the foals and yearlings would be observed for a few months. The best ones would be kept; the others would be let go.

The next morning Rafe's work began. He roped the gray mare that had caught his eye and led her into one of the breaking pens located behind the house. From the kitchen window, Caitlyn watched him work the mustang. His technique was vastly different from Wylie's. Abner roped a horse, blindfolded it, climbed into the saddle, and then, using a weighted crop, sharp spurs and fear, he broke the animal to ride, often breaking its spirit as well.

But not Rafe. He spent the first morning letting the mare grow accustomed to his presence. He brushed her coat until it gleamed like silver satin, and then he ran his hands along her back and legs, over her withers and down her neck. He picked up each foot and checked her hooves for cracks, and then he rested his shoulder against her right flank and smoked a cigarette. The mare, short-tethered to a stout post in the center of the corral, stood still, her dainty ears twitching back and forth. She did not seem to be afraid now, only curious.

"You gonna break that mare or teach her to smoke?" Abner hooked his arms over the corral fence, his voice derisive, his expression insolent. "Hell, if it's gonna take you this long to break one horse, we'll still be topping these broomtails when the snow flies."

"Why don't you mind your own business, Wylie?" Rafe replied mildly.

"The ranch *is* my business," Abner retorted. He glared at Gallegher and when he spoke, his words were bitter. "Hell, I was head wrangler here until you came along."

"Maybe you weren't doing the job right."

"Why you dirty half-breed bas—"

Rafe was over the fence, his hands closing around the other man's throat, before Wylie had finished speaking.

"I'd be careful if I were you," Rafe warned, his voice low and filled with menace.

"Get your filthy hands off me!" Abner demanded. If he was afraid, it didn't show on his face.

Rafe's mouth turned up in a wry grin as he tightened his hold. "I'd keep a tight rein on that tongue of yours, or you might wake up one morning and find it gone."

"Is that a threat?"

"Call it anything you like." Abruptly, Rafe released his hold on Wylie and returned to the corral.

Caitlyn felt her breath catch in her throat as she saw Abner's hand hover over his gun butt. For a moment, she feared Abner would shoot Rafe in the back, but after a moment Abner turned on his heel and walked away.

It was only a matter of time, Caitlyn thought again, only a matter of time before the barely concealed antagonism between the two men exploded into violence.

The tension between Abner and Rafe was a tangible presence at the dinner table that night. Caitlyn glanced at her father, sitting at the head of the table, and knew that he felt it, too.

They were lingering over deep dish apple pie and coffee when Brenden put his cup aside and cleared his throat. "There seems to be some confusion here as to who's in charge of the horses," Brenden remarked. "Perhaps there's confusion in other areas as well. Hicks is the foreman. Whatever he says, goes. Gallegher's in charge of breaking the mustangs. I watched him work this afternoon, and I've got no complaints. Wylie, you're in charge of the cattle, and since that's your job, I suggest you take a couple of the men and ride into the hills tomorrow, make sure none of our cows or calves are caught in the scrub. Also, I want a couple of men to ride the west fence and check for breaks. Luther, get someone to ride upriver and make sure there aren't any trees or rocks blocking the flow. The river looks a mite low and it shouldn't be, not this time of year."

Brenden's gaze moved from man to man. "Any questions?"

"The gray mare," Rafe said. "I'd like to have her."

One of Brenden's eyebrows went up. "In exchange for the black mare?"

Rafe shook his head. Black Wind was worth three times what Carmichael would get for the gray.

Brenden grinned. "Can't blame a man for trying. You can have the mustang for whatever the Army's paying for remounts." Brenden glanced around the table. "Anything else? If not, I'm going outside for a smoke."

There was the scrape of chairs and boot heels and murmured good nights as the cowhands took their leave.

Moments later, only Caitlyn, Abner, and Rafe remained at the table. Abner glared at Gallegher, willing the half-breed to leave the room, but Rafe sat back in his chair, one hand folded around his coffee cup, apparently in no hurry to depart.

Heaving a sigh, Abner turned his back on

101

the other man and smiled at Caitlyn. "The Fourth of July dance is next week," he remarked.

Caitlyn nodded. She knew what was coming and she dreaded it. At the same time, she wondered why Abner didn't take the hint and leave her alone. He had proposed to her three times, and she had refused him three times and still he persisted.

Abner cleared his throat. "I was, uh, wondering if you'd care to go with me."

"I'm going with my father, as usual, Abner, but thank you for asking me."

Abner felt the heat crawl up the back of his neck and he cursed himself for asking Caitlyn to the dance when Gallegher was in the room. He could almost hear the half-breed laughing at him.

"I guess I'll see you there," Abner muttered. Rising, he grabbed his hat and jammed it on his head. "Night, Miss Carmichael."

Rafe grinned as Wylie left the house. "Sounds like Abner's sweet on you."

Caitlyn shrugged. Abner was "sweet on her" but it was not to her liking, and it was certainly none of Rafe Gallegher's business.

"This dance a big affair?"

"Yes," Caitlyn answered, fidgeting with her napkin. "There's always a town picnic and games and races and fireworks on the

Fourth and then a dance at the Grange Hall. Everybody goes."

Rafe nodded thoughtfully. He hadn't been to a picnic or a dance in over six years, at least not the kind of dance Caitlyn was referring to. The Indians had danced often. There had been rain dances, war dances, scalp dances, friendship dances, and dances only the women participated in. But there were no dances where a man took a woman in his arms and held her close, no slow waltzes that afforded a man a chance to tell a woman that she had eyes as deep and green as the Missouri.

He drew his gaze from her face. "Sounds like fun."

"Yes." She willed her hands to be still, wondering why his presence upset her so. She never had trouble talking to Paulie or Rusty Jordan or Wishful Potter. Why did Rafe Gallegher leave her tongue-tied and uncertain?

The Fourth of July dawned bright, clear, and warm. Caitlyn woke with a smile on her lips, eagerly looking forward to spending a day in town. It was a long ride, almost two hours, and she didn't often have an occasion to make the trip. Her father wouldn't let her venture that far from the ranch alone, and so she had to wait until her father or Luther rode in for supplies, which they only did every other month or so.

She dressed with care, choosing a bright blue print that complimented her hair, eyes, and figure. It was her favorite frock, saved for special occasions. She spent twenty minutes fussing with her hair and finally left it loose, tied away from her face with a wide blue ribbon. Her shoes came next and after a final look in the mirror, she grabbed a white bonnet adorned with red, white, and blue streamers and left her room.

Her father was already at the breakfast table, looking quite handsome in a crisp white shirt, black leather vest, and black trousers.

"Where is everybody?" Caitlyn asked, taking a seat across from her father. She said everybody, but she meant Rafe.

"They've already gone," Brenden replied. "Left about a half-hour ago."

Caitlyn nodded as she reached for the platter of bacon and eggs in the center of the table. Her father hadn't mentioned Rafe and she couldn't bring herself to ask about him.

Caitlyn felt a surge of excitement as her father turned the buggy down the town's main street. Flags were flying, the buildings looked festive draped in red, white, and blue bunting. Children were playing games in the school yard, and she could hear the Cedar Creek Firehouse Band tuning up.

Caitlyn smiled and waved at her friends as they drove down the street. Minutes later her father reined the team to a halt near the church. Vaulting to the ground, he helped Caitlyn out of the buggy.

"See you at noon," Brenden said, winking at her.

Caitlyn winked back, knowing her father would head straight for the saloon to visit with his cronies and drink a few beers.

Lifting the hem of her skirt, Caitlyn went to join a group of young people who were milling about a long table that was laden with cookies, pies, cakes, and punch. Her best friend, Christine Barrett, called and waved and the two girls hugged as though they hadn't seen one another for years, and then spent the next half-hour getting caught up on all the latest news.

Several times, Caitlyn was tempted to tell Christine about Rafe, but each time she changed her mind, knowing that Christine would be shocked to learn that her best friend was infatuated with a man who was a half-breed.

The morning passed pleasantly, with Caitlyn renewing old acquaintances. Several of the young men who lived in town came by to spend a few minutes with her, promising to see her later at the dance.

She ate lunch with her father and Christine and then spent the rest of the afternoon watching the games and races, laughing with delight as she watched the pie-eating contest and the three-legged race. The older boys chased a greased pig, and then attempted to climb a greased pole to claim the five-dollar gold piece at the top.

At dusk, there was a pot luck dinner, and then the dancing began. Caitlyn saw several of the Circle C cowhands on the dance floor. Josh Turner was all spruced up and smelled heavily of lilac water and whiskey. Josh fancied himself as quite a ladies' man and he always danced with every unmarried female present, be she nine or ninety. Caitlyn was no exception and she laughed merrily as he whirled her around the floor.

She saw Marty Davis standing near the door, his big Texas hat pushed back on his head, his hands jammed in his back pockets. He was too shy to dance, but he liked the music.

Scott waltzed by with his fiancé, Naomi Wells. They made a striking couple, and Caitlyn looked forward to the day when they would marry and Naomi would move to the Circle C.

She saw her father glide by, a wide smile on his face as he looked down at the woman in his arms. Belinda Crocker was lovely, with dark chestnut hair and luminous brown eyes. Caitlyn knew her father stopped to visit Belinda whenever he was in town, and she also knew that Belinda hoped he would ask for her hand in marriage, but it would never happen. Her father had loved once and he would never love again.

Caitlyn danced with Rusty, and with Web, who was mighty spry despite his sixty-two years. She danced with her father, and with Hal Tyler, and even with Paulie, who rarely danced with anyone.

Luther did not dance, and neither did Wishful Potter. They stood side by side at the bar, each holding a foaming glass of beer in one hand and a fat black cigar in the other.

She saw Christine and waved at her as she twirled by. Christine was dancing with Riata Jones, one of the newer hands at Circle C, and they appeared to be having a wonderful time, spinning around the floor, laughing together as they went faster and faster. Christine smiled up at her partner and it was plain to see that she found him attractive. Perhaps Christine had finally found the man she was looking for, Caitlyn mused, though it was doubtful Christine's father would think a hired hand was worthy of his only daughter. Thornton Barrett owned the Cedar Creek Bank. They lived in the biggest house in town, gave the most lavish parties, and never bought anything unless it was the best.

Caitlyn lost sight of her friend in the crowd, and then she forgot about Christine as several of the young men she had seen earlier in the day came to claim a dance. Caitlyn gave each of her partners her full attention, laughing at their jokes, smiling at their compliments, and wondering if any of the men she danced with would one day be her husband. It seemed unlikely. Oh, they were all nice and polite, most were handsome enough, and they all had steady jobs in town, but none of them stirred her heart or warmed her blood the way Rafe did.

Rafe. As if summoned by magic, he appeared at her side to claim the next dance.

Caitlyn followed him onto the dance floor, bewitched by his nearness and his appearance. It was evident he had gone shopping earlier in the day. His buckskins were gone and in their place he wore a black silk shirt, tight black pants, and black boots. His hair, though still long enough to brush against his shirt collar, had been neatly trimmed. He did not wear a tie and his shirt collar was open, revealing a narrow vee of sun-bronzed skin.

Caitlyn cast about for something to say, but all she could think of was how devastatingly handsome Rafe looked. The black shirt was a perfect foil for his dark hair, ebony eyes, and swarthy skin.

With his arm around her waist, he guided her effortlessly around the dance floor, surprising her again, for he danced divinely, his steps light and smooth.

Rafe's teeth gleamed as he grinned down at Caitlyn. Her thoughts were as transparent as glass, and he was strangely flattered by her obvious approval at the change in his appearance. The fact that women found him attractive was something he had discovered long ago in New Orleans, though he had never given it much thought. Still, there had been distinct advantages to being tall, dark, and handsome—even when the dark part was caused by his Indian blood—the major advantage being that he had always had his pick of women along the waterfront.

Of course, it was that same dark appearance that made him unacceptable to the so-called nice ladies in town. They had shunned him on the streets, drawing their skirts aside as though touching him might bring disgrace. But he had seen the secret glances, the covert admiration when they thought no one was watching, and he knew they found him desirable, partly because of his appearance, and partly because he was forbidden.

He had occasionally seen a similar expression of desire in Caitlyn's eyes when she looked at him. He had burned with silent rage when other women looked at him like that, the longing in their eyes mixed with contempt. But Caitlyn was different. No matter how she felt about him deep inside, no matter if she harbored feelings of hate or revulsion, no hint of it ever showed on her face or in her voice and he was indebted to her for that, if nothing else.

Caitlyn was still searching for something witty or clever to say when the music ended. There was a brief pause and then the musicians began playing a slow waltz.

"May I?" Rafe asked, and without waiting for her reply, he swept her into his arms again.

They danced effortlessly, as if they had been dancing together all their lives. He held her just a little closer than was proper, enjoying how she felt in his arms, the pleasure that radiated from her eyes as they circled the floor, the way the lamplight turned her hair to liquid gold. She was like a feather in his arms, easily following his lead no matter how complicated the steps, her head tilted back so she could see his face, her lips curved in a smile that was his alone. He caught the faint fragrance of wildflowers in her hair, felt his desire stir at her nearness.

Caitlyn was wishing the waltz would last forever when the music ended and Abner

Wylie appeared at her side requesting the next dance.

"It's taken," Rafe said brusquely, then slid a glance in Caitlyn's direction to see if she had any objections. She didn't.

"The next one, then?" Abner persisted, ignoring Caitlyn's partner.

"They're all taken," Rafe said, his dark eyes issuing a challenge.

Caitlyn stared up at Rafe. *The gall of the man*, she thought indignantly, and yet, she was flattered, too, and relieved that she wouldn't have to dance with Abner after all.

Abner's face was livid as he turned on his heel and headed for the bar. He stood there, a drink in his hand, glaring at Caitlyn and Rafe.

Rafe was as good as his word. He stayed close to Caitlyn the rest of the evening, claiming her for every dance. Caitlyn overheard bits of gossip as the tall, dark-skinned man monopolized all her time. She saw the other single men watching Rafe, their eyes filled with confusion and disapproval, and she studied Rafe through the veil of her lashes, trying to see him as the men saw him. His incredible good looks were what she saw first and foremost. But then, looking past that, she saw the hardness in his face, the hint of violence that lurked behind his outwardly calm facade. It occurred to her that a

111

wise man would not make an enemy of Rafe Gallegher.

Once she caught Christine's eye, and saw her friend raise an inquisitive brow. Caitlyn smiled and shrugged.

Later in the evening she saw her father watching her with a speculative gleam. Rumors would be flying tomorrow, Caitlyn mused. The fact that she had spent the entire evening in the company of one man would no doubt be the main topic of conversation at every breakfast table in Cedar Creek.

At intermission Caitlyn and Rafe stood near the open doorway, waiting for the music to begin again. Then Rafe stepped in front of her. "Shall we go outside?" he asked, his voice low, intimate.

His eyes lingered on her mouth and Caitlyn felt her throat go suddenly dry. *He wants to kiss me*, she thought, flustered by the mere idea. *What shall I do?*

She could feel a quick heat climbing up her neck, staining her cheeks, and she was glad Rafe was standing in front of her so no one could see her face. She wanted to go outside with him, wanted to feel his arms close around her, to discover once and for all what it would be like to feel his lips on hers.

She wanted it very much, and he knew it. She could see the knowledge dancing in his eyes, in the slight curl of his mouth as he waited for her reply, certain she would say yes. His smug self-assurance piqued her anger.

"No, thank you," she replied coolly. "I'd rather stay in here."

"Liar."

The softly spoken word hung between them. Caitlyn lifted her chin and pursed her lips, irritated because he could read her thoughts so well.

"Excuse me," she said politely. "I think I'll go join my father and Miss Crocker."

"And I think you'll stay here."

She was about to argue with him when the music started. He did not bother to ask her permission this time, but swept her into his arms and out onto the floor.

He was insufferable, Caitlyn thought with a slight shake of her head, but she could think of no place she'd rather be than in Rafe Gallegher's arms as he twirled her around the dance floor. She liked the feel of his arms about her, the masterful way he executed the steps of the polka, the way he smiled down at her, his eyes filled with unspoken promises. His nearness made her heart beat fast and left her feeling breathless, as if she were on the brink of some exciting new discovery. She was sorry now that she had refused to go outside with him.

As the thought crossed her mind, she

caught Rafe's amused gaze. *I know what you're thinking*, his eyes seemed to say. *It isn't too late to take a stroll in the moonlight.*

She was glad when the song ended and the musicians broke into the Virginia Reel.

Too soon it was the last dance. Caitlyn followed Rafe's lead as they waltzed around the room, unaware of the picture they made as they glided across the floor: Rafe, tall and dark and handsome; herself, blonde and slim and radiant. They executed the steps of the waltz as though they had been dancing together for years instead of only one night.

It was the best Fourth of July she could remember, certainly the best dance, even though her partner had not spoken more than a few dozen words the whole night long.

She was about to ask Gallegher where he had learned to waltz so well when she felt his arm stiffen around her waist. He came to an abrupt halt, and it was then that Caitlyn saw Abner Wylie coming toward them, a surly expression on his face. It was evident he had been drinking, and drinking heavily. His eyes were red-rimmed, his steps unsteady.

"Mind if I cut in?" he asked, his words slurred and thick.

"She's with me," Gallegher said curtly.

"What's the matter, *Miss* Caitlyn," Wylie said, his tone insolent. "Ain't I good enough to dance with ya, or have you developed a

114

taste for darkies since this here 'breed came to work for yore pa?''

The couples dancing nearby gasped at Wylie's rude comment. The men, expecting trouble, quickly led their partners off the dance floor.

Caitlyn's cheeks heated with embarrassment. She glanced up at Rafe to see what effect Abner's crude remark had had on him and knew that Abner was as close to death as he had ever been. Rafe's face was dark with barely suppressed rage, his eyes narrowed to angry slits. He still had his arm around her waist, and it was as hard and unyielding as tempered steel.

There was a sudden hush in the hall as the musicians fell silent and now Caitlyn, Rafe, and Abner stood alone in the middle of the floor, a grim tableau in the midst of the brightly colored streamers and balloons that decorated the hall.

For the first time, Caitlyn understood why all the men were required to check their guns at the door.

"You will apologize to Miss Carmichael now," Rafe told Abner, biting off each word, "or you will accompany me outside."

"Apologize for what?" Abner asked with a sneer. "I just asked a simple question." Abner's gaze shifted to Caitlyn. "All I wanted was one dance," he whined. "You didn't have any objections to dancing with me last year."

"You weren't drunk then," Caitlyn replied, conscious of the crowd looking on.

"I wasn't drunk when I asked you earlier tonight, neither," Abner said, swaying.

Caitlyn looked at Rafe, and then back at Abner.

"I got no hard feelings against you, Miss Caitlyn," Abner said. "I just want to know why you're letting this half-breed make your decisions for you."

"I'm dancing with Mr. Gallegher because I wish to," Caitlyn retorted. She was angry now, furious with Abner for creating a scene. She clenched her hands at her side, wishing she had the nerve to slap Abner's face. Releasing an exasperated sigh, she glanced past Abner and saw her father striding toward her. Just what she needed, she thought irritably, another man!

Brenden came to an abrupt halt a few feet from where Caitlyn stood between the two men, and then he turned on his heel and returned to the sidelines. It was obvious that Rafe Gallegher didn't need any help, and from the look in Caitlyn's eye, neither did she.

"I'm waiting for that apology," Rafe said curtly.

"I'm sorry if I offended you, Miss Caitlyn," Abner said sarcastically, "but if you prefer dancing with this breed to dancing with decent folks, then I guess you're not the lady I thought you were."

Rafe's jaw tightened. His right arm fell away from Caitlyn's waist and before anyone in the room realized what was happening, he slammed his fist into Wylie's smirking face and knocked him out cold.

Then, as if nothing untoward had happened, he took Caitlyn by the arm and lead her off the dance floor. When they reached her father, Rafe lifted Caitlyn's hand to his lips and kissed it.

"Thank you for a lovely evening," he said. His eyes left hers and sought Brenden Carmichael's. "Do I still have a job?"

Brenden grinned. "For as long as you want it."

Rafe nodded, and then, without a backward glance, he walked out of the hall.

CHAPTER EIGHT

ABNER QUIT THE FOLLOWING MORNING AND Brenden accepted his resignation without an argument, saying only that Abner was welcome to stay on. But Abner refused. He had been humiliated before Caitlyn and half the town the night before and he had a large bruise on the side of his jaw as a constant reminder of that.

Brenden watched Abner stalk out of the house, knowing he probably should have fired Gallegher and kept Abner on the payroll. After all, Abner had been a part of the Circle C for several years. But Rafe Gallegher had the black mare, and as long as Gallegher was around, there was always a chance he would change his mind about selling the horse.

Caitlyn was glad to see Abner go. Wylie had never made any secret of the fact that he wanted her. His desire had burned deep in his pale blue eyes whenever he looked at her. She knew her father had been in favor of the match, but she could never warm up to Abner. The thought of his touch repelled her, the idea of becoming his wife was repugnant.

Brenden favored Gallegher with a speculative look as they sat down to breakfast later that morning. "You have any experience with cattle?"

Rafe shook his head. "Not much."

"Learn," Brenden said curtly. "Wylie was a top hand. You'll have to take his place if the boys need help."

Rafe nodded. "You're the boss."

"I wish more people around here would remember that," Brenden muttered. With a nod at Caitlyn, he grabbed his hat from the back of his chair and left the house.

Caitlyn stood up, prepared to leave the room, when Rafe caught her by the arm. "Can we talk?"

"About what?"

"Last night. I'm sorry for what happened."

Caitlyn shrugged. "Why should you be sorry just because you ruined my evening and made a scene in front of all my friends?"

Rafe's mouth thinned as he heard the sarcasm in her voice and Caitlyn felt a prick of guilt. Rafe hadn't been the one at fault. It had been Abner. But before she could examine her reasons for snapping at Rafe, he stood up, his eyes hard.

"If you wanted to dance with Wylie, why didn't you say so? I thought I was doing you a favor."

"Is that why you danced with me all night?" Caitlyn retorted. "To do me a favor?"

Rafe snorted, as if the question didn't deserve an answer.

"It was a dance," Caitlyn said. "You might have let me dance with someone besides you." Even as she spoke the words, she knew she was protesting too much. She had enjoyed dancing with Rafe. Once he had taken her in his arms, she had forgotten any other man in the room existed.

"Who'd you want to dance with?" Rafe asked, his voice slightly mocking. "Web? Wishful? Or that shy Texan? What's his name?"

"Marty Davis." She was breathless suddenly without knowing why. Rafe was still holding her arm and she took a step back. He released her, and she took another step backward, her eyes wary. Why was he looking at her like that, his eyes dark and amused? She took another step away from him, and then another. Too late, she realized he had maneuvered her into a corner.

Trapped, she drew herself up to her full height, her heart pounding as though she had just run a hundred miles uphill. His face filled her line of vision, blocking everything else from sight. She gave a little start when he reached out to draw her close, his strong arm imprisoning her waist while his other hand caressed her shoulder and slid provocatively down her arm.

And then he kissed her, a deep sensual kiss that drove all rational thought from her mind. She felt the length of his body against hers, hard, lean, and aroused. The evidence of his desire sent little tremors skittering down her spine and made her blood sing a song she had never heard before.

Her lips parted as she gasped for air and his tongue slid into her mouth. A quick heat flooded her being, as if the sun had exploded within her.

She felt lost when his mouth left hers, lost and confused. And shamelessly yearning for more.

Slowly, she opened her eyes.

He was grinning at her, his expression smugly satisfied. "I've been wanting to do that since last night," he admitted.

"Have you?"

He frowned at the glacial tone of her voice, the icy gleam in her eye.

"What's the matter? Didn't you like it?"

"Of course not," she lied, hoping to hang onto her dignity.

"Like hell! You've been wondering what it would be like for weeks."

"I have not!" she exclaimed, mortified that he had seen through her veneer of indifference so easily.

"Well, I have," he retorted.

He was still holding her close, and she was sorely tempted to ask him if he had enjoyed kissing her as much as she had enjoyed being kissed. His nearness and his mocking gaze made her extremely uncomfortable. She felt her heart slam against her chest as his gaze moved to her lips, felt her pulse race in anticipation. Without realizing it, she moved a little closer to him, lifting her head to give him easy access to her mouth.

Rafe grinned. Dropping a quick kiss on her forehead, he released her and walked briskly out of the room.

Caitlyn stared after him, his footsteps ringing in her ears, the taste and touch of his lips indelibly printed on her own.

Consuelo entered the room then, but Caitlyn was hardly aware of the other woman's presence, hardly aware of her surroundings, so shaken was she by Rafe's kiss, and her reaction to it.

Going to her room, she went to the window and gazed out, her glance automatically going toward Rafe who was working with one of the horses. She stood there for a long time, unaware of the passing minutes as she watched him swing a saddle onto a raw-boned buckskin mare, then vault effortlessly into the saddle. The horse began to buck as soon as it felt the man's weight, but Rafe stuck to the saddle like glue, his long black hair whipping about his face, his denim-clad thighs clamped around the horse's barrel. Caitlyn stared at Rafe, unable to draw her eyes away. His blue cotton work shirt clearly outlined the hard muscles in his back and arms. Sweat dampened the shallow valley between his shoulder blades.

It was a glorious battle, a battle of wills between a wild, range-bred mustang and a strong-willed man. The horse bucked and pitched for all it was worth, but in the end it stood subdued in the center of the corral, its head hanging, its heaving sides lathered with thick yellow sweat.

Caitlyn smiled as Rafe reached down to pat the weary buckskin on the neck, soothing the animal after its gallant effort.

Dismounting, Rafe led the mare from the corral; removing the saddle and blanket, he walked the horse up and down in front of the corral until it had cooled down. Then, with quick, deft strokes, he curried the horse until its coat was as smooth and shiny as polished bronze.

He had a way with horses, Caitlyn mused. And with women.

In the next few days, it seemed to Caitlyn that no matter where she went, Rafe was there. He was present at meals, of course, but, more than that, he turned up at other places, as well. If she went for a walk along the river, he was there. If she went to the barn to curry Red, Rafe was inside, mending a bridle or talking to Paulie or brushing Black Wind. If she sat on the porch at the end of a long day, she could be certain that, sooner or later, Rafe would join her.

His constant presence was unsettling, compelling, invigorating, and he was unfailingly polite. He never made a pass at her, never said anything remotely suggestive, and yet the tension between them was unmistakable. Each time he passed close to her, she felt her insides quiver in the most disturbing way. She waited for him to try and kiss her again so she could rebuff him with a scathing remark, but he never presented her with the opportunity. Perversely, that made her angrier, more anxious.

Each evening he bid her a polite good

night as she went to her room, and the sound of his voice and the promise in his eyes followed her down the hall like a shadow, infiltrating her thoughts as she prepared for bed, invading her dreams so that she often woke feeling warm and restless.

Wanting to get away by herself, she saddled one of the horses and rode away from the house early one Sunday morning. It was a beautiful day, warm and clear, and Caitlyn felt a sense of well-being as the mare trotted along. Occasionally, they passed a few head of cattle and once she saw a skunk nosing around a berry bush.

When she reached the pool at the far end of the valley, Caitlyn reined the mare to a stop and dismounted. After tethering the horse where it could nibble on the lush summer grass, she sat down near the edge of the pool to pull off her boots and stockings and let her bare feet dangle in the cool water.

It was a lovely spot. The pool was blue-green and clear, surrounded by trees and flowering shrubs.

Heaving a sigh, she fell back on the grass. Overhead, the leaves of the trees shaded her face like a lacy green umbrella, and she closed her eyes, letting the peaceful quiet soothe her.

She had been there only a few minutes when the sound of a splash brought her upright. Thoughts of wild Indians filled her mind and she hurriedly glanced around, fearful of what she might find.

But it was only Rafe, swimming in the water, his arms cutting through the water with long, clean, powerful strokes. He hadn't seen her yet, and she watched him with mingled feelings of pleasure and irritation. She had ridden away from the house to avoid him, yet she was not sorry he was there. Her insides fluttered with anticipation at his nearness and she was suddenly impatient for him to notice her.

As though sensing her gaze, Rafe turned his head toward her. She saw the recognition in his eyes as he changed direction and began swimming easily for the shore until he was only a few feet away.

Caitlyn watched him stand up in the waist-high water, her gaze drawn to his chest where rivulets of water coursed down his taut bronze flesh. The light sprinkling of curly black chest hair narrowed to a thin line before it disappeared from her sight beneath the water.

Shocked at the direction of her gaze and the images forming in her mind, she glanced up to find Rafe smiling at her.

"What are you doing here?" Caitlyn snapped, furious at the way her heart lurched and her pulse raced whenever he was near.

"Swimming," he retorted. "Do you mind?"

Caitlyn made a very unladylike sound of disgust. "Of course not. Why should I mind? It's just that you seem to be following me."

"Really?" Rafe planted his fists on his hips as he flashed her a roguish grin. "I thought *you* were following me."

"Don't be absurd!"

He shrugged, and she thought what an engaging picture he made standing there in the blue-green water with the bright azure sky behind him. She wished fleetingly that she were an artist so that she might capture his likeness on canvas, for she was certain she had never seen anything more beautiful, or more arrestingly male, in her life.

"You might as well come out and dry off," Caitlyn invited ungraciously.

"I don't think so."

"Why not?"

"Because I'm not wearing anything but water."

Caitlyn's face turned five shades of red as her imagination went suddenly wild.

"My clothes are across the way," Rafe remarked, amused by her stricken look. "If I go get dressed, will you still be here when I get back?"

"Of course," Caitlyn said. In truth, she wanted very much to flee, but she couldn't let Rafe think she was afraid of him.

He threw her a smile that seemed to say he didn't believe her before he turned and dove into the water. She watched him cross the pool, admiring the smooth natural way he moved through the water, the way the sunlight glinted in his thick black hair. She quickly lowered her head when he reached the other side and then, unable to help herself, she lifted her gaze in time to see him step onto the shore. His legs were long and straight, his buttocks small and firm, his back long and smooth, his shoulders broad and muscular.

A curious longing took hold of her as he moved out of sight behind a tree, and she had a sharp recollection of his kiss in the dining room only a few days earlier. What was happening to her?

A short time later he reappeared, mounted on the gray mustang. He rode the way he swam, she mused, easily and naturally, as though he had been doing it all his life. He was dressed in tight denim pants, a dark blue cotton shirt, and a black hat and she thought she had never seen anything more wonderful than Rafe Gallegher cantering toward her on the high-stepping mare.

Smiling, he reined his horse to a halt and swung agilely to the ground. "Still here, I see."

"I said I would be, didn't I?"

Rafe nodded. He was drawn to her in spite of all his intentions not to get involved with another woman. She was like a prickly pear, he thought, ripe for the taking but surrounded by thorns. With a sigh, he dropped down on the grass beside her, then stretched out on the ground, his hands clasped behind his head.

Caitlyn remained seated, her hands in her lap, her whole body tense at his nearness. No other man had ever affected her so, especially a man she knew so little about. She thought of what she did know: his name, the fact that he had lived with Indians, and nothing more.

"Who are you, Rafe Gallegher?" she asked. She glanced at him over her shoulder. "Who are you, really?"

"You know my name. What else do you need to know?"

"Where's your family? Are they still living?"

"My mother's dead. She died soon after I was born. My father is living with the Lakota. I have an Indian stepmother, and a five-year-old sister named Yellow Flower."

"Are you . . . have you . . . do you have a woman?"

Summer Wind's image flitted across his mind—her hair as black as onyx, her eyes so dark and beautiful, her sweet, lying lips. "No."

"You never told me why you left the Indians."

"Didn't I?"

"No."

"It's a pretty day," Rafe observed, changing the subject.

Caitlyn frowned at him, but she could see by the look on his face that he wasn't going to tell her why he'd left the Sioux.

Rafe sat up, stretching, and Caitlyn watched the play of muscles in his arms and shoulders. She clearly remembered those arms around her, waltzing her across the dance floor, holding her tight as he kissed her.

"Where did you learn to dance so well?" she asked, breaking the silence between them.

Rafe smirked wryly. "A madam in a whore-house back in New Orleans taught me," he answered, hoping such a shocking reply would make her keep her questions to herself.

"A madam?" Caitlyn croaked.

Rafe nodded. "Her name was Corinne, and she had the reddest hair I've ever seen." He chuckled. "She was a feisty woman, maybe sixty years old, and she'd been a madam for almost forty years."

"What else did she teach you?" Caitlyn asked, and then clapped her hand over her mouth, mortified by what she'd said.

One of Rafe's brows shot upward, and then he leaned toward Caitlyn, his dark eyes probing the depths of her soul. "Do you really want to know?"

Caitlyn shook her head vigorously. Scrambling to her feet, she ran for her horse and swung into the saddle. Lifting the reins, she pounded her heels against her horse's flanks and headed home.

Rafe's amused laughter followed her like the memory of a bad dream.

She saw the flames as soon as she topped the first rise. The barn was burning and she saw Paulie and Scott running in and out of the big double doors in an effort to rescue the livestock trapped inside. At least two dozen Indians were riding through the yard, their main goal the mustangs penned in the two corrals on the east side of the house. She quietly cursed the fact that the rest of the Circle C cowhands were out in the hills, checking the cattle.

Fear held her rooted to the spot for several minutes and when she finally summoned the nerve to ride closer, Rafe's voice stopped her.

"Stay here," he ordered tersely, withdrawing the Henry rifle from the boot of his saddle. "There's nothing you can do."

She would have protested, but he was already gone, riding hard for the house. The Indians had unlatched the corral gates now and the mustangs thundered through the gates, headed for the promise of freedom. The Indians followed the horses out of the yard, and the silence that followed in their wake seemed deafening.

Rafe turned his horse toward the barn, intending to help Paulie and Scott put out the fire, when he saw Carmichael lying near the front porch. He knew, even before he dismounted, that the owner of the Circle C was dead.

Caitlyn raced for home as soon as she saw the Indians riding away from the ranch. The loss of the herd seemed inconsequential when compared to the loss of the barn, the feed, and stock. She reined her mount to a dirt-scattering halt near the front of the house, and jumped from the saddle.

"Pa!" she called. "Pa, where are you?"

Seeing Rafe near the porch, she hurried toward him. "Rafe, have you seen my . . ."

The words died in her throat as Rafe stood up and turned to face her. She read everything she needed to know in his eyes. "No," she said, shaking her head as Rafe walked toward her. "No."

"I'm sorry, Caitlyn."

"No." She eluded his comforting hand and darted past him, her eyes growing wide when she saw the arrow lodged high in her father's back. "No!"

The last word was a sob, a heart-wrenching cry of denial.

"Caitlyn." Rafe placed his hand on her shoulder, knowing there was nothing he could say to comfort her.

"Don't touch me!" she shrieked, jerking away from his hand. "Don't you ever touch me again!"

Rafe recoiled from the hatred blazing in the depths of her deep green eyes.

"Indian!" She spat the word at him. "Your people killed my brothers and now my father. I hate you!" She shook her head, her eyes filled with loathing. And then, with tears streaming down her face, she dropped to her knees beside her father and drew his body into her lap. "Oh, Pa," she sobbed. "Oh, Pa. . . ."

Rafe watched her, his hands balled into tight fists. Her shoulders shook with the force of her tears and the sound of her cries tore at his heart. Pivoting on his heel, he walked toward the barn where Scott and Paulie were valiantly trying to put out the flames.

"Might as well let it burn," Rafe remarked. "It's past saving." He jerked a thumb in

Caitlyn's direction. "She needs you, Paulie. I'll look after things here."

"He's dead?" Paulie asked.

"Yeah."

"So's Luther." Paulie murmured as grief washed over his features. Luther had been like a father to Paulie, the only father he had ever known. With a heavy sigh, Paulie went to comfort Brenden Carmichael's daughter.

Caitlyn sat alone in the parlor, staring out the front window into the darkness beyond. The night was cold and black, like the room in which she sat, like the ache in her heart. Her father was dead. Luther was dead. Everyone she had ever loved was dead, and she was alone, so alone.

The tears came again and she was helpless to stay them. She had been sitting in the parlor for hours, just staring out the window. The barn had been destroyed, the milk cow and both draft horses had burned to death. All the mustangs had been stolen, including Rafe's gray mare. Luckily, Red, a couple of saddle horses, and Rafe's black mare had been saved.

Caitlyn laughed hollowly. What kind of luck was that, she mused bitterly, when horses were spared and people died? She would gladly have slaughtered every animal left on the place to have her father and

Luther alive.

Earlier, Scott, Paulie, and Rusty had loaded the blanket-draped bodies of her father and Luther into a wagon and taken them to Reitman's Funeral Parlor. Tomorrow, she would have to go into town and make arrangements for the funerals.

Tears burned her eyes and she pressed her forehead against the cool windowpane. "Oh, Pa," she sighed.

The cowhands had been stunned when they returned to the house that evening. They had offered their condolences, the words sticking in their throats, each of them thinking that Hicks and Carmichael might still be alive if more of the Circle C riders had been on hand to help fight the Indians.

Feeling the mantle of responsibility on her shoulders, Caitlyn had assured them that no one was to blame. They had been out doing their job. The burden of guilt lay on the heathen savages who had killed her father and Luther, killed them wantonly and in cold blood. Indians! She hated them all.

She had sent Rafe Gallegher packing earlier, and now she wondered if she had done the right thing. He had been an asset to the ranch; her father had liked and trusted him. But she could not bear the sight of him. He was an Indian, a constant reminder of how her brothers and father had died.

She closed her eyes and the memory of her brothers' deaths rose in her mind. How clearly she remembered that day! The Indians had come with the dawn, riding out of the east, with a blood-red sun at their backs and an ungodly shriek on their lips. They had struck quickly, lethally, stealing horses and cattle and killing six men. Arlo had been one of the first casualties; Morgan had been killed a short time later.

She recalled the sense of sadness and shock that had settled over the wagon train as six graves were dug, and six blanket-wrapped bodies were laid to rest in the bowels of the earth. A quick prayer had been said, and then they had moved on, fearful the Indians might return, but the rest of their journey had been uneventful. They had been bound for Oregon, but her father had fallen in love with the plains and they had settled there and life had been good. The Indians had never bothered them before. Yet now her father was dead.

Utterly weary, she drew the blanket around her shoulders and made her way to bed, only to lie awake for hours, wondering how she could go on. She could not hope to run the ranch alone but what else could she do? She couldn't sell it. Her father had loved this place, and so did she. Somehow, she would manage. Her father had never been a quitter, and neither was she.

Tomorrow, she would make Paulie the new foreman and have the men begin rebuilding the barn. Scott would have to take a couple of the hands and go into the hills and bring the cattle closer to home. Somehow, she would have to find a way to pay off the bank loan and she would have to go into town and arrange for her father's and Luther's funerals.

Reitman's Funeral Parlor was a small square building located at the far end of town. Caitlyn stood in the dreary office alone, her hands worrying a fold in her skirt as she tried not to think about what lay beyond the faded blue curtain.

Homer Reitman, a tall, somber man with dark gray hair and watery blue eyes, entered the office a few minutes later. Caitlyn could not help shivering as he invited her to take a seat. Somehow, she managed to choose caskets for her father and Luther, but it didn't seem real. None of it seemed real.

Leaving the funeral parlor, she went to speak to the Reverend Tobias Wilson about the funeral services. The minister was a kind and sympathetic man, sincere in his condolences, but she was relieved when the arrangements had been made and she could leave the small whitewashed church and step

138

out into the sunlight again.

She knew Mr. Reitman and the Reverend Wilson were being kind when they offered their sympathy, but the kind words, the gentle hugs, were almost more than she could bear. Her emotions were raw, close to the surface, and she was constantly fighting the urge to cry, to rail at fate, to close her eyes and hope that it was all a bad dream, a horrible nightmare that would end if she could only wake up.

Her head lowered to hide the tears that threatened to fall, she made her way down the boardwalk. She had not gone far when she bumped into someone. Looking up, she began to apologize.

"Well, well, if it isn't Miss Carmichael," Abner Wylie drawled, interrupting her in midsentence. "What brings you to town on this lovely day?"

She was in no mood to trade words with Abner Wylie. "Business," she said curtly. "Good day."

"Hold on a minute," Abner admonished, taking hold of her arm. "I heard about your old man. I'm sorry."

"Thank you." She glanced pointedly at his hand on her arm, but he didn't release her.

"What are you going to do now?" Abner asked solicitously.

"About what?"

"The ranch. Your old man's gone, and so's Luther. Who's gonna ramrod the place for you?"

"Paulie."

"Paulie!" He laughed, genuinely amused. "Paulie's a good man with animals, but he can't ride herd on the men. They'll walk all over him."

"I think he'll do fine and I'll be there."

"You? No self-respectin' cowboy is gonna work for a woman."

"There are several ranches in West Texas that are run by women," Caitlyn retorted. "And run quite well, too!"

"That's true," Abner agreed, "but those women aren't young and easy on the eye. They're women who grew up on ranches, married ranchers, and then took over after their husbands passed on. They aren't city girls who came West because their pa had itchy feet."

Caitlyn jerked her arm from Abner's grasp. "Good day, Mr. Wylie."

"Dammit, girl, will you listen to me for a minute?"

Caitlyn stopped in her tracks, not wanting to listen to Abner, but fearing she must, because what he had said so far was the truth.

Abner removed his hat and ran a hand through his hair. "You're gonna need a man

140

to help you run the place, and I'm offering to do the job."

"I have a foreman," Caitlyn reminded him.

"I'm not talking about being your foreman," he said. "I'm talking about being your husband."

"Husband!" Caitlyn exclaimed.

"Yes, ma'am. I'll make you a good husband, Caitlyn," he promised, "and I'll see that the ranch prospers."

Caitlyn stared at him, stunned by his offer. She was overcome with the urge to laugh and then, just as quickly, with the need to cry. She did neither.

"Thank you, Abner. I don't know what to say."

"Just say yes. You know I've always been sweet on you."

Caitlyn nodded, repulsed by the sudden flicker of desire that glowed in Abner's pale blue eyes.

"This is all very sudden," Caitlyn said at last. "I really can't think about it now. My father's and Luther's funerals are set for tomorrow morning, and I have a lot to do between now and then."

Abner nodded, certain she would accept his offer once she thought it over. Hell, what other choice did she have? "I understand."

Caitlyn held out her hand. "Good day, Abner."

He gave her hand a squeeze. "Think about what I said. You'll see it's the only answer."

Caitlyn nodded, then swept past him. Abner was right, she thought dismally. She *would* have to marry, and soon. But not him. Never him.

Brenden's funeral was well attended, for he had been well liked by his neighbors. He had been generous with his friends, willingly lending them whatever they needed, be it money or advice or feed to see them through a hard winter. He had been good to his hired hands, too, but as Caitlyn's gaze wandered over the Circle C cowhands, she wondered how long they would stay on. She was sure of Scott, Nate, and Rusty who had been with the Circle C since the beginning. And she knew Paulie would stay and Web. But what about the others? Hal Tyler, Wishful Potter, and Josh Turner. Riata Jones and Marty Davis had just signed on at the beginning of the year. Would they feel any loyalty to the brand, or was Abner right? Would the men quit rather than work for a woman?

She put such thoughts from her as the minister began to speak. He extolled Brenden Carmichael's virtues in glowing terms, neglected his vices, and commended his soul to heaven.

It was hard, standing there after the service was over, accepting the condolences of the mourners as they filed past. She fought back her tears as Belinda Crocker hugged her tight.

"We'll miss him," Belinda murmured.

Caitlyn nodded, unable to speak past the lump in her throat as the older woman patted her on the back. "I know it's hard to believe now," Belinda went on, "but there's better days ahead."

Caitlyn nodded again, and Belinda moved on as another of the townspeople came to shake Caitlyn's hand.

Abner was the last to pay his respects. He had dressed with care in a dark brown suit and striped cravat. His hair was slicked back, his boots were shined. Caitlyn had the distinct impression that he had purposefully hung back so that he might catch her alone.

"I'm sorry about your pa, Caitlyn," Abner said sincerely. "He was a fine man. I know how much you'll miss him."

"Yes, thank you, Abner."

"I know this isn't the proper time to bring this up, but I was wondering if you'd given any thought to what we talked about the other day?"

"Abner, please, I can't think about that now."

"Sure, sure, I understand." He took her hand in his and gave it a squeeze. "Call on me if you need anything. I'm staying here in town, over at Mabel's Boardinghouse."

"Thank you, Abner," she replied, wishing he would go away.

"Well, take care," he said, and settling his hat on his head, he walked down the hill, leaving her blessedly alone at last.

Caitlyn remained at the graveside long after everyone else had gone, bidding her father one last farewell. She also silently said good-bye to Luther. There had been no service for him. His wishes regarding a funeral had been found in his effects in the bunkhouse, and it had been his desire to be buried quietly, with no one in attendance other than the minister to bless the grave and say a final prayer for his soul.

Caitlyn brushed a tear from her cheek as she laid a primrose on her father's casket. "Rest well, Pa," she murmured. "I guess you're with Mother now. And Morgan and Arlo. I won't forget you."

Blinded by her tears, she turned away from the grave, then came to an abrupt halt as she saw a man striding toward her. It was Rafe Gallegher. She recognized his walk and the spread of his shoulders even before she saw his face.

Despite her vow to hate him forever, her heart felt a little lighter for the first time in three days.

Rafe nodded at Caitlyn as he closed the distance between them, his eyes taking in her tear-stained cheeks and red-rimmed eyes.

"I'm sorry, Caitlyn," he said quietly. "Is there anything I can do?"

She had sent him away with sharp words and a vow of everlasting hatred, and now he stood before her, hat in hand, offering his help. She stared up at him, at the dark bronze of his skin, the breadth of his shoulders, the strength in his arms, and she wished suddenly that she could rest her head on his chest and sob out all her sorrows, all her troubles and worries for the future. She knew intuitively that he would understand, that he could somehow turn wrong to right, but she remained rooted to the spot, the word "Indian" pounding in her brain.

Slowly, she shook her head. "I'll manage, thank you."

His jaw muscle twitched, and she regretted her brusque reply. He was being kind, and she had rewarded him with rudeness.

"I guess I'll be going then," Rafe remarked. "I just wanted to make sure you were all right."

"I'm fine," Caitlyn assured him but she wasn't fine. She was scared and alone.

Rafe nodded. She looked so small standing there, so vulnerable. The black dress out-

lined her tiny waist and full breasts, emphasized the pallor in her cheeks and the purple
shadows under her eyes. He had vowed never
to get emotionally involved with a woman
again, yet he was sorely tempted to draw
Caitlyn Carmichael into his arms and comfort her, to put himself between her and the
rest of the world so that she would never be
hurt again.

But he had offered his help and she had
turned him down flat. He couldn't really
blame her. Old hatreds and old hurts died
hard. When she looked at him, she didn't see
a man, all she saw was an Indian. And he
knew she'd never be able to forget that
Indians had killed her father and her brothers. He couldn't blame her, he thought
again, not really, but it hurt just the same.

He nodded in a gesture of farewell, and
then headed back toward town. He had
offered his help and she had refused it, and
that was that. When he reached the livery
barn, he'd saddle the black mare and ride
out of Cedar Creek.

Perhaps he'd go to California after all.

CHAPTER NINE

CAITLYN SAT AT THE HEAD OF THE KITCHEN table staring morosely into her empty coffee cup. The last two weeks had been the worst two weeks of her life. She had never really realized how much work was involved in running the ranch. Her father and Luther had handled everything so efficiently, she had never seen the hard work that went into their seemingly effortless decisions. Paulie tried hard, but after the first few days, she knew he wasn't cut out to ramrod the ranch. He lacked Luther's drive and authority. Already, the men were slacking off in their duties, letting little things slide, starting work later, leaving jobs undone, quitting early. She had discussed it with Paulie and he had spoken to the men, but nothing had changed.

No, Paulie wasn't qualified to run the ranch and neither was she. She knew she should turn the job over to Nate Jackson, but she lacked the courage to tell Paulie he had failed her.

The previous night, she had gone out to the bunkhouse and upbraided the men, reprimanding them for their sloppy work habits, insisting they do better, asking them to take pride in their work.

The cowhands had stared at her, shocked not only by her presence in the bunkhouse, which was strictly off limits to women, but by her words as well. Marty Davis and Riata Jones had quit on the spot, declaring they would not take orders or verbal abuse from a woman. Hal Tyler and Wishful Potter had started to leave, too, but then changed their minds, apparently willing to give her one more chance.

Two fat tears rolled down Caitlyn's cheeks. What was she going to do? There had been ten men on the payroll when she walked into the bunkhouse. Now two had quit. If Hal and Wishful decided to go, that would leave her with only six men. And she couldn't run the ranch with only six men. There were hundreds of cattle scattered over hundreds of miles, cattle that would have to be rounded up and herded closer to the house before winter came. The barn would have to be rebuilt, hay had to be put away to see them through the winter. There was a large leak in the kitchen roof that needed to be repaired before the rains came. There were fences to mend and crops to harvest. In the spring, there would be calves to brand and castrate, and she would have to find a buyer for the herd so she could pay off the bank loan.

A knock at the front door interrupted her dismal thoughts. She waited for Consuelo to answer the door, and then remembered that Consuelo had retired for the night.

Feeling utterly weary, Caitlyn pushed away from the table and went to the door.

"Rafe." His name slipped past her lips.

"Evenin', Caitlyn. Mind if I come in?"

She should have sent him away. It went against all the rules of propriety for her to entertain a man in the house at night, alone. But she was too pleased to see him, too eager for company, to turn him away.

"Please do." Caitlyn ushered him into the parlor. "Won't you sit down?"

"Thanks." He tossed his hat on the hall tree, then sat down in the chair that had been her father's, filling it, and the room, with his presence.

Caitlyn sat on the sofa, her hands folded in

her lap. "How have you been?"

"Fine. Yourself?"

"Fine." She dropped her gaze to the colorful rag rug at her feet, but even then his image filled her mind. He was wearing a dark brown shirt and black denim pants that cleanly outlined every beautiful masculine inch of him. She had thought of him often in the past two weeks, his face flitting across her mind at odd hours of the day and night. As the initial shock of her father's death passed, her hate and outrage lessened, and so did her anger at Rafe Gallegher.

And now he was here. She took a deep, nervous breath, her nostrils filling with the faint scent of brandy and tobacco. She could feel his eyes moving over her and when she looked up, she was trapped by his searching, dark-eyed gaze.

"I heard two of your men quit last night," he remarked. "What are you going to do?"

"I don't know." She lifted her chin and squared her shoulders. "You needn't worry. I'll manage."

"Yeah?" Rafe asked skeptically. "How?"

"One day at a time," Caitlyn retorted. She stood up, agitated by his blunt questions and her own inadequate replies.

"I saw Wylie in town earlier," Rafe said casually. Indeed, it was that little run in with Wylie that had sent Rafe riding hell for leather to the Circle C. "He was bragging in the saloon about how he was gonna marry you and take charge of the Circle C before the year was out."

Caitlyn's green eyes flashed like heat lightning. "Why, that miserable swine! I've never said or done anything to encourage him. How could he dare say such a thing? Why, I'd as soon marry a heathen savage as pair up with the likes of Abner Wylie!"

"That so?"

Rafe's words were as soft as dandelion fluff, and as penetrating as the cold wind that blew down out of the mountains on a dark winter night.

Caitlyn flushed from head to foot as she realized what she had said.

Rafe chuckled, amused by her crimson cheeks and stricken expression, relieved that Caitlyn had no intention of marrying Abner Wylie.

He shoved his hands into his pants pockets so Caitlyn could not see the tension building in him. He had fully intended to ride out of Cedar Creek the day after Carmichael's funeral, but each day he had found some new excuse to linger. He admitted now that it was Caitlyn Carmichael who held him here. They had shared little together, and he knew very little about her, but he wanted to know more. Much more.

His gaze moved over her and a slow heat spread through his loins. She was so lovely. Her hair was drawn into a tight knot at her nape, her eyes were shadowed, her cheeks pale, but for all that, she was lovely. Even the severe black mourning dress could not detract from her beauty. Instead, it accentuated her narrow waist and made her eyes seem darker than ever, like deep emerald pools.

He wanted her. He had wanted her from the first moment he saw her, when he was within a hair's breath of dangling at the end of a rope. He had wanted her then, and he wanted her now. Wanted her enough to make her an offer she would very likely refuse, one he would undoubtedly regret, but one he felt compelled to make just the same.

"Maybe you should take Wylie up on his offer," he suggested, knowing he'd kill Abner Wylie with his bare hands before he let Caitlyn marry him.

"Never!"

"You need a husband, Caitlyn, whether you like the idea or not. And you'd better find one soon. What about Scott?"

"He's engaged to Naomi Wells."

"Rusty?"

"He's too old."

Rafe shrugged. "What about Paulie? Or

Josh? Or Nate?"

"They're all too young."

"Wishful?"

"He's already been married three times," Caitlyn snapped, exasperated by his seeming urgency to see her married to someone else.

"Isn't there someone in town you've been seeing?"

"No."

Rafe nodded, his expression thoughtful, his eyes watching her intently. She lowered her gaze, aware of his nearness, of the attraction that was always between them.

He was silent for what seemed an eternity and when he spoke, his words caught her completely off guard.

"How about me? For a husband, I mean."

Caitlyn stared at Rafe, certain her ears were playing tricks on her. "You? You can't be serious!"

"Why not? I'm the right age. I'm healthy. And I'm willing."

"Don't be absurd."

"You said you'd rather marry a heathen savage than Abner Wylie," he drawled. "Here's your chance."

"No," Caitlyn said, but her pulse was racing like a runaway train and her heart was beating wildly in her breast, so wildly she thought she might faint. Marry Rafe Gallegher indeed! The very thought made her lightheaded. And yet, her choices were limited. There were few single men in this part of the territory. Most of the men in their twenties were already married, those still single were unsuitable for any number of reasons or undesirable. And those under twenty-five were too young, too immature. But Rafe . . . She remembered the press of his lips on hers, the strength of his arms when he rescued her from the path of the mustangs, the sight of him rising from the pool the day her father died. Marry Rafe . . .

A knock at the front door put an end to her turbulent thoughts, but her relief at the interruption was short-lived when she opened the door and saw Abner standing on the porch, hat in hand.

"Evening, Miss Caitlyn," Abner drawled, flashing her a smile as wide as Texas. "Mind if I come in?"

Caitlyn could only stare at him in dismay, wondering what he was doing there at such a late hour, wondering what she would do if the two men came to blows again, right there in the house.

Abner took Caitlyn's silence for an invitation and stepped into the parlor, only to stop dead in his tracks when he saw Gallegher lounging in the big overstuffed chair near the hearth.

Abner shot a questioning glance at Caitlyn.

"What the hell is *he* doing here?"

"He . . . he came to see how I was getting along," Caitlyn replied. "Won't you sit down, Abner?"

He shook his head.

Caitlyn drew a deep breath, and let it out in a soft sigh. "Why have you come, Abner?"

"I'd like to talk to you about that matter we discussed in town after your father died."

"I hear you've been discussing it quite a bit at the saloon," Caitlyn remarked, her green eyes bright, her gaze piercing.

Abner sent a murderous glance in Gallegher's direction. "I guess I know who you heard that from," he muttered.

"Is it true, what Mr. Gallegher said? Have you been telling everyone that we're to be married?"

"Not everyone," Abner hedged.

Caitlyn's gaze remained on Abner, and he fidgeted nervously. Of average height, with brown hair and pale blue eyes, his features were pleasant enough, Caitlyn mused, though his manner was a little gruff. She had never been sure what there was about him that she found distasteful, but the fact remained that he made her uncomfortable.

Her gaze moved to Rafe, still sitting in her father's chair, his long legs crossed at the ankles, his arms folded across his chest. He made her uncomfortable, too, but in a much different way. His hair was very black in the light of the lamp, his skin a deep bronze, his eyes like fathomless ebony mirrors holding secrets she longed to discover.

She made a decision then, one that made her mouth go dry and her palms begin to sweat as she faced Abner once again.

"I'm glad you haven't told too many people that we're to be married, Abner," she said, her voice barely audible. She clasped her hands to keep them from shaking. "Because, you see, I've decided to marry Mr. Gallegher."

It was a toss up as to which man was more surprised by her announcement. Rafe managed to keep his face impassive, but Abner stared at Caitlyn as though she had suddenly grown horns and a tail, and then he began to laugh.

"That's very funny," he said when his laughter died away. "Very funny. You, marrying a half-breed. I always wondered if you had a sense of humor and now I see you do, in spades."

"I'm quite serious," Caitlyn said. "You're the first to know."

Abner's face went pale, and then angry color flooded his cheeks and stained his neck. "You can't be serious!" he shouted. "Dammit, I—"

Rafe stood up in a smooth, effortless

movement and took his place at Caitlyn's
side. His arm went around her shoulders as if
it were the most natural thing in the world.

"Sorry you have to leave so soon, Wylie,"
Rafe said in a voice that left no room for
argument. "We'll let you know when we set
the date."

Abner looked at Caitlyn, unable to believe
his eyes and ears. She was actually going to
marry Gallegher! It was inconceivable.

He started to object again, but the look in
the half-breed's eyes stilled his tongue. Jam-
ming his hat on his head, Abner muttered a
hasty farewell and stalked out of the house,
the door slamming loudly behind him.

Caitlyn stood very still, aware of Rafe's
arm around her shoulder, of his presence at
her side. She had not looked directly at him
since she said she would marry him and now
she did so reluctantly, wondering what she
had gotten herself into. She had expected to
feel dismay, regret, even remorse, but all she
felt was relief. Rafe would find a way to make
everything right—the repairs that needed to
be made, the bank loan. She could now shift
all her problems to his capable shoulders.

Rafe grinned at her. "Well, ma'am, you
have but to name the day. I'm sure news of
our engagement will be all over town before
the sun sets tomorrow."

Caitlyn nodded. She had agreed to marry

this man, a man she knew almost nothing about, a man who was a half-breed, a virtual stranger. She would marry him, and in so doing, she would become his. He would make all the decisions regarding her ranch. His word would be law; the ranch would be his. She would be his, to do with as he pleased.

The relief she had felt only moments ago quickly turned to doubt. What had she done? A married woman had no rights other than those her husband gave her. He could abuse her, neglect her, beat her, and no one would lift a hand to stop him. She would be his property, like his horse or his saddle. She thought briefly of insisting that theirs be a marriage in name only, but she knew Rafe would never agree to such a thing. He was a man, with a man's needs, a man's desires.

Rafe took his arm from Caitlyn's shoulder and shoved his hands deep into his pockets. Her changing emotions were clearly reflected in the depths of her eyes, and he could almost read her thoughts. She was afraid of him, afraid to be his wife. He was a half-breed, after all. Tainted blood. Perhaps he should just forget the whole thing and ride on but he didn't want to leave her. If he stayed, he would finally have a place to call his own, a sense of security he had never known before.

"Change your mind already?" he asked sardonically.

Caitlyn saw the anger lurking behind his eyes, the muscle that twitched in his jaw. She hardly knew this man and she was suddenly certain she had made a dreadful mistake when she agreed to marry him. Perhaps she should have accepted Abner's proposal after all. Much as she disliked the man, they came from similar backgrounds, and he would be much more manageable than Rafe Gallegher.

"Well?" he asked impatiently, and waited, hardly breathing, for her answer. He watched the firelight playing in her hair like loving fingers, dancing among the honey-colored strands, turning it to gold. Her emerald green eyes were dark fathomless pools and her slightly parted, full lips were ripe for the taking. Her silky skin had been kissed by the sun, and her softly rounded figure cried out for a man's touch. His touch . . .

Caitlyn blushed under his bold scrutiny, felt her blood warm and her heart race. He wanted her, and if the truth be told, she wanted him.

"I haven't changed my mind."

Rafe let out a deep breath. "Name the day and I'll be there."

"Next Saturday morning," Caitlyn said. "I'll arrange it with Reverend Wilson."

Rafe nodded, his gaze lingering on her mouth. He knew he should go, but her nearness held him. Abruptly, he grabbed her by the shoulders and drew her up against him. Before she could protest, he covered her lips with his, his tongue invading the sweet warmth of her mouth, his hips grinding against hers.

She struggled for only a moment, and then she was kissing him back, her tongue darting out to taste his.

It was as if she had been asleep her whole life, she thought, dazed, and had only now awakened. Her blood was on fire, her skin tingling with awareness, as all her senses reeled under the onslaught of his tongue and lips.

She felt the press of his fingers digging into her arms, the rising warmth of his manhood against her belly. The shock of it made her stomach quiver, her insides fluttering as though a hundred butterflies were trapped inside, struggling to be free. She swayed against him, her breasts crushed against his chest, her arms twining around his neck.

Rafe groaned softly as Caitlyn melted against him. Sweet, he mused, so sweet.

He kissed her neck, let his tongue caress her ear. His hands slid down her arms, traveled over her back, then slid up her ribcage, his fingertips whispering against her breasts.

"You'd best let me go if you expect to be a maiden on your wedding day," he whispered huskily.

It took a moment for his words to penetrate the mists of passion. When they did, she let out a cry of indignation and wrenched out of his embrace.

"How dare you!" she sputtered. "I never . . . I wouldn't . . . Oh!"

Rafe shrugged, amused by the anger that flared in her eyes. "I just didn't want you to think I was easy," Rafe said, watching the sparks dance in her eyes.

"Oh, you . . . you . . . I don't care if I never see you again."

Rafe chuckled softly. "We've got a date Saturday," he reminded her, reaching for his hat. "Don't be late."

CHAPTER
TEN

CAITLYN STOOD AT THE ALTAR, WAITING. SHE
had told no one on the ranch or in town of
her forthcoming marriage to Rafe Gallegher,
and she was thankful now that she had kept
her wedding plans a secret, for it appeared
that Rafe had decided to leave her waiting at
the altar. She had sent him word that the
ceremony was to take place Saturday morning at eleven o'clock, and he had replied that
he would be there. Now, as the courthouse
clock struck the half hour, she decided he
had changed his mind.

Reverend Wilson cleared his throat, uncertain how best to handle what was rapidly
becoming an embarrassing situation.

Caitlyn felt the color climb in her cheeks as she faced the minister. "I guess he couldn't make it," she murmured, wishing the floor would open and swallow her. "I'm sorry for taking up your time."

"That's quite all right, Miss Carmichael, I . . ."

The reverend's voice trailed off as the church door swung open and Rafe strode briskly down the center aisle.

"Sorry I'm late," he apologized, his dark eyes on Caitlyn's face. He shrugged, grinning easily. "Took the tailor longer than he thought to lengthen these pants."

Caitlyn nodded as Rafe took his place beside her. It was a Rafe Gallegher she had never seen before. Wearing snug black trousers, a black broadcloth coat, a crisp white linen shirt, and a black silk cravat, he looked quite devastating. She was certain he was the most handsome man she had ever seen in her life. His hair was neatly combed, and his black boots were so shiny she could see her face reflected on the surface. A faint scent of lilac water tickled her nostrils.

"Are we ready, then?" the reverend asked.

"Quite ready," Rafe replied, taking Caitlyn's hand.

Caitlyn nodded, aware of Rafe's strong brown fingers threading through her own. She listened carefully to the words that made her Rafe Gallegher's wife, but it all seemed like a dream, hazy and not quite real. Her voice, when she responded, was faint and slightly uneven. And then, before she quite realized what she had done, the Reverend Wilson had pronounced them man and wife and Rafe was claiming his first kiss as her lawfully wedded husband.

His kiss, as light and soft as a whisper, ignited a fire within her that spread from the roots of her hair to the soles of her feet. She felt his mouth brand her lips. She was his now. Mrs. Rafe Gallegher. For better or worse. In sickness and health. Until death parted them.

Rafe took a step back, his eyes sweeping over his bride. Caitlyn looked beautiful, beautiful but slightly stunned, as if she could not quite accept the reality of what had just happened. Her hair, as soft and yellow as cornsilk, was swept into a soft chignon at her nape. Her eyes, as green as a new leaf, were wide and filled with a faintly bemused expression as she gazed up at him. Her dress was of pale pink silk, the style rather old-fashioned but very becoming.

He smiled at her, hoping to reassure her, and then he gave her hand a squeeze. "Shall we go, Mrs. Gallegher?"

Caitlyn nodded, her heart beating a mile a minute as Rafe pressed money into the reverend's hand before escorting her from the church.

Rafe paused outside. "Hungry?"

"A little," Caitlyn admitted, though she wasn't sure she could keep anything down, her stomach was fluttering so.

"Good." Taking her arm, he steered her down the street toward the town's only restaurant.

People turned to stare as Rafe and Caitlyn passed by. Saturday was a busy day in town, a time when the women did their weekly shopping and the men lingered over the seed catalog or stopped at the smithy to have plows or wagon wheels repaired. The sight of a man in a black Sunday-go-to-meeting suit and a woman in a pink silk gown drew every eye, and the townspeople nodded sagely as they put their heads together. So, the rumors had been true. Caitlyn Carmichael had married one of the hired hands.

The women looked at Caitlyn with quiet envy, for Rafe Gallegher was a very handsome man and one to be admired despite his Indian heritage. Looking at him, they could almost forgive her for marrying a half-breed.

The men looked at Caitlyn and shook their heads in disapproval. No matter how much she needed a husband, she should have married a man of her own kind, not some dirty half-breed.

At the restaurant, Rafe ordered an enormous lunch, then pulled a long black cigar from his coat pocket, and bit off the end.

"Do you mind?" Rafe asked.

"I'd rather you didn't," she admitted candidly. "I don't care for the smell of cigars."

With a nod, Rafe laid the Long Nine aside. "Caitlyn Gallegher," he murmured, trying the name, trying to believe it was real, she was real.

Caitlyn's gaze dropped to the red-checked tablecloth. There was something intimate in the way he said her name, in the pull of his eyes when he looked at her. She was glad when the waitress served their meal.

Rafe ate without tasting anything, all too conscious of the woman seated across the table. She was his wife now, lawfully and legally his to do with as he pleased.

He studied her face, the smooth peach-colored skin, now lightly powdered, the tilt of her nose, the graceful curve of her cheek, the delicate brows, and incredibly long lashes. Desire rose within him, hotter than any flame, shaking him to the core of his being. Lord, how he wanted her, warm and willing, in his arms.

Caitlyn glanced up suddenly, and he wondered if she had somehow divined his thoughts. He held her gaze for a long time, saw the confusion in her eyes, the faint hint of what might have been fear, or perhaps regret.

Rafe clenched his jaw. Was it possible she was already sorry she had married him? "What is it?" he asked gruffly.

Caitlyn nodded toward the front window. Outside, a group of townspeople had gathered on the boardwalk. "I think our secret's out."

Rafe glanced over his shoulder, frowning when he saw the crowd.

"I guess by now everyone knows that I married a . . . that I married you."

"Married a half-breed, you mean," Rafe muttered. "Go ahead, say it."

Caitlyn flushed guiltily. "I'm sorry. I never thought about what people would think, what they'd say, when they found out."

"What *will* they say?"

"I'm not sure. I suppose they'll be shocked."

Rafe stood abruptly and tossed a handful of coins on the table top. "Come on, Mrs. Gallegher, let's go satisfy their curiosity."

He grabbed her hand and practically dragged her outside. The crowd parted to let them pass, but Rafe stood on the boardwalk, his dark eyes sweeping the crowd.

"You heard right," he said loudly. "We were married this morning." He smiled at Caitlyn, a hard smile that did not reach his eyes. Then he swung her into his arms and carried her down the street to where she had left the carriage. Effortlessly, he placed her on the high spring seat, vaulted up beside her, and shook out the reins. "Giddap, horse," he growled, and they drove out of town at a lively trot.

It wasn't until later that he realized he'd left the black mare at the livery barn.

Caitlyn sat silent beside her husband, her hands balled into tight fists. How dare he embarrass her before her neighbors! What made him think everyone would frown on their marriage, on her choice of a husband? Perhaps the townspeople had gathered around to wish them well. And perhaps not.

She grunted softly as she recalled the way the crowd had looked at her, the faces strong with disapproval, shock and outrage.

Caitlyn shook her head. She had never considered how others would view her marriage to Rafe. She had spent her whole life doing what was proper, what was expected, trying to be the kind of daughter her father could be proud of. In town, she had always behaved as a proper young woman should, never doing anything to call attention to herself, never stepping beyond the bounds of propriety even when she yearned to do so. And now, in one fell swoop, she had outraged a whole town. She had married a man

169

who was a half-breed, a man who would, in all probability, never be accepted by any of her friends. Indians were hated and feared by the people of Cedar Creek; half-breeds were regarded with suspicion. How could you trust a man who had mixed blood? How could you be sure where his true loyalty lay?

As they pulled into the ranch, it occurred to Caitlyn that the cowboys might not accept her new husband any more readily than the townspeople. In an effort to keep the ranch together, she had foolishly done the one thing that would no doubt drive all the help away.

A wave of hopelessness swept over Caitlyn. How could she have been so blind? Even though she disliked Abner, she realized now that he would have been accepted as a suitable husband by the townspeople, and viewed as a suitable boss by the cowhands.

She slid a glance in Rafe's direction. His profile was clean-cut, like a statue cast in bronze. His cheekbones were high and well-defined, his nose straight, his jaw square and strong.

Caitlyn lifted her head, her expression changing from defeat to defiance. Despite what anyone else might think, she would rather be married to Rafe Gallegher than to a man like Abner Wylie. She had never liked Abner, never trusted him. Rafe might be a half-breed, and considered inferior by many, but she knew deep in her heart that she could trust him, that he had her best interests in mind. Perhaps he would never love her, perhaps he would forever be a stranger to her, but he would never cheat her, never abuse her.

Her heart felt suddenly light as Rafe reined the horse to a halt near the front porch. With lazy grace, he swung to the ground. Walking around the carriage, he placed his hands around her waist and lifted her down. Their eyes met and held as they had so often that day, and Caitlyn felt a little thrill of excitement dance along her spine.

"Welcome home, Mr. Gallegher," she murmured shyly.

"Welcome home, Mrs. Gallegher," he replied, and sweeping her into his arms, he carried her up the steps and over the threshold.

Caitlyn nudged the front door closed with her toe and then felt suddenly warm all over as he continued to hold her close. She could no longer meet his eyes and she lowered her gaze to his mouth. It was a nice mouth, very masculine, very inviting. She remembered how he had kissed her the night they agreed to be married. The memory was enough to heat her blood and she wondered what it would have been like if he had not stopped with just a kiss . . . A sudden flush crept up her neck and into her cheeks. She would find out soon enough.

"Aren't you going to put me down?" Caitlyn asked, risking a look at Rafe's face.

Rafe nodded, though letting her go was the last thing he wanted to do. Her hair was soft where it brushed his chin, and the scent of her perfume lingered in his nostrils. He was tempted to carry her down the hall to the bedroom and satisfy the yearning that had plagued him since he first saw her standing at the altar. He took a deep breath, reminding himself that he had all night to hold her, to touch her. All night.

Caitlyn felt abandoned when he released her. Running a hand over her hair, she glanced around the parlor. Everything looked the same as it had that morning, yet everything was different now. She was Mrs. Rafe Gallegher and nothing would ever be the same again.

"I guess I'll go change," she remarked.

Rafe nodded, sensing her need to be alone. "Do you want to tell the men about our marriage, or shall I?"

Rafe smiled wryly. "I don't think it'll make any difference, but it might be better coming from you."

"Very well." She felt awkward standing there and she hurried out of the room and

172

down the narrow hallway to her bedroom.

Closing the door behind her, she stood there for a long moment, gazing at her bed and dresser, the knickknacks on the shelf, the stuffed doll on her bed. She had been a girl when she left home this morning, but she was a married woman now.

She quickly changed out of her pink silk and donned a blue cotton print. For the next hour, she moved her personal belongings and clothing into the room her father had shared with her mother. She changed the sheets on the large brass bed, plumped the pillows, hung her clothes on one side of the wardrobe, then stood there imagining Rafe's clothes hanging next to hers.

Turning from the wardrobe, her gaze fell on the bed and a sudden heat engulfed her as she thought of the coming night, of slipping into bed beside Rafe. It seemed shameful to contemplate such things in the light of day and she hurried from the room.

Night would come soon enough.

CHAPTER
ELEVEN

CAITLYN SAT ACROSS THE DINING TABLE from Rafe, the remains of a roast beef dinner between them. The house was quiet, and the quiet engulfed them.

Caitlyn sipped a cup of coffee, wishing she could think of something light and airy to say. The silence between them filled her with anxiety and unrest. What was *he* thinking? Why didn't he say something?

The meal had started on a light note. He had complimented her cooking, and they had chatted about the ranch while they ate. Caitlyn had told him of her visit to the bunkhouse, unable to mask her surprise that none of the hands had quit on the spot.

Gradually, they had run out of conversation, leaving only a taut silence.

She put her cup aside and rose smoothly to her feet. Preferring to do her own cooking and cleaning now that she was married, she had asked Consuelo to stay on to cook and do the washing for the cowhands.

She was conscious of Rafe's eyes watching her as she moved from the dining room to the kitchen. He was leaning back in his chair, one hand shoved into his pants pocket, the other holding a long black cigar. He had not asked her permission to smoke this time, and it had not occurred to her to object. This was his house now.

Rafe felt the tension build in him as he watched Caitlyn clear the table, her skirts rustling as she moved. He watched the tantalizing sway of her hips, the way her breasts pushed against the fabric of her bodice when she reached over her head, the graceful lift of her hand as she brushed a stray lock of hair from her forehead.

He followed her into the parlor when the dishes were done, and sank into the chair that had been her father's favorite and was now his. It was an odd feeling, knowing that he had a place to call his own. He had never owned a home before, never owned a piece of ground—or a woman.

In New Orleans, he had lived in hotels and

rooming houses with his father; they had taken their meals in restaurants. With the Cheyenne, he had owned only the clothes on his back, his weapons, and a couple of horses. But now he was a man of property. A married man with a virgin bride.

His eyes sought Caitlyn. She was sitting on the sofa, mending a tear in the hem of one of her dresses. The firelight played across her features and danced in her hair, and he knew he had never seen anything more lovely, more desirable, than the woman sitting across the room.

He glanced at the clock, willing the time to pass so that he could take her to bed and love her as he so longed to do. He wondered what she would do if he swept her into his arms and made love to her on the floor in front of the fire. Would she be shocked, or pleased?

If theirs had been a love match, he would have made her his by now, but she did not love him. In truth, he doubted if she even liked him very much. She had married him because she needed a husband and he was the best of a bad lot. And he had married her because he wanted her as he had never wanted any woman.

Caitlyn looked up from her mending, her eyes drawn to his. The dress fell from her fingers as she read the raw hunger in Rafe's steady gaze. The tension stretched between them, as taut as a Lakota bowstring, as vibrant as the fire that crackled in the hearth.

She felt his gaze on her face, saw the way his hands balled into tight fists as his eyes traveled over her breasts and then back to her face to linger on her mouth. She licked lips gone suddenly dry, and felt a peculiar tingle in the pit of her stomach as Rafe stood up and walked toward her.

"Caitlyn."

She couldn't speak, couldn't think. The moment she had dreaded, and anticipated, had come.

Rafe knelt before her, his dark eyes heavy-lidded with passion. "Don't be afraid," he murmured as he reached up to remove the pins from her hair. "I won't hurt you."

Caitlyn nodded, mesmerized by the feel of his hands in her hair, by the intensity of his gaze. She closed her eyes as he leaned forward to kiss her. His lips were like fire, his hands like flames as he removed her clothing. He kissed her until she was breathless, mindless, and then he drew away from her to shed his own clothes.

Shy, yet curious, she opened her eyes to watch him. The firelight cast reddish-orange shadows across his chest and face, reminding her of the flames that had consumed the barn the day her father had been killed.

Indian.

She stared at Rafe and all she saw was her father's body lying face down in the dirt, an arrow protruding from his back. Her ears rang with the sound of heathen war cries, the acrid smell of smoke and gunpowder filled her nostrils.

Indian.

She saw her brothers lying dead in the dust. Arlo had died from an arrow in his throat. A lance had pierced Morgan's heart. There had been blood everywhere.

Indian.

She shook her head as Rafe knelt beside her. "No."

"It'll be all right, Caitlyn," he assured her, thinking it was only a case of wedding-night jitters that made her hesitant.

Caitlyn stared at him. His skin was dark, his hair long, straight, and black, as black as the heathen war paint the Indians had worn the day they killed her father.

Guilt and remorse swept the passion from her heart. Indians had killed her brothers and her father, and she had married one. What had she been thinking when she agreed to marry Rafe? How could she have let her desire for a man blind her to what he was?

Rafe reached out to stroke her cheek and she recoiled from his touch. His hands were large and brown and strong. She thrust her hands against his chest to hold him away.

"Don't," she whimpered. "Please don't."

Rafe swore softly as he imprisoned both her hands in one of his. "Don't fight me, Caitlyn," he said, his voice husky with desire. "I'm not going to hurt you."

"Don't touch me," she cried, her voice rising hysterically. "Don't ever touch me again!"

Rafe drew back as though she had slapped him. His face was hard, his jaw rigid, his eyes like flint. *Tainted blood*, he thought bitterly. He should have known better.

He dressed quickly, his hands shaking with anger, his breathing ragged. He should have known better than to get involved with another woman, especially a white woman.

He left the house without a word, knowing he had to get away from Caitlyn before he did something they'd both regret.

Once outside, he breathed deeply of the cool night air as he reminded himself of Summer Wind's treachery, of his vow never to love or trust another woman as long as he lived. He swore a vile oath as he gazed up at the moon. Caitlyn was like the moon, he mused bitterly, bright and cold and out of reach.

Damn! How could he live in the same

house with her, sit across the table from her morning and night, and not touch her? He was a man, not a monk. Damn!

A wry grin twisted his lips. If his wife would not have him, there were other women who would. Women who were well versed in the art of pleasing a man, women who could make every time seem like the first time. Women who loved the color of his money more than they despised the color of his skin. With that in mind, he saddled one of the horses and rode into town.

Frenchy's was located at the north end of Cedar Creek. A large, two-storey white house with bright yellow shutters, and a red lamp in the front window, it stood a good distance away from the other buildings. There were at least a dozen horses tethered to the long hitching post out front.

A little Negro boy took the reins from Gallegher's hand and smiled a knowing smile. "Have a good time, Mistuh," the boy called as Rafe went up the steps.

The inside of Frenchy's looked exactly the way decent, God-fearing women imagined with heavy red paper on the walls, lots of gilt-edged mirrors, and cozy little red velvet settees just big enough for two. A large crystal chandelier shimmered from the ceiling in the parlor, the glow from the candles softening the hard lines on the faces of the women who reclined in the parlor, waiting for their next customer.

It was the room beyond the parlor that drew Rafe's interest. A long mahogany bar ran the length of the room, and rows of shelves with fancy lead crystal glasses and goblets lined the wall. Two dozen tables were scattered around the room, each ringed by four or five leather-bound chairs. A heavy layer of smoke floated over the heads of the gamblers, and the clink of coins and the soft whisper of cards being shuffled by expert hands could be heard as he entered the room.

He took a place at one of the poker tables, sat back in his chair, and concentrated on the game at hand. Winning was easy, but, more than that, it was necessary. He did not want to have to take money from Caitlyn, and the wages her father had paid him were almost gone.

He won the first three hands, let the fourth one go because the other players were beginning to murmur about his luck. And it was luck. So far. He doubled his bets with each hand and when he left the table two hours later, he had won over a hundred dollars.

He went to the bar and ordered a shot of whiskey, which he tossed off in a single swallow, and then he wandered into the parlor to take a look at what Frenchy had to offer in the way of a good time.

Caitlyn stood at the front window, a feeling of despair winding around her heart. Where was Rafe? She shied away from the obvious answer, not wanting to believe it even though she knew it was true. He had gone into town to buy what she had refused him. Pain tore through her heart, a pain so severe, so sharp, she thought she might die of it.

Fighting back tears, she went into her room and donned her nightgown, then slipped into her cold lonely bed, only to lie there for hours, unable to sleep. This was her wedding night. It should be the happiest night of her life. Instead, she was home alone, wondering where her husband was.

Rising, she drew on her robe and went into the parlor. Stirring the ashes in the hearth, she placed a log on the coals and sat in the chair by the window, staring out into the darkness. Tears of misery welled in her eyes. They should not have married so soon, she thought unhappily. She was still mourning her father, still trying to sort out her feelings for Rafe. She was attracted to him and she knew she could trust him. But she had not yet come to terms with the fact that he was half Indian. Perhaps she never would.

"Oh, Lord," she murmured. "What have I gotten myself into?"

She could not deny her attraction for Rafe, she mused again. And yet, the same thing that attracted her also frightened her. He was half Indian, and she was afraid of Indians. It was all so confusing!

It was well after midnight when she saw him ride into the yard leading Black Wind, and she felt a sudden flicker of relief. Perhaps he had not gone into Cedar Creek for a woman, after all, but only to retrieve his horse.

She stood up, uncertain of what to do. Should she go to bed and pretend she knew nothing of his excursion into town? Or should she confront him and demand to know where he had been?

She was still undecided when the front door swung open and Rafe entered the room.

"Caitlyn," he murmured, surprised. "Why aren't you in bed?"

"I couldn't sleep," she replied honestly. "Where have you been?"

"I went into town," he answered, his voice giving nothing away.

"To pick up Black Wind?"

"Yeah."

"Nothing else?"

Rafe quirked one dark eyebrow at her.

"Like what?"

She felt the back of her neck grow hot but she had gone too far to turn back now. "I thought you might have gone to Frenchy's place." She held her breath as she waited for his answer.

"That's just where I've been, *Mrs*. Gallegher." His voice was soft, but the emphasis he placed on her married title cut Caitlyn to the quick. He would not have gone to such a dreadful place if she had not refused him his husbandly rights.

A cold hand curled around her heart, leaving her hurting and speechless. She wanted to scream at him, to reproach him for his infidelity, but she had no one to blame but herself. He was a man, after all, not a gelding, and if she would not have him, there were other women who would.

"Any objections?" Rafe asked.

Caitlyn shook her head. She had many objections, she thought furiously, but the words froze in her throat. How could she admit she wanted him now, when he had been to Frenchy's? He smelled of tobacco, whiskey, and cheap perfume. In her mind's eyes, she could see him smoking and drinking and carrying on with some cheap tart. The image hurt more than she would have dreamed possible, and she bit down on her lower lip to keep from crying.

Rafe nodded curtly. He had hoped to spark her jealousy, to make her admit she cared for him a little, but he was wasting his time. She didn't want a husband, only someone to run the ranch.

"Good night, *Mrs.* Gallegher," he said caustically, and stalked out of the room.

Caitlyn stared after him, stung by his philandering and his abrupt good night. She was a married woman now, she thought ruefully, and she had never felt more utterly alone.

Rafe's presence could be felt everywhere in the days that followed. Though he had been in charge for only a few weeks, changes were already taking place. Fences had been mended; the cattle were being branded; calves had been castrated; and the hole in the kitchen roof had been repaired. A couple of trees near the house had been cut down for firewood; debris had been dragged from the river so the water didn't back up and stagnate; and the horses had all been newly shod. What was left of the barn had been removed and the ground cleared in preparation for the building of a new one.

Caitlyn knew the hands grumbled about Rafe. He demanded a day's work for a day's pay, allowed no slacking off, no drinking in the bunkhouse after work. What he asked was no more than her father had asked, but the men resented taking orders from a half-breed. Paulie had told her the men talked constantly of quitting, but so far none of them had turned in his time.

If only things between herself and Rafe were running as smoothly as the operation of the ranch, she mused as she hung a load of wash on the line. Rafe had moved into the spare bedroom and rarely spoke to her except to advise her about the affairs of the ranch. They ate their meals in virtual silence, the tension between them growing stronger with each passing day. And each Saturday night he put on his good shirt, shined his boots, and rode into town.

Those hours that Rafe was in town caused Caitlyn agonies of distress as she imagined her husband in the arms of another woman, touching her, kissing her, wooing some cheap tart with the sweet words that Caitlyn so longed to hear. But Rafe had made no move toward her, said nothing to indicate he cared. Indeed, he seemed perfectly happy with the way things were, and she could not humble herself to beg for his touch.

And now, worst of all, she was dreaming about him at night, her sleep haunted by shadowy images of his handsome face, by dark phantom fingers that caressed her skin and caused her to awaken, her breath ragged, her skin covered with a fine layer of perspiration.

There had been so many times when she thought he would take her in his arms. So many times when his eyes met hers, when the tension hummed between them. Sometimes, when he passed close by her, she felt all her nerve endings reach out for him. She would not have rebuffed him if he had reached for her then. Indeed, she would have welcomed his touch as a flower welcomed the sun. But he never laid a hand on her, never suggested they alter their sleeping arrangements.

And yet, he wanted her. She knew it. She could see it when he looked at her, feel it in the words that went unsaid. Sometimes she wanted to scream at him for ignoring her. Couldn't he understand the awful strain she had been under the past few weeks? She'd buried her father and gotten married in such a short time. All she'd needed was a little time to adjust to the enormous changes in her life. She longed to explain her actions on their wedding night, but the longer she put it off, the harder it became, and now it was impossible.

She hated him, she thought as she plucked the clothespins from his shirt and dropped it in the laundry basket at her feet. Hated him with a passion. A wry grin turned up the corner of her mouth. Passion, she mused, that was the operative word. He had stirred her desires with little more than a few kisses on their wedding day, making her yearn for more, so much more. Despite the fact that she didn't love him, that he was part Indian, she longed for his kisses, for the touch of his hands in her hair, the press of his body turning her limbs to jelly, making her stomach quiver with anticipation.

She dropped the last article of clothing into the basket, lifted it onto her hip, and carried it toward the back door. It was then she saw Rafe. He was exercising Black Wind, riding the horse at a trot around the corral. The beautiful horse moved fluidly, long legs reaching out, neck arched, head high, tail flowing like black silk. And Rafe . . . The sun glistened on his naked back and broad shoulders, and touched his hair with blue highlights. She admired the taut muscles in his legs as he guided the horse with the pressure of his knees.

If only she were an artist, she thought for the second time since she had known Rafe, so that she might capture the beauty of man and beast as they circled the corral, two magnificent creatures made one for this brief moment.

The laundry basket, balanced on her right hip, was momentarily forgotten as she watched Rafe rein the mare into a tight rearing turn and circle the opposite way.

Rafe saw Caitlyn out of the corner of his eye as he reined the horse around. He circled the corral one more time, then drew Black Wind to a halt and slid to the ground. Removing the bridle, he gave the horse an affectionate slap on the neck and vaulted over the corral fence.

He felt his heart beat a little faster as he approached Caitlyn. It was amazing the effect she had on him. He had only to look at her to want her. The fact that she had been watching him pleased him more than it should have.

"I'll carry that," he said, taking the laundry basket from her.

"Thank you," Caitlyn murmured, trying not to stare at his naked chest, or at the narrow trickle of sweat making its way toward his flat belly.

She turned on her heel and opened the back door, deeply aware of the man behind her. He smelled of sweat, horse, and tobacco. Masculine smells, she mused, and not at all unpleasant.

Rafe placed the basket on the kitchen table, then straddled one of the chairs, his arms folded across the latticed backrest.

"Would you like some lemonade?" Caitlyn asked.

"Yeah." He watched her bustle about the kitchen, enthralled by her beauty, by the grace of her movements as she took a glass from the cupboard, filled it with cold lemonade, then sliced him a piece of chocolate cake. How many nights had he lain awake, wanting her? How many times had he left his lonely bed and gone outside, breathing in the crisp air, letting it cool his fevered flesh?

He drew his thoughts away from the desire that plagued him like an old wound. "What's for dinner?"

"Chicken and dumplings."

Rafe nodded. She was a good cook, but his mind was not on food. If she were truly his wife, he would take her in his arms and kiss her soundly, perhaps make love to her there, on the kitchen floor, in the full light of day. If she were truly his wife, he would tell her of the nights he had dreamed of her, confess that he found her the most desirable woman in the world. If she were truly his wife, he would not have to tell her, he thought wryly. She would know.

He muttered an oath under his breath as he stood up. Draining the glass in one long swallow, he wiped the back of his hand over his mouth. "See you at dinner," he said gruffly, and left the house.

Dinner was a strained, silent meal. It was Saturday night, and Rafe was going to town.

Caitlyn ate without tasting her food, her imagination already picturing him in the arms of another woman, holding her, laughing with her, making love to her. Unbidden, unstoppable, the tears came.

Rafe chanced to look up at that moment, the food on his plate forgotten as he saw the silent tears tracking Caitlyn's cheeks.

"What is it?" he asked, troubled by the quiet misery he saw reflected in her eyes. "What's wrong?"

"It's Saturday," Caitlyn wailed.

Rafe frowned. "So?"

Caitlyn wiped the tears from her eyes with the corner of her napkin. "So you'll be going into town and I'll be here all alone." *There*, she thought, *I've said it*.

"I'd stay home if I had a reason," he said gruffly. His eyes were hard when he looked at her, hard and unyielding. He wanted her, but he had vowed never to touch her again, not until she could come to him, willing and ready to be his wife.

Caitlyn swallowed hard. She wanted him, but she couldn't admit it, not out loud. And what if she agreed to let him make love to her and then couldn't go through with it?

"Rafe, I . . . can't you give me a little more time to . . ."

"Take all the time you want," he said curtly, and with a disgusted frown, he rose from the table and went to his room.

Moments later he emerged looking devilishly handsome in a pair of black twill pants and a dark red shirt.

"Don't wait up," he muttered caustically, and then he was gone.

The next five hours dragged as though time had stopped. Caitlyn cleared the table, washed and dried the dishes, and mopped the kitchen floor. She lit a fire in the hearth when she ran out of chores, picked up a book and tried to read, but the words made no sense and she tossed the book aside.

Filled with dismay, she gazed into the fire. The dancing flames were hypnotic, lulling her to sleep. As always, Rafe's dark image paraded through her dreams, his smile roguish, captivating. But this night her dreams turned to nightmares, his smile to a grimace, and suddenly there wasn't just one Indian in her dream, but dozens, all painted for war. They swarmed over the ranch, killing her father and Luther, killing the cowhands, burning the barn and the house. And then they were chasing her. She heard a voice calling her name, felt rough hands shaking her. . . .

"Caitlyn! Dammit, Caty, wake up!"

Rafe shook her, his eyes filled with concern as he saw the tears coursing down her cheeks, heard her soft cries of pain.

He drew her into his arms as her eyelids fluttered open. "It's all right," he murmured, dropping to the floor before the hearth, his arms tight around her. "It's all right." His hand stroked her hair, and his breath was a whisper against her cheek, soft, warm, and scented with brandy.

Caitlyn snuggled against him, grateful for the strong arms that held her tight, for the solace of his touch, for the sound of his voice, low and husky, assuring her there was nothing to fear.

"I was having a nightmare," Caitlyn said. "I was dreaming about the day my father was killed . . ." Her voice trailed off and her eyes searched his face, so handsome, so obviously Indian. Unconsciously, she stiffened in his embrace.

Rafe felt her body tense and though she didn't move, he felt her withdraw from him as he saw the accusation in her eyes. He could almost hear the disdain in her voice as she thought the word "Indian" in her mind.

"You okay now?" he asked, his voice cold.

Caitlyn nodded, her eyes trapped in the web of his gaze. She saw the hurt lurking in his eyes, felt his unspoken anger in the arms that still held her close.

"How long are you going to blame me for what happened to your father?" he asked brusquely. "How long will you go on hating me because I'm Indian, and hating yourself because you married me?"

"Rafe . . ."

"I'm not a savage, Caitlyn. I've never murdered anyone, red or white. I'm not a savage," he repeated, his ebony eyes hot on her face. "If I were, you'd be a woman now, and, oh, hell," he muttered, "maybe I am a savage."

His mouth covered hers in a kiss that was almost brutal in its intensity, his lips grinding into hers, his tongue sliding over her lower lip, demanding entrance to the honeyed sweetness within.

It never occurred to Caitlyn to object. Her arms went around his neck, and her mouth opened to his invasion as she kissed him back. The heat from the fireplace was nothing compared to the quick heat that ignited between them. She groaned low in her throat as his lips trailed down her neck, his tongue searing a path along the delicate skin of her throat before returning to her lips. Her heart was pounding like a blacksmith's hammer as Rafe's hands slid along her ribcage and down her thigh. Without taking his mouth from hers, he stretched out on the floor, taking her with him, so that their bodies were now pressed together, thigh to thigh, heat to heat.

His hand found its way under her nightgown and moved slowly, provocatively, over her ankle and calf to her thigh. She felt her breath catch in her throat as his hand stroked her bare flesh and her arm went around his neck, holding him close, as her tongue mated with his.

From far away she heard a distant sound, insistent, irritating. She whimpered softly when Rafe drew his lips from hers, and only then did she realize someone was knocking on the front door.

Rafe muttered a vile oath as he left Caitlyn and went to the door, his hand reaching for the Winchester rifle above the lintel.

He drew a deep breath, then exhaled in a long frustrated sigh. "Who is it?"

"Paulie."

Rafe opened the door, frowning. "What the hell are you doing here at this hour?"

"There was some trouble down at the corral," Paulie explained. "A mountain lion attacked Caitlyn's stud."

"Oh, no," Caitlyn exclaimed. Rising to her feet, she hurried to Rafe's side. "Is Red . . . is he still alive?"

"Yes, ma'am, but I think you should come down and take a look at him."

"Yes, of course."

The big red stallion was down on its side in the corral. Long gashes ran along its neck and flanks and it seemed to Caitlyn that there was blood everywhere. But the lacerations were not the worst problem. Somehow, in fighting off the mountain lion, the stallion had broken its left foreleg.

The stallion whickered softly as it caught her scent, and Caitlyn blinked back her tears as she knelt beside the horse.

"How bad is it, Paulie?" she asked, stroking the stud's forehead.

"Real bad, Mrs. Gallegher."

"Will he have to be destroyed?"

"I don't know. It's your decision, not mine."

"What would you do?"

"I'd try to save him, if he was mine."

Caitlyn nodded. "Is there anything I can do to help?"

"Stay by him. I think your presence soothes him some."

She sat by Red for the next two hours while Paulie set the stallion's broken leg, then carefully stitched up the numerous cuts and gashes in the animal's neck and flanks. Rafe remained with her, holding the stallion's head so it couldn't stand up.

It was near dawn when Paulie got up, his face lined with fatigue, his forearms bloody. "I've done everything I can do, Mrs. Gallegher. We'll just have to wait and see."

Caitlyn rose slowly to her feet, the muscles in her legs and back aching from sitting for so long. "Thank you, Paulie."

"We'll have to keep him in one of the stalls until his leg heals. I don't want him walking around on it."

"He won't like that," Caitlyn remarked, smiling faintly. "And he'll be a bear to ride when his leg is better. You know how he is if he isn't exercised every day."

Paulie nodded. There was no guarantee she'd ever be able to ride the blood bay stallion again and they both knew it.

"Let's go, Caitlyn," Rafe said, draping his arm around her shoulders. "You need some sleep. And I think Paulie does, too."

She didn't argue, but willingly followed Rafe out of the barn and back to the house. His arm slid down to her waist as they made their way down the narrow hallway to Caitlyn's bedroom. He took his arm from her waist when they reached the door and a sudden awkwardness rose between them.

They had been so close earlier, Caitlyn thought, wishing she knew how to recapture the intimacy of those moments before the fire. She almost asked him to stay the night with her so she might enjoy the comfort of his presence, discover what it would be like to fall asleep in his arms. But then, unbidden, came the thought of Frenchy's women, painted, powdered, and perfumed, sharing a bed with Rafe, holding him as she had been holding him, their hands more familiar with the hard planes and textures of her husband's body than she was.

"Good night, Rafe," she said curtly. How could she have let him kiss her earlier? How could she have forgotten that he preferred other women to his own wife?

"Caitlyn." There was a wealth of unspoken desire in his voice, a need to hold her, to comfort her.

For an endless moment they stood close, not quite touching.

She wanted him, Caitlyn thought, regardless of how many other women he had known. She wanted him, and that thought shamed her.

Rafe waited, hoping Caitlyn would ask him to stay, and when she didn't, he shoved his hands into his pants pockets and turned away. His voice was cold and bitter when he bid her good night and left her there, alone, untouched, and empty inside.

The following Saturday Caitlyn told Rafe she needed to go to Cedar Creek to get supplies, but all she really wanted was to get away from the ranch. She needed to see Christine, to talk to someone who would listen without sitting in judgment.

She dressed carefully that morning as appearances were important now, more important than ever. No one in town must ever suspect she was less than happy, that her marriage was far from perfect.

She chose a green dress with tiny white flowers embroidered on the scooped bodice. A wide white sash spanned her waist, and black kid boots hugged her feet. She took a last quick glance in the mirror before leaving the room. The dress complimented her hair and eyes and flattered her figure. She wondered if Rafe would notice how nice she looked, and then scolded herself for caring.

He was waiting for her in the parlor. He had gone shopping since their marriage, purchasing several pairs of trousers and shirts, as well as a pair of dress boots and a broad-brimmed black Stetson. Today he wore black pants and a dark blue shirt. His hat was pushed back on his head.

"Ready?" he asked curtly, and when Caitlyn nodded, he opened the door for her and followed her outside.

His hands were strong and sure as he helped her into the buckboard. Vaulting up onto the seat beside her, he took up the reins and clucked to the horses.

Caitlyn was hardly aware of the trip to town, so conscious was she of the man beside her. She felt her heart quicken each time his thigh brushed against hers, each time the jostling of the buckboard caused his arm to bump hers.

From the corner of her eye she studied his profile. Was it possible he had grown more handsome since they first met? Had his shoulders always been so broad, his legs so long?

She thought of the nights she had lain awake wanting him and yet, even as she desired him, she could not forget the nights he went to town. The image of Rafe making love to one of Frenchy's whores haunted and tormented her, making her own desire for him seem cheap, tawdry.

Rafe kept his eyes on the road. Since the night of Caitlyn's nightmare, he had waited, hoping she would admit she wanted him, hoping she would be able to forget he was half Indian and see him as a man and nothing more. But she seemed content with things the way they were, and he refused to beg for her favors. Indeed, he cursed himself for caring. Women were nothing but trouble, and yet he could no longer deny that he cared for her, that he wanted more than just a few quick kisses and an hour in her arms to relieve the awful ache that plagued him day and night. He wanted to share his thoughts with her, his dreams, his doubts.

He glanced at her, admiring the unblemished beauty of her skin, the gold of her hair, the blush in her cheeks. Her hands were folded in her lap and she seemed totally absorbed in the passing scenery.

He was glad when they reached town. Her nearness was a constant torment, and he left her at the Mercantile Store, saying he would meet her back there at three o'clock sharp.

Caitlyn smiled and said that would be fine, then watched as he walked across the street and entered the Cattlemen's Saloon. With a sigh, she hurried down the street to Christine's house. She had two hours to visit with her friend and get her shopping done before Rafe came to pick her up.

Christine was surprised to see Caitlyn, and they spent a few minutes exchanging pleasantries before Christine's curiosity got the best of her. Taking Caitlyn's hand in hers, she squeezed it.

"Enough about the price of yard goods and the weather," she said candidly. "What's bothering you?"

"Am I that transparent?" Caitlyn wailed softly.

"No, but then, I've known you long enough to know when something's troubling you. What is it?"

"It's Rafe," Caitlyn admitted.

"Does he beat you?" Christine asked, only half joking. The man was an Indian; nothing he did would surprise her.

202

"No, it's nothing like that. Oh, Chris, everything is such a mess!"

"I'm listening."

Caitlyn drew a deep breath and then, her eyes downcast, her voice low, she told Christine about what had happened on her wedding night.

"I behaved badly," Caitlyn finished. "I hurt him, I know I did."

"And now you're sorry."

Caitlyn nodded. "What should I do? I can't just sashay up to him and say, 'I'm sorry, let's go to bed.'"

"Why not? You're married."

Caitlyn stared at her friend in amazement. "How would it sound? What would he think? What if he refused me?"

Christine shrugged. "I think you're making too much of this. You want him. He seems to want you. What have you got to lose?"

My pride, Caitlyn thought to herself, but she didn't say the words aloud.

"Pride's not much company on a cold night," Christine said, her impish grin in place once more.

"You amaze me, Chris," Caitlyn muttered. "You're not even married, yet here you are, giving me advice. I'm shocked."

Christine laughed and Caitlyn joined in. The laughter released some of Caitlyn's tension and she felt better than she had in a long time.

"Anyone can give advice," Christine said. "I suppose I should be appalled to discuss such an intimate problem, but sometimes I think people make more out of marriage and mating than's necessary."

"Well, don't let anyone else hear you say that. Your reputation would be ruined," Caitlyn muttered.

"It certainly would be." Christine laughed. "Let me know how things turn out."

"I will. Thanks, Chris."

Caitlyn was smiling when she left Christine's house almost two hours later. Perhaps her friend was right. Perhaps she should take a chance and admit she had been wrong.

She entered the Mercantile Store and placed her order, chatting with the owner's wife while her things were loaded in the back of the buckboard. There were several women in the store and Caitlyn felt them watching her, wondering. *Married to a half-breed*, she could almost hear them thinking. *What is it like? Is he as savage as his Indian ancestors are known to be? Does he abuse her, beat her, degrade her?*

Turning from the counter, Caitlyn pasted a smile on her face, hoping she looked like a woman who was happily wedded and bedded. She nodded to several of the ladies as she left the store, felt her cheeks burn with rage when she overheard one of them whisper loudly that Caitlyn Gallegher had a lot of nerve, coming to town to mingle with decent, God-fearing people.

Outside, Caitlyn stood on the boardwalk, her gaze fixed on the saloon across the street, willing Rafe to come for her.

Instead, she saw Abner Wylie walking toward her.

"Afternoon, Mrs. Gallegher," Abner said, tipping his hat.

"Mr. Wylie."

"Fine day."

"Yes, it is."

"You're looking well," he said as his gaze slid over her, lingering on her breasts before returning to her face.

"Thank you," Caitlyn replied tersely. She kept her hands at her sides, resisting the urge to cross her arms over her breasts. "If you'll excuse me, I'm supposed to meet my husband at the post office."

It was a bald-faced lie, told in hopes of ridding herself of Abner's company. It didn't work.

"I'll just walk along with you," Abner said, and there was nothing for Caitlyn to do but start down the street toward the post office.

"How's everything at the ranch?" Abner asked.

"Fine."

"I heard a couple of your boys grousing at the saloon last Saturday night. Seems they ain't too happy about working for a breed."

Caitlyn pursed her lips, refusing to rise to the bait.

"Can't say as I blame them none," Abner went on. "You can't trust them redskins. They'll steal you blind."

Caitlyn scowled, wishing the earth would open and swallow Abner Wylie whole, though she thought that would be a mouthful, even for Mother Earth to accomplish.

"Well, here we are," Abner remarked when they reached the post office at the far end of town. "Seems as though your husband is late."

"Yes."

"You should have married me, Caitlyn," Abner said, his voice low and hard. "How could you sell yourself to that bastard? I'd have taken good care of you, and the ranch, too. You knew I was sweet on you. Your pa knew it, too, and he approved. You had no right to leave me for that damned breed. No right at all!"

Caitlyn stared at Abner, stunned by his words. The jealousy blazing in his pale blue eyes made her uneasy.

"I didn't leave you," Caitlyn said quietly. "There was never anything between us."

"I asked you to marry me three times!"

"I don't love you. I'm sorry."

"Do you love that breed?"

"That's none of your business."

"Like hell! If it wasn't for that damned Injun, I'd still be head wrangler at the Circle C, and you'd be my wife."

"That's not true!"

"The hell it isn't! Your old man liked me fine until that Injun came along."

"My father never stopped liking you, Abner," Caitlyn said. "You quit the Circle C, remember? He never asked you to leave."

"You were meant to be mine, Caitlyn," Abner said passionately, and before Caitlyn could guess what he had in mind, he pulled her into the alley between the post office and the Cedar Creek Bank and Trust and kissed her, his arms imprisoning hers at her sides while his body pinned her against the wall of the bank.

Caitlyn struggled furiously, repulsed by his kiss. She nearly gagged as his tongue forced its way into her mouth. An angry roaring filled her ears as his kiss grew deeper and then, recalling herself, she brought her knee up hard and fast.

Abner gasped and reeled backward as her

knee slammed into his groin. "You bitch!" he growled. "You'll be sorry for that."

"Don't you ever touch me again," Caitlyn warned. "I'll tell Rafe if you ever come near me again, and he'll kill you."

Abner grinned at her through the layers of pain that wracked him. Slowly, he caressed the butt of his gun. "I hope he tries."

Caitlyn felt a twinge of unease. Abner was fast with a gun. She had often seen him practicing behind the barn, matching his draw against that of the other cowhands. Abner never lost. His draw was sure and smooth and very, very fast. It was an odd talent for a cowboy, but he was good. Very good.

And Rafe didn't wear a gun.

With a small cry of dismay, Caitlyn ran out of the alley, her hand smoothing her hair as she went.

Abner watched her go, his narrowed eyes glinting with rage and unfulfilled desire. It galled him to know she had chosen a half-breed over him, and he vowed someday he would make her pay. Someday, somehow, he would find a way to have the ranch and Caitlyn, too. And if he had to kill the breed somewhere along the way, so much the better. He would like nothing more than to see Rafe Gallegher in his gun sights.

Abner laughed softly as he left the alley.

He had never realized he possessed such a deep vengeful streak, but the thought of taking vengeance against Caitlyn for her ill-treatment of him was sweet indeed.

Rafe was waiting for Caitlyn outside the Mercantile Store when she arrived, looking breathless and pale.

"Where've you been?" he asked, frowning.

"I stopped by the post office to see if there was any mail."

"You look like you ran all the way," he observed. "Did you get all your shopping done?"

"Yes. Shall we go home now?"

"If you're ready."

"I am."

He sent her a questioning glance, but when she said nothing more, he shrugged. Women, he thought. There was no understanding any of them. She'd been so eager to come to town, and now it seemed she couldn't wait to get home.

Caitlyn didn't mention the incident with Abner, thinking she'd tell Rafe later, at home. For now, she sat staring at the road, wondering if there wasn't some way she could hang onto her pride and still let Rafe know she wanted him.

The knowledge that it was Saturday night didn't help. What if he'd rather spend the night at Frenchy's than at home with her?

209

She fidgeted through dinner, knowing if she didn't do something that night, she never would.

As soon as dinner is over and the dishes are done, she thought, *I'll tell him I was wrong, that I didn't mean all the terrible things I said*.

Rafe stood before the small oval mirror propped on the highboy in his bedroom, shaving. He was getting tired of spending every Saturday night at Frenchy's, he thought, when what he really wanted to do was sit in the parlor and share a few quiet hours with Caitlyn. But he knew he couldn't stay in the same room with her and not touch her, not any more. Just being in the same house with her was torture. It wasn't too bad during the week; there was enough work to keep him busy outside. But Saturdays, the men quit early to go into town.

He slipped into a clean shirt, picked up his hat, and left the room. Except for the tension between himself and his wife, life at the Circle C was good. He had a home to call his own, three meals a day, and money in his pocket. Caitlyn's stallion was recovering rapidly. The wounds in Red's neck and flanks were healing, and Paulie was confident the stud's leg would mend in time.

Caitlyn was in the parlor, a basket of mending in her lap. As always, he was struck by her beauty. She wore a pink dress with a high lace collar and puffed sleeves. The tight bodice outlined her breasts; the wide sash emphasized her narrow waist. Her hair, as gold as the sun, fell in soft waves down her back, held away from her face by a narrow pink satin ribbon. Her profile was soft and feminine, her neck slender and inviting.

Caitlyn looked up as Rafe entered the room, her expression morose. "I guess you're going to town," she said, forcing a smile.

Rafe nodded curtly.

Now, Caitlyn thought. *Tell him now*. "Have a good time."

"Thanks."

He started to turn away, but something in her eyes held him. She looked sad, somehow, and he suddenly felt guilty for leaving her home alone every Saturday night. Then he shook his guilt aside. She could keep him home if she wanted to.

Caitlyn's throat felt tight. *It has to be now*, she mused, but somehow she couldn't form the words. *I'm sorry for the way I behaved on our wedding night*, she thought, rehearsing the words in her mind. It was a simple apology, long overdue. Why couldn't she say it?

Instead, to her horror, she blurted, "Do you have a special girl at Frenchy's?"

Rafe stared at her, appalled that a decent,

God-fearing woman would ask such a question, and then he began to laugh. "A special girl?" he exclaimed. "Hell, Caitlyn, I don't have *any* girl."

"I don't understand."

"I've never touched any of Frenchy's whores, Caitlyn," he confessed.

"Never?" Her heart felt suddenly light and carefree.

"Never."

"Why, Rafe?"

"Don't you know?"

Caitlyn's eyes were wide, as clear and green as the Pacific on a calm summer day. Slowly, she shook her head. "Why, Rafe?" she asked again, hoping he would say the words she suddenly longed to hear.

"Because of you." His voice was quiet, his dark-eyed gaze intent upon her face. "I thought about trying one of Frenchy's girls the first time I went there." He shrugged. "A couple of them aren't so bad to look at, but then I'd think about you, here, alone, and I couldn't do it. It's you I want, Caitlyn. No one else."

They were not the words she longed to hear, but they filled her with a bubbling sense of joy. He'd never made love to any of Frenchy's girls. Relief was sweeter than honey, chasing away the dreadful images her imagination had conjured up each Saturday night when Rafe left home.

"Caitlyn . . ."

She heard the question in his voice, saw the yearning in his eyes, and knew she could no longer deny her heart's desires.

Rising, she let the mending basket fall to the floor and walked into Rafe's arms. She pressed her face against his chest, suddenly shy and uncertain. She could feel the rapid beat of his heart beneath her cheek, feel the coiled tension within him as he held her close, his arms almost crushing the breath from her body. She felt his lips move in her hair.

"Caitlyn," he whispered as his hand began to stroke her back. "I've wanted you for so long, waited so long."

"Don't wait any longer, Rafe."

"Caty!" He scooped her into his arms and carried her swiftly down the hallway to her bedroom, his mouth raining kisses on her forehead and cheeks and finally her lips.

Gently, he placed her on the bed, his eyes blazing with an ebony fire as he stretched out beside her.

Caitlyn's heart was pounding erratically as she returned his kisses. She slid her hand under his shirt, her fingertips exploring the hard planes of his back. His skin was smooth, like satin over steel, and she marveled at the muscles that bunched beneath her hand.

Rafe's lips trailed down her neck as his fingers unfastened her dress. He pulled the bodice down, slipping it over her shoulders and down her arms. Her chemise came next and then he was dropping feather-light kisses on her shoulders, her throat, her breasts.

Caitlyn's breath caught in her throat as his lips nuzzled her flesh. She had never known such excitement, such wonder. Her skin flamed wherever he touched her, and she felt vibrant, alive, and terribly vulnerable. Her fingers threaded through his hair as she writhed beneath him, driven by a need she didn't quite understand.

But he understood. His hands were trembling with desire as he removed her clothing and then his own.

He was beautiful, she thought, perfectly proportioned. His skin was reddish brown all over, with a light sprinkling of fine black hair on his arms, legs, and chest. He had a small scar on his left thigh and she wondered what had caused it, but there was no time for such questions now, not when he was gathering her into his arms again.

She moaned with unbridled pleasure as her bare skin rubbed against his, whispered his name as he began to kiss her again, his hands gently massaging her back, stroking her thighs. His tongue was a dancing flame against her own. She was weightless, mindless, drowning in sensations she had never experienced, never imagined. Why had she waited so long to let him love her? Why had she wasted so many days, she lamented, so many nights, when she might have been here in his arms, touching him, tasting him, exploring his hard muscular frame?

His breath was warm against her face as he murmured her name, telling her that she was beautiful, desirable. And then he was atop her, his long body covering her own, fanning the fires between them.

She gazed up into his face, her arms wrapped around his neck, her body arching to receive him. There was a sharp stabbing pain and then, incredibly, only waves of pleasure as he moved deep inside her. She was dying, she thought vaguely, for surely no one could survive such heat, such ecstasy.

Time lost all meaning, reality faded away, and there was nothing but the two of them joined together in a blissful embrace as they moved to the ancient rhythms of love.

"Rafe, oh, Rafe!" she cried as bright rainbow waves of fulfillment washed over her. She felt his body shudder a moment later and then he lay still, his face buried in the hollow of her neck, his breathing labored and erratic.

215

She held him close, wishing the moment would never end. She was a part of him now, and he was a part of her. For this brief span of time they were truly one flesh. She had never felt so content, so utterly at peace.

Rafe continued to hold Caitlyn close, his hand absently stroking the curve of her breast as his lips nuzzled her neck. She was his now, truly his.

They lay close for a long time, and then Caitlyn shifted her weight, the movement innocently provocative, and Rafe found himself wanting her again. His blood warmed, his heart began to pound, and he rose over her once more, his dark eyes aflame.

"Caty?"

She nodded, surprised that he wanted her again so soon, and equally surprised to discover that she wanted him, too. He made love to her gently, tenderly, his hands and lips trailing fire as he aroused her.

His skin tasted of salt now, and his hair was damp beneath her hands. She let her palms slide over his arms, glorying in their strength. The heat in his eyes thrilled her even as desire coiled within her, drawing her toward the brink of fulfillment once again.

It was even better the second time, and Caitlyn was smiling with pleasure when Rafe's life spilled within her.

216

"My husband," she whispered the words, delighting in them, and in the sense of well-being that swelled inside her heart.

Rafe chuckled softly, his breath tickling her ear. "My wife," he murmured huskily. "At last."

CHAPTER TWELVE

CAITLYN WAS STILL SMILING WHEN SHE woke the next morning. Turning her head, she gazed tenderly at the man who had brought her such pleasure the night before. Her husband. She had never realized what a wonderful word that was: husband.

Her heart beat a quick tattoo as she studied his face. How handsome he was! She glanced at his long form outlined by the blankets. He was handsome all over, she thought, blushing. Last night she had explored his body with bold abandon, pleased beyond words with what she saw and touched. Her fingers had stroked and caressed each inch of him, surprised that her untutored hands could bring him pleasure.

She felt her cheeks grow warmer as she recalled how his hands had roamed freely over her own flesh, and how much she had enjoyed it. And suddenly she could not face him. Her feelings were all so new, so unexpected, she felt the need to be alone.

Slipping out of bed, she drew on her wrapper and tiptoed from the room. Going to the kitchen, she began to prepare breakfast. Soon the aroma of frying bacon and fresh-brewed coffee filled the room.

She was standing at the stove scrambling eggs when she felt his arms slip around her waist, felt his lips on the side of her neck.

"Good morning, wife," he murmured.

"Good morning, husband," she replied. Her voice was all aquiver, her hands trembling at his nearness. She took a deep breath and his scent filled her nostrils, stirring a sudden hunger that had nothing to do with food.

Rafe's hands slid upward, his fingers sliding over her stomach, until his hands cupped her breasts. Lowering his head, he buried his face in her hair, loving the womanly fragrance of her, the way she leaned against him, the soft sigh of contentment that escaped her lips.

"Caitlyn."

"Are you hungry?"

"Famished." He wasn't talking about breakfast and they both knew it.

"The eggs are almost done," she remarked.

"Leave 'em."

Nodding, she put out the fire, then turned to face him. She gave a little gasp, her cheeks turning crimson, when she saw that he was naked and fully aroused.

"Is that how you plan to come to breakfast every day?" she asked, smothering the happy laughter that welled in her breast.

Rafe grinned. "Do you mind?"

"Oh, no," Caitlyn replied, slowly shaking her head. "It's very becoming."

He grinned broadly as he scooped her into his arms and carried her back to bed.

They missed breakfast that day. And lunch.

Rafe let out a long contented sigh as he sipped a cup of hot black coffee. Caitlyn stood at the kitchen counter preparing an enormous meal. Her hair was still mussed, her lips slightly swollen from his kisses, her cheeks rosy, her eyes still warm with the afterglow of their lovemaking. She had never looked more beautiful.

He grinned as he felt the faint stirrings of desire. He had thought his yearning for her would wane once he had possessed her, but it seemed the opposite was true. Once had not been enough. Twice had only whetted his appetite for more. The third time had been exquisite, and still he longed to hold her again, to bury himself within her and never let go.

Caitlyn set a plate before Rafe, heaped high with sliced roast beef, potato salad, fresh corn, and buttermilk biscuits dripping with honey.

"I hope you're hungry," she said, smiling at him, and then, seeing the look in his eye, she shook her head. "You can't be serious!" she exclaimed. "Not again. Not so soon."

"Are you refusing me?"

"No, but couldn't we have something to eat first? I'm awfully hungry."

Rafe picked up his fork and speared a slice of roast beef. "Better eat up, then," he advised with a roguish grin. "You're gonna need your strength."

Late that night Rafe and Caitlyn sat on the sofa before the hearth. Her head rested on Rafe's shoulder, and her hand lay on his thigh. She felt very married sitting there beside him clad in nothing but a blue cotton wrapper. Rafe wore only a pair of trousers.

A fire blazed merrily in the fireplace, casting long shadows on the walls. Her stomach was full, her heart content, her lips slightly bruised from their last bout of lovemaking.

Once they had let the barriers down, it seemed they couldn't get enough of each other.

Caitlyn glanced up so she could see her husband's face. She loved his profile, and she loved him. It still surprised her, the way she felt about Rafe. She had waited so long to fall in love, had dreamed of a lean, wiry golden-haired man who would court her with candy and flowers and sweet words until, at last, she accepted his proposal, offered on bended knee, and became his wife.

But this was better, Caitlyn mused with a little sigh. Rafe was tall and broad-shouldered, darkly handsome, with a roguish smile that could make her forget everything else.

It occurred to her that she knew very little about the man who was now her husband in every sense of the word. And now, having discovered him physically, she wanted to know everything—his past, his hopes for the future, his dreams.

"Rafe, where were you born?"

"Georgia."

"How old are you?"

"Twenty-five."

"When's your birthday?"

"April 10."

She filed the date away for future use.

"Full of questions tonight, aren't you?" he

asked. He stroked her thigh, his hand dark against her alabaster skin, but Caitlyn would not be sidetracked.

"What's your father like?"

Rafe shrugged. "He's a wanderer, always was. That's why he likes living with the Lakota. They never stay in one place long, and my pa's always had an itch to see new places."

"Do you look like him?"

"Some, only his hair is brown."

"Do you think I'd like him?"

"Probably. Most women do."

"Would he like me?"

"Definitely."

Caitlyn was silent for a long moment, and Rafe wondered if she'd finally run out of questions. But she'd only been gathering her nerve for the next one.

"Did you ever ride to war with the Sioux?"

"A time or two," he admitted, knowing what her next question would be before it left her lips.

"Did you ever fight against your own people?"

"You mean *your* people, don't you?" Rafe asked sardonically. "They're both my people, Caitlyn. I'm as much Indian as white. But, no, I never rode against the Army, or the settlers, either. Only against the Crow when they raided our village."

"Did you wear war paint and feathers?"

"Yeah."

"It seems so . . . uncivilized." She tried to imagine him in a skin clout and moccasins, his hair in braids, his face streaked with vermillion. She was unsettled by how easily the image came to mind.

"It is uncivilized," Rafe replied, "but no one ever accused the Indians of being civilized, only savages." And yet, for all their primitive ways, they were the only people who had ever accepted him for what he was, the only people who hadn't cared about his mixed blood. He had been a good fighter, a capable hunter, and they had admired and respected him for that. And when he told them he would not fight against the whites, they had respected that decision, as well. No warrior was ever forced into battle; each man followed the dictates of his own conscience. If he wanted to fight, he did, and if he wanted to stay home, that was all right, too.

"You never told me why you left the Indians," Caitlyn remarked quietly.

Rafe's jaw clenched and for a moment she was sorry she had asked the question, for it seemed to have spoiled the companionable silence between them. But then Rafe took her hand in his and gave it a squeeze.

"I was banished from the tribe for killing a

man," he explained. "We'd both been courting the same girl, and . . ."

"What was her name?"

He had not meant to go into detail. "Summer Wind."

"Was she pretty?"

"On the outside."

"What do you mean?"

"I thought I was the only man she was
interested in, but she was courting Hump
Back Bear at the same time, letting us both
believe there was no one else." Rafe shook
his head. "Hump Back Bear was furious
when he found out about me. I would have
walked away, but he wouldn't let it go. He
was mad and spoiling for a fight, and the next
thing I knew, he was dead."

"Did you love her?"

"I thought I did at the time."

"Did you ever make love to her?"

"No."

"I'm glad," Caitlyn said. She could not
abide the thought of him making love to
another woman.

"Any more questions?" Rafe asked, his
voice lightly teasing.

She pretended to think about it, then
shook her head. "No, not right now," she
murmured, "except maybe one."

Rafe cocked an eyebrow at her. "Well?"

"Do you think you'll ever want to go back

226

to the Lakota?"

"I can't."

"Because you were banished?"

"Yeah."

"Not even to visit your father?"

"Banishment is like death, Caitlyn. I can't ever go back. It could mean my life at the most, a severe beating at the least. The Indians don't have very many laws, but the ones they have are strictly enforced."

Rafe yawned widely, a smile playing about his lips as he stretched his arms overhead. "I think I'm ready to turn in, wife," he remarked. "How about you?"

Caitlyn's heart skipped a beat as his gaze touched her lips. "Me, too," she agreed. "I'm terribly tired."

Rafe quirked an eyebrow at her as he reached for her hand.

"Not that tired," she amended, blushing prettily.

"I'll never see the outside of this house again if you don't stop looking at me like that," Rafe muttered as he dropped his arm around her shoulder. "I'm not complaining, though," he added, chuckling. "You're a lot prettier than those mangy cows."

"Thanks," Caitlyn retorted dryly.

His hand slid up and down her ribcage as they walked down the hall to the bedroom. Inside, he closed the door and then, very leisurely, he began to undress her.

"Damn," he breathed as he unfastened her robe. "You're the most beautiful thing I've ever seen."

His hands spanned her waist as he dropped his head to nuzzle her breast. Caitlyn gasped as little shock waves of pleasure rippled through her. She drove her fingers through his hair, her lips brushing the top of his head.

She heard his breath quicken as he slid the robe from her shoulders and quickly stepped out of his trousers.

"You're beautiful," she murmured fervently. "I never knew a man could be beautiful, but you are."

Rafe felt his neck grow warm at her unexpected compliment. Other women had remarked on his virility, his physique, his ability to satisfy them. But no one had ever told him he was beautiful.

He took her hand, led her to the bed, and gently pulled her down beside him. He meant to make love to her slowly, tenderly, but her nearness and the love in her eyes filled him with a sense of urgency and he took her masterfully, powerfully, his hands arousing her to fever pitch as he found release in her sweet womanly warmth.

* * *

They spent three days in the house, loving one another, getting to know each other. Rafe went out only once to assure Paulie that all was well, and to inform him that it would be business as usual the following week.

Paulie grinned knowingly. "Sort of a delayed honeymoon, huh?"

"You could call it that," Rafe agreed.

"I'll take care of everything," Paulie said, his grin growing wider by the minute.

Rafe nodded. He could feel Paulie grinning at his back as he returned to the house.

He found Caitlyn in the bedroom changing the sheets on the bed. Watching her, all thoughts of Paulie and the ranch left his mind.

Caitlyn shrieked as Rafe grabbed her from behind and dumped her unceremoniously on the bed. He began to tickle her, laughing when he discovered she was ticklish everywhere.

"It isn't fair!" she wailed as his finger tickled the bottom of her foot. "Stop it, Rafe! Please stop."

"Yes, ma'am," he said contritely, and releasing her foot, he folded his hands in his lap.

"What are you doing?"

"I'm stopping."

"Oh." She sounded disappointed.

"You told me to stop, didn't you?"

"I told you to stop tickling me," Caitlyn said, looking up into his eyes, a provocative smile playing over her lips. "Can't you think of anything better to do?"

"I'll work on it," he said solemnly.

And he did.

It wasn't until Thursday morning at breakfast that Caitlyn remembered her encounter with Abner Wylie. She stewed about it all day, wondering if she should tell Rafe what had happened. She tried to recall exactly what Abner had said as she prepared dinner that night.

"What is it, Caty?" Rafe asked, noticing her frown as she sat down across from him.

"Nothing, I . . ."

"Come on, Caty, spit it out."

"Do you remember when we went to town last Saturday?"

"Yeah."

"I saw Abner Wylie."

Rafe's dark eyes narrowed slightly. "Where?"

"Outside the Mercantile Store."

"What did he want?"

"He said that I should have married him, that I *would* have married him if you hadn't come along."

"What else?"

She hesitated. "Nothing."

"Don't lie to me, Caty."

"He tried to kiss me, and I kicked him . . . there. You know. I told him you'd kill him if he ever touched me again, and he said he hoped you'd try."

"Dammit, I will kill him!"

"No, Rafe! Promise me you won't do anything. Please. It will only cause trouble."

"Caty . . ."

"Please, Rafe, promise me."

"All right," he agreed reluctantly. "I promise. But if he ever lays a hand on you again, I'll skin him alive." Rafe's eyes glittered savagely. "And I know how it's done."

Their days fell into a pleasant routine in the next few months. They rose early, had breakfast together, then Rafe went out on the range with the hands while Caitlyn took care of the household chores. Sometimes he came home for lunch, sometimes Caitlyn rode out with a picnic basket and they shared a quiet hour under a shady tree.

Dinner was Rafe's favorite time of the day. Caitlyn proved to be an excellent cook and he complained that he was gaining weight. But it wasn't the food itself he enjoyed the most, it was Caitlyn. She was a constant joy. He delighted in her smile, her laughter, the way she spoiled him. After dinner, they would sit in the parlor. Sometimes they didn't say much; Caitlyn would be busy with the mending or a piece of embroidery while Rafe went over the ranch accounts.

But bedtime was the best time, and it came earlier and earlier each night as their passion for one another grew stronger. Rafe's need for Caitlyn continued to amaze him. She was his now, in every way, and still his desire for her raged like a fire out of control. Holding her only made him want her more, possessing her offered only a brief respite.

And Caitlyn felt the same. She could not seem to get enough of Rafe. She needed his touch as she needed air to breathe and water to drink. His smile charmed her, his touch left her breathless.

And so the days passed swiftly. Summer gave way to fall as the leaves turned, clothing the trees in magnificent gowns of burnt orange, gold, and crimson. The horses grew shaggy, the cows grew fat with calves that would be born in the spring, and Black Wind's belly began to swell. The barn had been rebuilt, bigger than before.

Hal and Wishful had decided to stay on through the winter and Caitlyn knew it was because of Rafe. They no longer considered him an outsider. He was good with the men, fair and honest, as her father had been, willing to listen to their complaints and suggestions.

They harvested the last of the crops, filled the barn loft with winter hay. Caitlyn put up the last jars of fruits and vegetables and felt a surge of pride in a job well done when she looked at her cupboards, each shelf filled with neatly labeled bottles.

Winter came in a rush of wind and rain that shook the last of the autumn leaves from the trees and flooded the rivers. Rafe spent long hours outdoors when the weather permitted, checking on the livestock, making certain the fences were still standing, that the river was clear of debris.

The first snow covered the land in a mantle of pristine white. The river froze, and the cowhands began hauling hay to the cattle. It was hard work. Caitlyn hated to see Rafe go out in the bitter cold, but he wasn't the sort of man to send his help out to do a job he wasn't willing to do himself.

It was the best thing he could have done, Paulie told Caitlyn one evening at dinner. Rafe worked as hard as anyone else, and the men respected him for it.

A few days before Christmas Caitlyn said she wanted a tree. Rafe looked at her kind of funny for a minute, and then he grinned.

"A Christmas tree," he drawled. "That *would* be nice."

"You act like you've never heard of one before," Caitlyn remarked, frowning at him.

Rafe chuckled. "Well, the Lakota weren't much for celebrating Christmas," he reminded her. "The last Christmas tree I saw was in a New Orleans brothel."

"Rafe!"

"It's true. The girls took Christmas Eve off and decorated the tree and then they sat around reminiscing about their favorite clients."

"Did they mention *your* name?" Caitlyn asked, her voice faintly sarcastic.

"You bet," Rafe said, winking at her.

"You're not serious!"

Rafe stared at Caitlyn, uncertain how best to answer. If he told her the truth, he knew she'd be angry. A lie would be better, he thought ruefully, but he wanted no lies between them.

"It was a long time ago, Caty," he assured her, the laughter gone from his eyes.

She had known the kind of life he had led in New Orleans; he had mentioned it before. But they were married now and knowing that he had made love to other women hurt dreadfully.

"Caitlyn, I'm sorry."

"It's all right," she said, not meeting his gaze. "I knew you weren't a saint."

"Caty, don't be angry." His fingertips caressed her arm, making shivers of delight skitter down her arm.

"I'm not."

"You are. You're jealous, aren't you?"

"Of course not."

"Admit it, Caty mine. You're jealous because I made love to other women. But it wasn't like what we have, Caitlyn. It was never like this."

"Truly, Rafe?"

"Truly."

She snuggled into his arms, her head on his shoulder. Outside, the snow fell in large lacy flakes, but inside it was warm, so warm. He had not said the words she longed to hear, but he would. She knew he would.

The lamp burned low, and Rafe began to caress her, his eyes holding more heat than the hearth, his lips telling her better than words that he wanted her, needed her.

She surrendered her lips to his, vowing she would never be jealous again, never doubt his love. She would be the only woman in his future, the only woman he would ever want or need.

CHAPTER THIRTEEN

IT WAS SPRING, AND THE TREES STRETCHED their arms toward heaven, their branches sprouting new growth. The grass poked its head through the last patches of snow, and the birds seemed to sing a little more brightly as they raised their morning hymns to the sky. Black Wind's belly was swollen with the life she carried, and Caitlyn began counting the days until the foal would be born.

Scott and Paulie and the others began to ride into the hills and canyons to round up the cattle, driving the animals to the ranch where the calves would be branded and castrated before driving them to market. Her father had made a deal to sell eight hundred head to Fort Laramie, and Rafe was making plans for the drive. Those plans did not include taking Caitlyn along, but she had other ideas, ideas she wisely kept to herself for the time being.

Rafe spent long hours out on the range and she threw herself into a fit of spring cleaning, scrubbing the floors, washing the windows, shaking out the rugs, and airing the bedding.

There had been some losses during the winter, Rafe told her one night at dinner. So far, they had found fourteen dead cows and a couple of dead calves. Most of the animals had been caught in a blizzard up country and froze to death.

But such losses were normal and Caitlyn did not dwell on them. She spent a part of every day at the holding pens, watching the cowhands brand the calves. It was hot, dirty, noisy work. Dust filled the air, clinging to the cowboys' sweaty arms and faces. The calves bawled for their mothers, the mothers bawled for their young, and the cowhands cursed long and loud as they wrestled frightened calves to the ground, burned the Circle C brand in their flesh, and castrated the males.

Usually, Caitlyn avoided the branding, but Rafe's presence in the pen drew her like a magnet. He had quickly learned the ins and outs of handling a branding iron and she watched with pride as he worked alongside Scott, Nate, and Wishful. Unlike the other cowhands, Rafe worked without a shirt, his muscles rippling beneath his sun-bronzed flesh, igniting little fires of desire within Caitlyn's breast. He was such a handsome man, such a joy to watch, tall and lean and rugged.

She made sure she had plenty of food waiting for him at the end of the day. He didn't seem to care what she served him for dinner so long as there was plenty of it and lots of hot coffee to go with it.

After dinner, she heated water for his bath while she washed the dishes. More often than not, she washed his back, and that always led to his front, and the next thing she knew, she was in the tub with him, or lying on the parlor floor on the rug in front of the hearth. No matter how many hours he worked, he was never too tired for her.

He told her with words and kisses and long slow caresses that she was beautiful, desirable. She gloried in his touch, in the power of his body, in the sweet romantic words he whispered in her ear, in the way he cried her name as their bodies came together in the final throes of passion.

Oh, yes, she thought, marriage was a wonderful thing, and Rafe Gallegher was everything she had ever dreamed of even though he never said the three words she longed to hear.

It was on a cool spring night that Black Wind went into labor. Paulie summoned Rafe and Caitlyn and the three of them took a place inside the barn near the mare's stall where they could watch her without being in the way.

The mare paced for about an hour, occasionally laying down, her legs thrust straight out, then rising to pace again.

Just when Caitlyn thought Paulie had made a mistake, Black Wind stretched out on the ground, straining mightily. There was a gush of water and then two tiny hooves slid into view, followed a moment later by a dark muzzle, and then the head and shoulders. Black Wind took a breather once the foal's head had emerged, and then, exerting herself one last time, she expelled the rest of the foal from the birth canal.

Caitlyn felt tears well in her eyes as she beheld the miracle of birth.

"It's beautiful, isn't it?" Rafe murmured. He took her hand and squeezed it as the mare whickered softly to her foal. Scrambling to her feet, Black Wind sniffed the foal, then began to lick the filly's neck.

"She's as black as the ace of spades," Rafe remarked.

Caitlyn grinned. "And those legs must be three feet long."

"She's a beaut!" Paulie declared.

Caitlyn and Rafe stayed until the filly had gained her feet and began nursing, then they bid Paulie good night. He would stay until Black Wind passed the afterbirth. While he waited, he daubed some iodine on the filly's navel to guard against infection, and then he made a hot bran mash for Black Wind.

Caitlyn was subdued as they made their way back to the house.

"What is it?" Rafe asked.

"The filly's beautiful," Caitlyn said, choking back a sob. "Pa would have been so pleased."

"Caty." He took her in his arms as she began to weep.

"Oh, Rafe, I miss him so!"

"I know, Caty, I know."

She pressed her face against his chest as her tears came faster, releasing some of the hurt in her heart. She had been close to her father. After her mother died and her brothers were killed, she and her father had turned to each other like two lost souls. They had grieved together and comforted one another, and in so doing they had forged a deep bond.

Gradually, Caitlyn's sobs decreased and she became aware of Rafe's hands stroking her hair, his strong, capable hands gentle as they soothed her.

"Pa had such big dreams when we started out," Caitlyn said, sniffing. "He wanted to raise the best horses in the territory, to make a new home for my brothers and me after my mother died. He wanted to make the name Carmichael stand for something, build something he could be proud of. But he never got to see his dreams come true, Rafe. He died a little when the Indians killed my brothers, but he still had his dream. With Red and Black Wind, he found a new hope for the future and he began to think it wasn't too late, that his dream of raising the best horses in the territory might still come true. And then those filthy savages killed him in cold blood." Hatred filled her voice and dried the last of her tears. "I wish they were all dead, Rafe. Every last one of them." Her anger vanished as quickly as it had been born. "I wish he could have seen the filly . . ."

She was suddenly aware of Rafe's arms around her, of the fact that his muscles were taut, his jaw tight. For a moment she wondered what was wrong, and then she knew. The words "filthy savages" screamed inside her head.

She glanced up, her eyes begging for his understanding. She no longer thought of him as an Indian, but as her husband, the man she loved. But she could find no forgiveness in her heart for the savages who had killed her brothers and murdered her father and Luther. The West would be a better place if every Indian on the face of the earth was wiped out once and for all.

"Rafe . . ."

"It's all right, Caitlyn."

His words offered little comfort, not when she saw the anger in his eyes. He was half Indian and she knew intuitively that he could not separate himself from her words.

"I didn't mean you were a savage," Caitlyn said, wanting to erase the barely suppressed fury in his eyes. "I don't think of you as an Indian any more, I . . ." She bit off her words, knowing she was only making things worse. He was proud of his Indian heritage, proud of who and what he was.

Rafe released her and went to the hearth where he rolled and lit a cigarette. He could not blame Caitlyn for her hatred of Indians. She had ample reason to hate and fear them and yet, her words had filled him with anger and pain. People had scorned him and looked down on him his whole life because of the Indian blood in his veins. He had endured numerous insults, felt his anger rise when men called him a dirty half-breed. The women hadn't been so bad. They had been fascinated by his Cherokee blood, titillated by the fact that he was a savage, forbidden, mysterious. He knew if he'd been short, fat, and ugly, they would have shunned him. But he had inherited his mother's dusky skin, black hair, and ebony eyes, and Killian Gallegher's charm and rugged good looks.

Rafe scowled as he gazed out the window. He was not unaware of his looks. Women had always fawned over him because they liked his long, lean frame and rugged countenance. He was not vain about his appearance; it was a fact of life, and if it had made him more desirable to the ladies, well, so be it.

He had thought himself past hurting, now that he had Caitlyn for his wife and a home to call his own. But her words had cut like a knife. Filthy savages. Was it possible that, deep down, that was how she thought of him, too?

He tossed his cigarette into the fire, watched it flame and die. He didn't really have a home to call his own, he mused. The ranch belonged to Caitlyn; the deed was in her name. He was no more than a ramrod, making sure the men stayed in line, the work was done, things ran smoothly. Being married to the boss was just an extra bonus.

He was surprised at how bitter he was.

"Rafe." He heard the uncertainty in her voice, the sadness, the regret.

"Go to bed, Caitlyn," he said curtly.

She hesitated for a moment, wanting to go to him, to make things right between them again. But she could not bring herself to cross the short distance between them. He looked so angry. So unforgiving. So hurt.

She murmured a quick good night and left the room. She sat on the edge of the bed for a quarter of an hour, idly brushing her hair as she listened for the sound of his footsteps in the hall. But she heard only silence.

Slipping under the covers, she stared up at the ceiling, refusing to cry. Why was he being so sensitive and unreasonable? Surely he knew she didn't think he was a savage! After the last few months, he must know that she loved him wholly and completely.

She heard the clock chime the hour and still he did not come to bed. Her eyelids grew heavy, heavier, until sleep claimed her.

When she woke the following morning, she was alone in bed. Glancing at the pillow beside hers, she was dismayed when she saw he had not come to bed at all.

Rising, she drew on her wrapper and hurried into the kitchen, hoping to find him. But the kitchen was empty. A lone coffee cup bore mute evidence that Rafe had been there earlier.

Discouraged, Caitlyn poured herself a cup of lukewarm coffee, then stood at the kitchen window, staring out. Darn her thoughtless tongue! He had every right to be offended.

Moments later she saw him ride out of the yard mounted on a big bay gelding.

A sense of depression settled over Caitlyn as she watched Rafe ride away. He'd be gone all day, riding the south range with Scott and Rusty Jordan. Why hadn't he stayed for breakfast so they could settle the problem between them?

It was an effort to do the chores that day. Usually she made the bed and cooked and cleaned with a song on her lips, but today black depression followed her from task to task. She had no appetite so she skipped lunch, wondering if Rafe's pride would fill his empty belly. He'd had no breakfast and would get no midday meal unless one of the hands had packed enough for two.

Late in the afternoon she went into the barn to see Black Wind and the filly. The filly was asleep on a pile of straw, but she woke up as Caitlyn leaned over the stall door. Caitlyn could not help smiling as the day-old foal scrambled to her feet and began to nurse.

"She's a beautiful baby," Caitlyn told the mare as she scratched her forehead. "Just beautiful."

She spent another few minutes in the barn, then wandered outside. Red whickered as she passed his corral and she decided to take the stallion out for some light exercise. Perhaps an hour or two in the open would make her feel better.

Twenty minutes later she was riding away from the ranch.

It was a lovely day. The air was turning cool as the sun began to slide behind the mountains, but the heavens were a cloudless blue, the trees gorgeous in their new spring green. Scattered patches of wildflowers added spots of color to the greening hills, and the river was running high and wide.

She passed several head of cattle as she rode toward the pool and she made a mental note to tell Scott so he could round the animals up.

The pool was still, ringed with a carpet of new grass. She saw several squirrels scampering between the trees, heard the raucous cry of a jay.

Dismounting, she pulled off her boots and stockings and dangled her feet in the cold water. Red grazed beside her, enjoying the fresh grass. After a few minutes, Caitlyn took her feet out of the water. She had been contemplating a swim, but the pool was too cold.

She wondered if Rafe would be in a better mood when he came home that night. What could she say to appease him? She'd slept badly last night, missing his arms around her, missing his kiss that sent her off to sleep each night and woke her each morning.

She turned at the sound of hoofbeats and saw Scott, Rusty, and Rafe riding toward her, herding a dozen head of cattle. She felt her heart quicken as she saw her husband. Would he acknowledge her presence, or simply ride on?

She stood up so he would be sure to see her, saw him gesture for Scott and Rusty to go on ahead. Then he was riding toward her.

Caitlyn's heart was beating rapidly by the time he reined his horse to a halt beside the pool, and she stared up at him, wishing she could think of something to say that would heal the rift between them.

Rafe let out a long sigh. He was tired and dusty and hungry, yet just looking at Caitlyn made him forget all that. She was wearing a blue cotton shirtwaist and a calico skirt that was damp around the hem. Her hair was tied back with a blue ribbon, though several strands had escaped to curl around her face. But it was her eyes that held him. They were as green as the grass at her feet, filled with a silent plea for his forgiveness.

He mouthed a vague obscenity as he swung from the saddle and took her in his arms. She melted against him, her eyes welling with tears.

"Forgive me," she murmured. "I never meant to hurt you."

"I know." Drawing back a little, he cupped her face in his hands, his fingertips wiping away her tears. He felt his heart catch as she gazed up at him, her cheeks damp, her eyes filled with love.

"Caty."

"I love you, Rafe. I never meant to offend you."

"I know." It wasn't her fault she hated Indians anymore than it was his fault he was a half-breed.

Gently, tenderly, he kissed her and the touch of her lips drove away all the hurt, all the hard feelings.

"Come on," he said huskily. "Let's go home."

Caitlyn nodded, her heart light as Rafe lifted her onto Red's back, then swung aboard his own bay gelding.

Side by side, they rode toward the Circle C.

CHAPTER FOURTEEN

Rafe LET OUT A SIGH OF EXASPERATION. "Dammit, Caitlyn, you're not going and that's that. The trail's no place for a woman."

"You sound just like my father," Caitlyn retorted.

"Well, he was right. Now I want your word that you'll stay here until I get back."

Caitlyn's eyes flashed with defiance, shooting green sparks at him. "I'm going, and *that's* that. You seem to forget those are my cattle. I have every right to ride along."

"You have no rights at all except the ones I give you," Rafe snapped. "You're my wife, and I'm telling you to stay here, at home, where you belong."

Caitlyn glared at her husband, too angry to speak. How dare he talk to her like that! No right, indeed! The ranch was hers, the cattle were hers, and she would do as she darn well pleased. And if he didn't like it, that was just too bad.

Rafe swore under his breath. He had tried to reason with her, he had tried to threaten her, and now he had tried to bully her, and nothing had worked. One way or another, he knew Caitlyn was determined to accompany the herd to Fort Laramie and short of tying her to the bedpost, he couldn't think of any way to make her stay home.

"Caty, please do as I ask."

She felt her anger drain away at his soft-spoken request. She almost agreed but then she shook her head. "I'm going."

He knew when he was licked. "We're leaving at first light. Be ready, or we'll go without you."

It was an empty threat. He wasn't about to leave her behind. Knowing Caitlyn, she'd just follow him, maybe get into trouble, maybe get lost. He couldn't take that chance. Besides, he didn't really want to spend the next couple of months sleeping alone, wondering if she were all right at home.

Caitlyn smiled triumphantly. "I'll be ready."

* * *

They were on the trail shortly after dawn the following morning, eight hundred head of belligerent cattle, six men, and one woman who could hardly suppress her excitement. Paulie and Rusty were staying behind to look after the ranch.

Rafe rode up beside Caitlyn. "Are you sure you won't change your mind? This isn't an overnight ride, Caty. We'll be gone for weeks."

"I'm going."

Rafe nodded. Removing his hat, he swung it over his head and Scott started the herd moving down the trail. It would take a week or more until the herd was trail-wise and until then they were in for a lot of hard work.

An hour later, Caitlyn was wondering why she'd been so determined to accompany the herd. The cattle bawled continually, loudly protesting each step of the way, almost as if they knew what fate awaited them at the end of the trail. Great clouds of dust choked the air, and only the kerchief tied over her nose and mouth kept her from choking on the thick powdery dust. Added to the bawling cattle could be heard the shouts of the men as they tried to keep the herd moving in the right direction, the occasional whinny of a horse, and the constant rumble of hundreds of hooves jarring the ground.

The cowhands pushed the herd hard that

first day, wanting to get them as far from familiar territory as possible. Tired cattle, Caitlyn knew, were less inclined to wander away from the herd, and less likely to try and turn back toward their home range. Later, when the herd was trail-wise, they would travel slower, covering twelve to fifteen miles a day, giving the cattle time to graze and fatten up along the way.

Her father's cowhands knew what to do; they had done it several times in the past. Scott and Nate rode point that first day. Hal rode the line, while Josh and Wishful, who had been the last to hire on, rode drag, urging the herd along.

The cattle were nervous on the trail at the beginning of the drive, ready to bolt at the slightest provocation. Brenden Carmichael had always included a few old bulls in the herd to help calm the other animals and counteract the antics of the young steers. Caitlyn saw that Scott had done the same.

They rode hard for five hours, pausing only briefly for a quick meal at noon, and then they were on the move again.

Another six hours passed before Rafe called a halt. By then, Caitlyn was certain she would never be the same. She was positive her legs were permanently bowed, just like Web's. Every muscle in her body was stiff and sore and she was more than a little relieved to be off the back of her horse and standing on solid ground. It took the last bit of her energy to strip the rigging from her mount and then she dropped to the ground, sitting cross-legged on her saddle blanket, too weary to pay any attention to what was going on around her.

Web had volunteered to do the cooking on the trail. Caitlyn knew she should offer to help him prepare the evening meal, but she couldn't seem to make her legs move. She was vaguely aware of the cowhands settling the herd for the night and heard Rafe issuing orders designating who would take the first watch, who would take the second, and so on. The smell of woodsmoke tickled her nostrils as Web lit the cook fire, and she heard the men gather round, talking about the day's events. But, by then, she was almost asleep. Hardly aware she had done so, she lay down, curled into a ball, closed her eyes, and fell asleep.

Rafe shook his head when he found her asleep beneath a lacy cottonwood. If he'd had a man to spare, he would have sent her back home, but it was too late now. He debated waking her for supper, but decided she needed rest more than food. After covering her with a blanket, he swung into the saddle and rode out to check on the herd, making sure the nighthawks were in place

before he returned to the fire. Web had
cooked up a mess of chili and beans and
sourdough biscuits that met with everyone's
approval, and Rafe let out a sigh of relief.
There was nothing worse than the prospect
of spending weeks on the trail eating grub
that wasn't worth chewing. A good cook
meant one less thing for the men to grumble
about.

Gradually, the fire burned low and the
men turned in. Then Rafe sought his own
blankets. Caitlyn was still asleep, one hand
tucked under her cheek, her hair a golden
frame for her face. He felt the familiar
longing well inside him when he looked at
her, but this was not the time or the place.

Wrapping a blanket around him, he
stretched out beside her, his head pillowed
on his saddle, his hat pulled over his eyes. Yet
even then he was aware of the woman lying
beside him. He could hear the soft sound of
her breathing, smell the faint fragrance that
clung to her hair. He was still awake when
Scott shook his shoulder to inform him it
was his turn to ride herd on the cattle.

It was a dark night, peaceful and quiet.
Rafe rode around the herd, passing the other
nighthawk with a nod and a low-spoken
greeting. Most of the men sang softly as they
circled the herd, but Rafe wasn't familiar
with the mournful cowboy songs and so he

rode silently, his thoughts on Caitlyn and their future together.

The next week went by in a haze of dust and long hours in the saddle. Caitlyn took to riding with Web in the chuck wagon when the long hours on horseback got to be too much for her. The old man didn't say much, but they got along well enough, and she began helping out with the cooking, although Web insisted on making the coffee and the biscuits, complaining that her coffee was too weak and her biscuits a mite heavy.

"Heavy, indeed!" Caitlyn had muttered under her breath, but she didn't argue. He was the cook; the chuck wagon was his domain.

She didn't get to spend much time with Rafe, though she saw him often and slept near him at night. She hadn't realized how much she had enjoyed going to sleep in his arms until it was denied her. Now she was lucky if he kissed her good night. She knew his feelings for her hadn't changed; it was only because they were surrounded by cowhands that he kept his distance, but she missed his affection just the same. He had shown her what passion was, had aroused desires she had never dreamed existed, and now she could not even touch him. And he was so desirable. Her eyes followed him whenever he was near, admiring the way he rode the buckskin gelding he had chosen from the remuda, the way his shirt molded itself to his shoulders and back, the way his jeans hugged his long muscular legs. He was good with the men, heeding their complaints, settling their disputes, and laughing at their bawdy jokes.

They had been on the trail for over two weeks when they saw the Indians, a half-dozen braves mounted on calico ponies. Caitlyn stared at them, fear choking her throat as she stared at their hideously painted faces, the feathers tied in their long black hair, and the weapons in their hands.

Rafe rode to the chuck wagon and told Web to stop the wagon, then he rode out to meet the Indians. Caitlyn felt as though the breath had left her body as she waited for Rafe to return. Would he return? Or would the Indians kill him and then massacre her and the others?

After what seemed like an eternity, Rafe rode back to the wagon. "They're Cheyenne," he said curtly. "They want some of our cattle. If we give them a couple head, I think they'll ride on. If we refuse, I think they'll fight."

"Give them what they want," Caitlyn said. "Anything to get rid of them."

Rafe nodded. He called to Scott, who was

riding drag, and they rode through the herd, cutting out six head of prime cattle, and then Rafe went to talk to the Indians again.

Fifteen minutes later the Indians were gone, and so were six head of Circle C cattle.

"They had a hard winter," Rafe told Caitlyn, his eyes gazing into the distance. "Their children are hungry and their old ones are dying. Their shaman has told them the gods are displeased with his red children, and that the buffalo will not come this year."

"That's silly," Caitlyn said, frowning.

Rafe shrugged. "Some of the Indians believe that the coming of the white man is a punishment from *Wakan Tanka*. And who knows, they could be right. The white man's diseases have already wiped out some of the tribes. And now the buffalo are growing scarce. And if the buffalo disappear, the Indians will disappear right along with them."

Rafe shook his head, as if to clear it of bad thoughts. "Move her out, Web. We've got some catching up to do."

They camped near a river a few days later, and as soon as her horse had been tended, Caitlyn slipped away from the camp and sought out a secluded place where she could bathe. She was sure she had never been quite so dirty in her entire life. Her hair was layered with dust, and her skin was gritty with dirt and dried sweat.

At the river's edge, she slipped out of her riding skirt and shirt and made her way into the water, gasping as the cold wetness closed over her. Taking a deep breath, she plunged into the river, fighting down a shriek as the coldness penetrated her skin.

She was floating lazily sometime later when Rafe's voice split the peaceful silence.

"What the hell are you doing?" he demanded, his voice harsh and filled with anger.

Caitlyn stood up, her arms automatically folding over her breasts. "I'm taking a bath," she replied mildly. "What's wrong?"

"What's wrong?" he exclaimed. "I'll tell you what's wrong . . ." His voice trailed off as his eyes swept over her. Her hair was wet and shiny, like liquid gold. Her skin was pink, adorned with hundred of tiny water droplets that caught the amber rays of the setting sun and sparkled like a web of diamonds across her skin. He let his gaze slide over her, dropping lower, lower, until the water shut off his view of her sleek flesh.

Caitlyn felt suddenly warm all over as Rafe's eyes wandered over her damp skin. It had been so long since he had held her close, so long since she had felt his body next to her own, felt his breath warm upon her face.

As if drawn by an invisible thread, she left the water and walked into his arms, sighing as he drew her close. She felt his lips move in her hair, and then he was lifting her in his arms and carrying her away from the river toward a copse of trees that were sheltered in the lee of a craggy boulder. Gently, he placed her on her feet and then, wordlessly, he began to undress.

Caitlyn felt her heartbeat quicken at the sight of him, felt her cheeks grow hot as he drew her down onto the ground and began to cover her face and neck and breasts with the softest of butterfly kisses. His hands were impatient as they sought her secret places, his lips insistent as he covered her mouth with his own. His tongue slid over her lips, tantalizing, persuasively demanding entrance, and she felt her bones turn to butter and her blood to flame as his tongue slid into her mouth.

"Wife," he groaned, his voice hoarse with longing. "It's been too long."

"Too long," she agreed, her own voice throaty with desire.

She felt his weight as he rolled onto her, his knee spreading her thighs, and she welcomed the burden. She lifted her hips to receive him, sighing with pleasure as he filled her, making her complete. They were perfect together, she thought exultantly, like two halves of the same whole.

It was only later, when their desire was spent and she lay curled in his arms, that Rafe remembered his anger. Lifting himself on one elbow, he gazed down into Caitlyn's face.

"Never again," he said, speaking each work slowly and distinctly. "Never again are you to leave camp alone. Is that understood?"

"Yes sir," she answered petulantly.

"Dammit, Caitlyn, you're not at home now. There are Indians out here, in case you've forgotten. Wild animals, snakes, and who the hell knows what else. It isn't safe for you to go wandering off alone."

He was right and she knew it. "I'm sorry, Rafe," she said contritely, "I guess I just didn't think."

She lifted her hand to caress his cheek, smiling a little at the scratchy stubble that tickled her fingertips. Rafe let out a long breath as he turned his head and kissed her palm. He had been furious when he returned to camp and found her gone, furious and terrified. They were out in the middle of nowhere, surrounded by endless miles of untamed country and hostile Indians. His imagination, usually none too colorful or creative, had conjured up a dozen horrible fates that might have befallen her.

"Caty, I didn't mean to shout at you. I . . ." He lacked the words to tell her how he felt, and so he bent down and kissed her instead.

But Caitlyn saw the love and concern in his eyes, and her answering kiss told him she understood.

The next few days passed peacefully enough. Caitlyn stayed close to camp, ever aware of Rafe as he went about his duties. She had chosen her husband well, she thought proudly, for he was quite capable at bossing a trail drive, even though she knew he had never done it before. He owed part of his success to the fact that he wasn't too proud to ask Scott or the other men for their opinion if he wasn't sure about something. He took his turn as nighthawk and at riding drag, which was the worst position on the trail. No one liked riding at the end of the herd, eating dust for hours at a time.

They had been on the trail almost three weeks when they reached the North Platte River. Caitlyn felt a twinge of apprehension as she watched the cowhands drive the herd across.

Fording a river was always dangerous, even if the water was low. But on this day, the North Platte was running high and wide. Caitlyn held her breath as Scott, Nate, and Wishful urged the lead steers into the water.

The cattle plunged into the river, swimming with their heads just above the water. Caitlyn said a silent prayer that none of the steers would try to turn back. Many a cowboy had lost his life in the midst of a herd of swimming cattle that had suddenly tried to turn back the way they had come.

She felt her mouth go dry as she watched Rafe put his horse into the water, urging a few stragglers toward the far bank.

It seemed to take forever, but, at last, the entire herd was safe on the other side. Rafe had crossed the river several times and now he came back to help her across, while Scott and Nate helped Web get the chuck wagon to the other side.

Caitlyn kept her horse close to Rafe's buckskin gelding as they forded the river. With anyone else, she would have been afraid, but not with Rafe. He would take care of her.

She was about to breathe a sigh of relief when a burst of gunfire rent the air, followed by a shower of arrows. The cattle took off in a dead run, stampeding across the broken hills. Caitlyn's horse panicked, lost its footing in the sandy river bottom, and began floating downriver.

Rafe swore under his breath as all hell broke loose. He seemed to see everything at once: the cattle running at breakneck speed, the Indians rising up out of nowhere, and the cowhands quickly unholstering their guns and firing at the Indians. But there was no time to worry about anything or anyone but Caitlyn, and he yanked on his horse's reins, intending to follow her, when an arrow pierced the buckskin's neck. The horse reared up in the water, then toppled over sideways, forcing Rafe to kick free of the saddle or be swept away under a thousand pounds of dead weight.

He cast a quick glance at the shore. All the men were out of sight except Web, who had taken cover behind the wagon and was rapid-firing a rifle in the direction of the attackers.

A bullet whistled dangerously close to Rafe's head and he went underwater, letting the current carry him downstream after Caitlyn.

He remained underwater until he thought his lungs would burst and when he surfaced, he was far downriver. He climbed onto the riverbank, shaking the water from his eyes as he searched the riverbank on both sides, his gaze sweeping up and down. Away in the distance, he could hear the sound of gunfire and the faint shouts of the men. But here, there was only a taut silence.

He felt the short hairs prickle along the back of his neck as he drew his knife. Crouching, he studied the ground at his feet, then swore softly as he saw the trail of a shod horse veering away from the riverbank. Two other horses, both barefoot, had closed in on the shod horse almost immediately. All three sets of tracks led into the trees some twenty yards away.

His mouth set in a grim line, Rafe reached back into his memory, summoning everything that the Lakota had taught him about tracking an enemy. He stripped off his wet shirt, removed his boots and sodden socks and began to move forward, his footsteps as silent as the whisper of the clouds dancing across the sky. All thought of the cattle and the fate of the Circle C cowhands was forgotten. Only Caitlyn filled his thoughts.

He moved noiselessly, his eyes and ears straining for any sight or sound that would guide him to his woman. Occasionally, he paused, his head lifting, his nostrils testing the wind like a wolf on the scent of prey.

He had been on the trail for about forty minutes when he heard it: a faint feminine cry laced with terror.

A cold smile peeled Rafe's lips back in a feral grin of satisfaction. His quarry was near.

Another few yards, and he came to their horses, tethered to a sturdy sapling. Going to ground, he snaked his way through the tall grass.

Caitlyn struggled wildly as two Indians wrestled her to the ground. Fear added strength to her limbs, but she was no match for two men driven by lust.

Tears of fear and frustration burned her eyes as one of the Indians yanked her riding skirt down to her knees. A brown-skinned hand passed before her eyes and she lunged forward, sinking her teeth into the man's palm. Blood filled her mouth and she felt a fleeting moment of triumph as the brave uttered a cry of pain and jerked his hand away.

It was a small victory and accomplished nothing. She heard her shirt and chemise rip, felt a breath of cool air brush over her exposed breasts. The Indians leered down at her, their eyes hot, their paint-smeared faces like something out of a hideous nightmare.

"Oh, God, help me," she murmured aloud, knowing in her heart that no help would come. She was lost and alone, totally at the mercy of the two savages who were tearing away the last of her undergarments.

The warrior on her left grabbed both her hands and pulled her arms over her head, while the second warrior straddled her hips. Unable to move, she closed her eyes as he began to unfasten his breechclout.

Time seemed to slow, emphasizing every movement and sound. She felt the Indian's hands on her belly, heard a low gutteral laugh as his companion urged him on. The wind rustled the leaves on the trees, cooling the sweat on her skin and she began to shiver.

Two fat tears slipped under her closed eyelids. They would rape her and kill her and she would never see Rafe again. She felt suddenly sorry for her husband. He would come looking for her, find her body, abused and scalped. Poor Rafe.

She gasped as she felt the Indian's hands on her breasts and she was glad she was going to die. Rafe would not want her after this. No man would want a woman who had been defiled by savages.

The Indian squeezed her breast painfully and she began to weep, crying for the pain, crying because she didn't want to die.

She heard a soft grunt, felt a sudden weight on her chest as the Indian straddling her hips fell forward.

Caitlyn's eyes flew open and she felt her stomach churn as she saw the haft of a knife protruding from the warrior's back. The remaining Indian released his hold on her hands and scrambled to his feet, his narrowed eyes searching the trees.

Disbelief widened Caitlyn's eyes as she saw Rafe step into the open. He was unarmed, and Caitlyn heard the Indian behind her laugh softly as he drew a knife from his belt.

Rafe spared hardly a glance at Caitlyn, who was trying to wriggle from beneath the dead weight of the Indian sprawled across her chest. All his attention was focused on the tall Crow warrior grinning at him.

The Indian held out his left hand, gesturing for Rafe to come closer. Rafe smiled in reply, silently cursing the fact that he had lost his rifle in the river. He glanced around, hoping to find a weapon he might use, but he saw none save for a bow lying beside the dead brave, the knife in the warrior's hand, and his own knife sticking out of the dead man's back.

With a sigh of resignation, Rafe stepped forward, his arms outstretched, his chin tucked under.

The Crow went forward to meet the white man. Certain of an easy victory, he lashed out with his knife, slashing at the white man's chest. Rafe jumped out of the way, trying to maneuver closer to the dead man and the blade in his back, but the Crow grinned and shook his head.

With a supreme effort of will Caitlyn managed to extricate herself from beneath the dead Indian. It took her a moment to catch her breath, and then she rolled over and scrambled to her knees, her eyes riveted on the two men circling each other only a few feet away.

The Crow's blade had made contact with flesh and there were several shallow cuts on Rafe's arms. And even as Caitlyn watched, the Crow opened a wicked gash in Rafe's side while managing to avoid being entangled in Rafe's grasp.

He needs a weapon, she thought frantically, and cursed the fact that the Indians who had attacked her were armed with nothing but a bow and a knife.

Choking back the bile that rose in her throat, she grasped the handle of the knife lodged in the dead man's back. Closing her eyes, she tightened her grip and jerked the blade free.

Rising to her feet, she called Rafe's name and when he risked a glance in her direction, she tossed him the knife. Drops of blood sprayed through the air like drops of red rain.

Rafe caught the knife in mid-air, grinned broadly as his fingers curled around the handle.

The smile left the Crow's face when he saw that his opponent was armed. The contest was no longer a game he was sure to win, but a fight in which there could only be one victor.

The Crow was a skilled fighter, agile and

fearless, but Rafe had learned to fight in the back streets of New Orleans, and he used every dirty trick he had been taught.

Caitlyn watched, breathless, her hands clenched against her breasts, her heart beating erratically. It seemed as though hours had passed instead of mere minutes. Both men were sweating profusely, and bleeding from numerous minor cuts on their arms and chests. She looked at Rafe, momentarily repelled by the fury in his eyes, by the feral expression on his face. His lips were slightly parted, his eyes narrowed to slits, his whole being centered on the man glaring at him across two feet of ground.

And then her momentary revulsion was swept away by a wave of pride. He was her husband, her man, and he was fighting for her life.

The two combatants came together in a rush and when they parted, Rafe was bleeding profusely from a long gash in his lower left side. The Crow smiled triumphantly, certain the battle was won.

Rafe clenched his teeth against the searing pain in his side. He felt a sudden urge to lie down, to close his eyes and slide into oblivion. But then, out of the corner of his eye, he saw Caitlyn, her face deathly pale and afraid, and he shook his head, fighting the urge to surrender to the darkness that seemed to hover all around. He could not pass out now. To do so would leave Caitlyn at the mercy of the Crow.

Marshalling all his strength, he advanced on the warrior. In a last desperate move, he feinted to the left, dropped into a crouch, and, pivoting on the balls of his feet, brought his knife upward in a short quick jab as the Crow lunged toward him. His knife sank into the warrior's chest.

The Crow grunted as the ten-inch blade pierced his heart. For a moment he looked faintly surprised and then, expelling a last breath, he spiraled to the ground.

Rafe's eyelids felt heavy, and the knife was like a lead weight in his hands. He gazed at Caitlyn, trying to smile, to reassure her, but the strength was draining from his body. He heard her cry of distress as he dropped to his knees, the knife slipping from his fingers.

Caitlyn ran to his side, more frightened than she had ever been. Rafe's face was pale and drawn, blood covered his left side and soaked his trousers.

"Rafe. Rafe!"

With an effort, he lifted his head, his dark eyes seeking her face, and then he slid to the ground, unconscious.

Frantic, Caitlyn ran to her horse and removed the canteen from the saddle horn. Grabbing her chemise, she hurried back to

Rafe's side and began to wipe the blood from his side, then she pressed the cloth over the ugly wound, pressing hard to stop the bleeding. And all the while she sent urgent prayers to heaven, praying that God would spare her husband's life.

And even as she prayed, the cloth under her hand was turning red with blood. So much blood. How could a man lose so much and still live? The warm smell filled her nostrils, making her stomach queasy.

She whispered his name, felt a flicker of hope as his eyelids fluttered open.

"Caty?"

"I'm here."

"We've got to get out of here. Might be others . . ."

"Lie still."

"No. Got to get you out of here."

"Rafe, you're bleeding and I can't make it stop."

He gazed into her eyes for several moments. The pain and the weariness made it difficult to understand what she was saying. Her face blurred, and he blinked several times, trying to clear his vision.

Caitlyn's heart went out to him. She could see in the depths of his eyes that he was in terrible pain, and yet his only thought was for her safety.

His teeth clenched, Rafe lifted his head

and gestured at the blood-soaked cloth. "Let me see it."

Carefully, Caitlyn removed the bandage, revealing a jagged gash oozing with blood.

"Knife," Rafe said, his voice unsteady. "Heat the blade . . . slap it over the cut."

She nodded, swallowing back the nausea that rose in her throat. Rising, she went to her saddlebag. She had a box of sulphur matches wrapped in a piece of oilskin, along with a change of clothes and some beef jerky.

Removing the matches, she built a small fire, rinsed the blood from the knife with water from her canteen, and then held the blade over the flames until it glowed a brilliant white. She stared at the hot metal for a long time. She couldn't do it, she thought helplessly. She could not place that heated strip of metal over living flesh.

"Rafe . . ." She knelt beside him, the knife in her hand.

"Do it, Caty." He forced a smile. "It can't hurt any worse than it does now."

He turned on his side, his face pressed against her knees, his hands grasping her thighs, his whole body tense with dreadful anticipation.

Biting down on her lower lip, Caitlyn uncovered the ghastly wound. She felt a shudder pass through Rafe's body as the heat from the blade neared his flesh.

Teeth clenched, Caitlyn pressed the white-hot blade over the wound. Rafe groaned and his fingers dug into her thighs. His body convulsed as the heated blade seared his torn flesh, and then, mercifully, he passed out.

The stench of burning flesh filled Caitlyn's nostrils, mingling with the scent of blood and death. Tossing the knife into the dirt, she turned her head to the side and began to vomit. She retched until her stomach was empty and her throat ached, sickened by what she had done, by what surely would have happened to her if Rafe had not come along when he did, by the presence of the two dead Indians.

After a long while, she stood up. She rinsed her mouth with water, and washed her hands and face. For the first time since Rafe had killed her attackers, it occurred to her that she was naked. She dressed quickly, then stripped the saddle from her horse and covered Rafe with the blanket. He was still unconscious. Hopefully, he would stay that way for some time. She gazed at him for several minutes, wishing there was something more she could do for him, praying that the wound in his side would not become infected.

Too restless to sit still, she spent the next half-hour dragging the two dead warriors further into the trees, covering their bodies with leaves and branches. After that, she went through their war bags, but found little except for a few pots of war paint, jerky and pemmican, and a bladder of water.

Returning to Rafe's side, she sat down beside him, wondering what had happened to the herd and to the Circle C cowhands. Were the two dead Indians part of the raiding party who had attacked the herd? For a moment, she considered going in search of Scott and the others, but such a move seemed ill-advised. She had no idea where the rest of the Indians were, no way of knowing if any of the cowhands were still alive.

And she could not leave Rafe out here alone. She gazed at him intently, wishing he were unhurt. He would know what to do. Blinking back her tears, she brushed a lock of hair from his brow. He was badly wounded. Perhaps fatally.

The shadows grew long, and the sky turned to flame as the sun slid toward the horizon. She watched the changing colors of twilight, felt the air grow cold as the sun slipped out of sight. She tucked the blanket securely over Rafe's shoulders, and wrapped another around herself.

Rafe stirred restlessly, but he did not wake up. His skin was hot when she touched it and she bathed his body with cool water in an effort to bring down the fever. For a time, he murmured incoherently, and then he fell silent, his breathing shallow, his skin still much too warm.

Caitlyn took his hand in hers, willing him to get better, quietly begging him not to die. She had known him such a short time and yet he was her whole life.

"Caty?"

"I'm here."

Blindly, he reached out for her and she cradled his head in her lap, her hand stroking his forehead. The heat radiating from his body frightened her.

Hours passed. The moon rose high in the sky, and the woods were filled with the sounds of the night—the rustle of the wind playing in the trees; the distant baying of a wolf; the soft whoosh of an owl's wings as it passed overhead in search of prey.

Rafe had told her some Indian tribes believed owls brought bad luck. The Apache believed the presence of an owl was an omen of impending death.

In the daylight, safe at home, she would have dismissed such a belief as superstitious nonsense. It was not so easy to ignore such a belief now, with Rafe lying in her lap, badly wounded.

She held him all through the night, her

heart aching for the pain that troubled him even in sleep. Tremors wracked his body, and quiet tears slipped down her cheeks. Her eyelids grew heavy, fluttering down as she curled up beside Rafe, one arm draped protectively over his chest. With a sigh, she crossed the threshold from consciousness to slumber.

He ran a fever for the next two days, and Caitlyn stayed close to his side, bathing the sweat from his body, giving him as much water to drink as he could hold, urging him to eat when he was awake for more than a few minutes. Sometimes he clung to her, refusing to let her go, his fingers occasionally bruising her flesh as pain and fever tormented him.

Fear was Caitlyn's constant companion. Fear that the wound would fester. Fear that he would die. The ever-present fear that more Indians would come.

She had resigned herself to the fact that he was not going to get better when, miraculously, his fever broke and he fell into a deep, peaceful, healing sleep.

Caitlyn's smile was brighter than the rising sun as she offered a quiet prayer of heartfelt thanksgiving. Relief and weariness washed over her like a cleansing tide. Thank God, she thought as she curled up beside Rafe to sleep, the worst was over.

CHAPTER FIFTEEN

Rafe woke to a nagging pain in his left side and a terrible thirst. For a moment, he stared up at the cloudless sky, his breathing heavy as he fought to conquer the throbbing ache that seemed to be as much a part of him as his hands and feet.

He felt Caitlyn's warmth pressed against his right side and when he turned his head, he saw her lying beside him, her head pillowed on her arm. There were dark shadows under her eyes and a smudge of dust on her forehead.

Moving carefully so as not to awaken her, he eased the blanket back, removed the bandage from his side, and studied the wound. The gash was ragged and ugly, the skin surrounding it singed and black, but he could detect no sign of infection. He was lucky to be alive, he thought wryly. Damn lucky.

He drew the blanket up over his chest again, disgusted because he was too weak to move without becoming winded. It would be several days before he would be strong enough to travel.

Muttering an oath, he closed his eyes and drifted to sleep again.

He was not a good patient. He fretted constantly because he had to lie there, helpless as a newborn babe, when he was anxious to find out what had happened to Scott and the others, and to the herd. It was all Caitlyn could do to keep him immobile and after three days of trying, she gave up. The wound was healing, and there were no telltale red streaks or other signs of infection. His temper was vile, but his color was good, and so was his appetite for food and for her.

Though he was too weak and too sore to engage in anything strenuous, he was strong enough to hold her close and kiss her, strong enough to caress her until she yearned for his complete recovery.

On the fourth day after his fever broke, he insisted on getting up and walking around, saying that lying down made him feel weak. Caitlyn thought he looked a little shaky, but his determination won out and later that afternoon, after he had rested again, they packed up and headed for the river. They were out of water; it was time to move on.

At the Platte, they filled their canteens and then rode upstream until they located the tracks of the herd. The ground was badly chewed up by hundreds of head of stampeding cattle, leaving a trail that was wide and easy to follow.

They had gone less than a mile when they found the body of Wishful Potter. It was barely recognizable. The Indians had scalped him, and scavengers had preyed on the corpse. Caitlyn turned away, her stomach heaving, and saw a second body lying in the underbrush. It was Hal Tyler. Were they all dead?

"Let's go," Rafe called.

"Go?" Caitlyn repeated weakly. "We've got to bury them first."

Rafe shook his head. "I'd like to Caty, but I don't have a shovel or the strength."

"Please. We can't just leave them out here."

"They're beyond caring," Rafe said gently.

"Please."

He looked into her luminous green eyes and he could not refuse her. "All right," he agreed, dismounting. "We'll gather up some branches and rocks and cover them with that. It's the best we can do."

It took the better part of an hour to gather enough fallen limbs and rocks to cover both bodies, but Caitlyn felt better when the job was done. Until she looked at Rafe. His face was pale, his skin sheened with sweat though the day was cool. How foolish she had been to worry about the dead when her only concern should have been for her husband's health.

She saw him wince with pain when he stepped into the saddle, and her conscience pricked her. Just because he stubbornly insisted he was well enough to go on didn't mean it was true.

They found Josh Turner's body a short time later. When Rafe started to dismount, Caitlyn told him to stay put, that she would take care of covering the body. Nevertheless, Rafe insisted on helping her. There were tight lines of pain around his mouth by the time they had finished and Caitlyn hoped they wouldn't find any more bodies. She murmured a brief prayer over the makeshift grave, then mounted her horse, her heart heavy.

Moving on, they saw where the herd had slowed in its headlong flight. Rafe reined his horse to a halt and followed the trail with his eyes. He frowned as he studied the prints. The hooves of the horses were shod. And Indians didn't ride shod ponies.

"What is it?" Caitlyn asked, riding up beside him.

"Nothing," Rafe replied absently. Dismounting, he hunkered down on his heels for several minutes, studying the ground and then he began to walk, following the trail on foot. He swore softly when, some yards away, the trail of the herd divided.

He stared into the distance, his expression thoughtful. The shod horses bothered him. Of course, they might have been Circle C horses, but some sixth sense told him otherwise.

Mounting, they continued toward Fort Laramie.

They found no more bodies that day.

At dusk, they made camp near a shallow stream. Rafe caught a couple of speckled trout and Caitlyn cooked them, wondering if she'd be able to eat after the carnage they had seen that day.

She picked at her food, even as she urged Rafe to eat his. In the end, neither of them ate much, and Rafe threw the scraps a good distance from camp.

"Do you think they're all dead?" Caitlyn asked later, when they were lying close in each other's arms.

283

"Probably."

Caitlyn gazed up at the star-studded sky. All dead. Hal and Wishful. Josh and Nate. Old Web. And Scott. How could she tell Naomi that Scott was dead?

They were on the trail early the next morning. Caitlyn looked at Rafe, dismayed by the pain she saw reflected in his eyes. Why was he pushing himself so hard? she wondered bleakly. The cattle were gone, and the men were dead.

"Why don't we just turn around and go home?" she asked as they traveled steadily toward Fort Laramie.

"Some of the men might have survived. They might even have saved part of the herd. If they did, they'd go to the fort to sell the stock and recuperate."

"Maybe," Caitlyn agreed dubiously. But she doubted if any of the men were alive. Still, when they found no more bodies that day, she felt a faint thread of hope take root in her heart. Perhaps some of the men *had* survived; perhaps all was not lost after all.

The next two days passed without incident, but Caitlyn could not help growing more and more nervous. Each day that passed took them deeper into Indian territory, and she knew they were ill prepared to meet, much less survive, another attack. They had no weapons other than the bow and arrows and the knives Rafe had taken from the two dead warriors. She was not much impressed with their scanty arsenal until the morning she saw Rafe use the bow.

They had camped near a winding stream the night before and now Rafe stood behind a fat tree trunk, downwind of the three does and two fawns drinking from the edge of the stream.

Caitlyn held her breath as Rafe put an arrow to the bowstring and sighted down the shaft. The arrow was made of cane, fletched with three feathers from a red-tailed hawk. The bow was made of mulberry wood, the string fashioned from sinew.

It seemed an eternity passed as Rafe took aim and then he let the arrow fly. She supposed it was a beautiful shot. The arrow flew straight and true, killing one of the does instantly. The other deer bounded away and Caitlyn felt a keen sense of regret that such a beautiful animal had to be killed so that they might have food.

She watched as Rafe quickly skinned and quartered the deer. He sliced a good portion of the meat into thin strips for jerky, then roasted a couple of steaks. For all her sorrow at seeing the doe killed, Caitlyn had to admit that the meat was the best she'd ever tasted.

Later, while Rafe prepared the rest of the meat for their journey, she walked a short distance downstream where she found a berry bush. She also found a wild plum tree and she filled her skirt with fruit.

By the time Rafe had finished with the venison, it was dusk and they spent the night near the stream, feasting on fresh venison, berries, and cool clear water. She watched Rafe continually, ever thankful that he was still alive. She was lucky, she thought, lucky to have such a strong, resourceful man for a husband.

They rode into Fort Laramie two weeks later.

Caitlyn relaxed on the big brass bed, her eyelids heavy, her hair squeaky clean for the first time in weeks. Rafe lay beside her, his eyes closed, one arm thrown across his forehead. They had arrived at the fort earlier that afternoon. Rafe had reported the Indian attack, and been informed that three of his men had reached the fort. One had died, and the other two were in the infirmary.

"Looks like you could use a couple of days there yourself," the commanding officer had remarked, but Rafe had refused.

They had spent a few minutes with Scott and Nate. Scott had taken an arrow in the shoulder and another in his left thigh, and Nate had sustained a nasty head wound. Web had been unconscious when they reached the fort, Scott said, and he had never recovered.

Caitlyn had insisted Rafe let the doctor examine his wound while they were there, and only when the doctor announced that everything was coming along fine did she truly believe Rafe was out of danger.

Caitlyn glanced out the window. A flag waved in the distance, and she felt a sense of pride as she gazed at the bright red, white, and blue stars and stripes. She had been impressed with what she saw when they rode into the clay and brick fort. Groups of houses were built near the fifteen-foot-high walls, leaving a center compound of about a hundred feet square. Originally erected as a trading post thirty years ago, in 1834, it was located on the left bank of the Laramie River, about a mile above its junction with the North Platte. But thirteen years later the Army, wanting to establish a fort in the area, purchased the Laramie Trading Post, and called it Fort Laramie.

Whatever its origins, Caitlyn was glad the fort existed. It served as a place of refuge for westbound travelers, a haven of safety in the midst of warring Indian tribes.

She glanced at Rafe again. Was he asleep? Her gaze wandered over his bare chest, admiring the vast expanse of copper-hued skin, the narrow ribbon of curly black hair that disappeared beneath the sheet. Her gaze lingered on the wound in his side, just above his waist, reminding her again of how near she had come to losing him.

A small sigh escaped Caitlyn's lips as she snuggled under the covers. The room was dim and quiet and she felt a sudden longing for home, even though home would never be the same again. A part of the ranch had died with her father.

But Rafe was here. Rafe, who had strong arms to hold her, courage to protect her. Rafe, who had been wounded because of her.

She turned to look at him again and found herself gazing into his eyes. *Rafe*, she thought, surprised she had not realized it before. *Rafe was home.* No matter where they were, she would always be home if he were there beside her.

"Caty." His voice was low, deep and husky, washing over her like gentle waves.

Her heart seemed to stop for an instant, and when it started again, its beat had accelerated. She felt her skin grow hot where his hand rested on her thigh.

"You're awake," she said inanely.

Rafe nodded. "And hungry."

"But we just ate," Caitlyn said, frowning, and then she smiled because he was not talking about food.

288

"Your wound," Caitlyn murmured, but her protest died in her throat as his arms slipped around her waist and he drew her against him. Her breasts were flattened against his chest, her legs twined with his. She felt the heat of his length against her own, felt the flame of his manhood rise against her thigh.

Desire unfolded within her like a flower opening to the sun. Her eyelids fluttered down and she took a deep breath. His scent filled her nostrils, his touch surrounded her, setting her pulse racing. Their lips came together, fire meeting fire. Her tongue dipped into his mouth, as gently as a hummingbird sipping from a vine, and she tasted him, savoring the silky texture of his mouth, the heat of his tongue. A slow heat uncoiled deep within her, spreading outward like the ripples in a stream as his hands played over her body, kneading her flesh, sweetly stroking the curve of her hip, the satin smoothness of her thigh, the warm swell of her breast.

With a seductive smile, she straddled his hips while her hands drew invisible designs over his chest. She bent to kiss him, her fingers threading through his hair, the tips of her breasts brushing against his chest. The sensation of her smooth skin sliding across the hair on his chest excited her and she moved against him, teasing him, tempting him, until he groaned with desire.

In one quick movement, Rafe rolled over, sweeping Caitlyn with him, and now he was in control. He stroked her breasts, watching the way her eyes grew heavy-lidded with passion, the way her lips parted as her breathing grew more rapid, more erratic.

She was beautiful, so beautiful. Just looking at her was enough to arouse him; touching her took him to the very edge of heaven.

She arched beneath him in silent invitation and they came together, her warmth enfolding him, surrounding him, as he filled her, completing her, until fulfillment broke over them in undulating waves of pleasure.

Rafe woke early the following morning. Caitlyn was sleeping soundly, her face wearing the look of a woman who had been well-satisfied the night before.

Dressing in the buckskins he had bought the day before, he left the room and walked into the morning sunshine. The soldiers were already up and about. Some were drilling in the center of the compound, others currying their horses or cleaning their weapons.

Nearing the Army hospital, he decided to go in and pay Scott and Nate a visit. Early as it was, he found the two cowhands already awake. They had pushed their beds together and were engaged in a lively game of five-card stud when he entered the room.

They exchanged the usual greetings, and then Scott and Nate exchanged worried glances.

"I think you should tell him," Nate told Scott. "He's got a right to know."

"Tell me what?" Rafe asked.

"After the attack, me and Nate found Web in a ditch. He was in a bad way, all shot up, arrows sticking out of him like quills on a porcupine." Scott's face paled with the memory.

"Go on," Rafe urged.

"He was in a bad way," Scott repeated. "Just before he passed out, he said he'd seen a white man with the Indians. He said it looked like Abner Wylie."

"Wylie!" Rafe exclaimed.

Scott nodded. "We didn't want to say anything the other day when Miss Caitlyn was here, didn't want to worry her none."

Rafe nodded.

"Anyway, me and Nate have given it a lot of thought. Supposin' old Web was right? Supposin' Wylie was behind that attack? What are we gonna do?"

Rafe shook his head. "I don't know. You boys didn't see him, did you?"

Nate shook his head. "No."

"You were right not to mention this in front of Caitlyn," Rafe remarked. "Let's just keep it to ourselves for now."

Scott and Nate exchanged looks and then both men nodded.

"You're the boss," Scott said.

"Yeah. Thanks for telling me about Wylie."

Rafe stayed a few more minutes, and then left.

Abner Wylie. Rafe grunted thoughtfully. Was it possible that Wylie had somehow teamed up with the Indians, that he had offered them as much beef as they could run off if they would help him attack the herd? Was Wylie so mean-spirited, so set on revenge, that he would not only put Caitlyn's life in danger, but see innocent men killed? And if it was true, how could he prove it now that Web was dead?

Troubled, he wandered across the compound and out through the gates of the fort until he found himself in the midst of the Crow encampment that was set up adjacent to the fort.

A muscle worked in Rafe's jaw. The Lakota and the Crow were ancient enemies, the hatred between them growing stronger and more virulent when the Crow started scouting for the Army. Rafe could understand the Lakotas' hatred. He, too, despised the Crow for leading the white men against the Indians.

Farther on, Rafe saw a pair of lodges set up a good distance from the others. As he watched, he saw a lanky, red-headed corporal emerge from one of the lodges, a satisfied smirk on his face as he adjusted his trousers. A short time later, a Crow warrior stepped out of the second lodge, a bottle of amber liquid half-hidden in the folds of a blanket.

Rafe frowned. Apparently someone was selling women and whiskey to red men and white men alike, and no doubt making a hefty profit from both.

"What's your pleasure?"

Rafe glanced over his shoulder to see a tall man with greasy black hair and stained teeth coming up behind him.

The man smiled. "Your pleasure?" he repeated. "Whiskey to warm your belly, or a woman to warm your blood?"

"Neither," Rafe retorted.

"Too early in the day for ya?" the man asked amiably. Digging a toothpick from his shirt pocket, he began digging around in his back teeth.

"Yeah," Rafe agreed. "Too early."

"That's a shame," the man said. "I got me a pretty lil Injun gal. She don't have much fight left in her, but she's as soft as her name. Summer Wind—"

"What?" Rafe grabbed the man by the front of his greasy buckskin shirt. "What did you say?"

"I got me a pretty lil Injun—" the man began.

"Her name!" Rafe demanded. "What did you say her name was?"

"Summer Wind." The man's face paled at the fury building in the half-breed's eyes. "Forget it," he said, trying to free himself from Rafe's grip. "You wouldn't like her."

"Where is she?"

"Tent on the left." The man grinned wolfishly at the thought of selling the Indian girl again so soon. "Hey!" he hollered as Rafe released him and started toward the lodge. "Payment in advance."

But Rafe didn't hear him. His face taut, he walked to the lodge and ducked inside.

She was sitting on a pile of filthy buffalo robes, her long black hair falling in a tangled mass over her bare shoulders and breasts. Even in the dim light, he could see the ugly bruises and welts on her arms and neck, the dark shadows under her eyes. She didn't look up when he entered the lodge, only fell back on the furs and closed her eyes, a resigned expression on her face.

"Summer Wind."

She shuddered at the mention of her name, but did not look at him.

"Summer Wind."

She recognized his voice then and her eyelids flew open. She stared at him for a long time, and then shame flooded her eyes with tears. Grabbing one of the robes, she drew it over her nakedness. "Go away."

Muttering an oath, Rafe lifted her into his arms and held her close. "What are you doing here?" he demanded gruffly.

"Please, Stalking Wolf, go away. I am ashamed to have you see me like this."

"I'm not leaving until you tell me what the hell you're doing here."

"I ran away from our People," she said, her voice muffled against his shoulder. "After you were banished, no one would speak to me. My own father would not acknowledge me, and so I ran away. It was a foolish thing to do, I know that now. But I thought if I could find our brothers, the Cheyenne, they might take me in."

Summer Wind shuddered convulsively. "Instead, the man, Beech, found me wandering across the plains, half-dead. He nursed me back to health and then brought me here."

"How long have you been doing this?"

"I do not know. It seems like a very long time."

"Do you want to stay here?"

"No!"

Rafe nodded. "Let's go then."

Summer Wind shook her head, fear evident in her expression. "Beech will not like it."

"I don't give a damn what he likes. Where are your clothes?"

"I have none."

"He can't keep you naked all the time."

"No, but he keeps my clothes in his lodge so I will not run away."

Rafe touched the ugly bruise on her arm. "Did he do this?"

"Yes."

He swore softly as he lifted her to her feet, then removed his shirt. "Here, put this on."

Summer Wind did as she was told. His shirt was warm and fell almost to her knees and as it covered her nakedness, she felt a rush of hope. Stalking Wolf was there. He had come to save her from a life of shame. Her eyes moved over him. She had forgotten how very handsome he was, how tall, how strong.

She frowned when she saw the bandage swathed around his middle. "You're hurt."

"It's nothing. Let's go."

Beech was waiting outside, his arms folded across his chest. He frowned when Rafe stepped out of the lodge, followed by Summer Wind.

"Hey," Beech exclaimed. "Where do you

think you're going with my whore?"

"She's not yours any longer," Rafe said curtly. "Now, get the hell outta my way."

"Not so fast, half-breed. You can't just waltz in here and walk away with my livelihood."

"Watch me."

"They got laws against stealing," Beech whined.

"They've got laws against what you're doing, too," Rafe retorted sardonically.

"They do not!"

"Then I'm making one."

"Like hell!" Beech reached behind his back, withdrawing a long-bladed knife from the sheath on his belt.

Summer Wind's eyes grew wide as Beech advanced on Stalking Wolf. Her eyes flew to the bandage at his side. He had been wounded, she thought, and not long ago, else he would not still be wearing a bandage.

Rafe swore under his breath. Every time he got involved with Summer Wind, someone came after him with a knife. But this time he was unarmed.

He grabbed a stout stick from the ground, using it to parry the other man's knife thrusts. Beech attacked and retreated, attacked and retreated, his thin lips pulled back to expose his rotting teeth.

And then Beech got careless. It was the

moment Rafe had been waiting for. He swung the stick in a high arc, and brought it crashing down on Beech's wrist.

With a howl of pain, Beech dropped the knife and Rafe was on him, his fists swinging relentlessly, driving into the man's face and throat. There was a sharp crack as Beech's nose broke and blood washed over Rafe's hands. Beech went limp and Rafe released him and stood up. As he struggled to catch his breath, he saw that a crowd had gathered.

"What the hell's going on here?" The question came from a short, barrel-chested soldier wearing captain's bars.

Briefly, Rafe explained what had happened, and the captain nodded. "You'd best get the squaw out of here," he suggested. "My men won't be too happy about your making off with their only source of entertainment."

Rafe nodded.

"All right, men," the captain said. "Let's break it up. The show's over."

Rafe let out a long breath, wondering what he had gotten himself into. He saw the gratitude in Summer Wind's eyes, and behind the gratitude he saw the stirrings of old feelings. For the first time since he had heard Summer Wind's name on Beech's lips, he thought of Caitlyn.

He doubted if all the fast talking in the

world would be enough to get him out of this.

Caitlyn stared at the Indian girl who stood near the window clad in Rafe's shirt. She was at a loss for words. She had listened patiently to Rafe's explanation, hardly aware of what he was saying as she took in the girl's bare brown legs, the way her breasts filled the front of the shirt, the way her black eyes adoringly followed Rafe's every move. She could hardly believe her ears when Rafe said Summer Wind would be going back to the Circle C with them.

Because she could not quite handle this startling bit of news, Caitlyn changed the subject.

"I went to see Scott and Nate," she said. "They're both looking much better, but the doctor wants to keep them in bed for another week." Ordinarily, the fact that her men were recovering so well would have made Caitlyn smile, but she could not smile now, not with Summer Wind standing there, looking vulnerable and in need of comfort.

Rafe nodded. "Caty, why don't you sit down. You look a little pale."

"I'm fine," Caitlyn said. She looked at Rafe, her eyes searching his. *Why have you brought her here?* she wanted to cry. *Why is she looking at you like that?*

"I'm going to take Summer Wind over to the infirmary and have the doc take a look at her," Rafe said. "We'll be leaving tomorrow, early."

Caitlyn nodded, too numb to speak. It was easy to see the Indian girl still cared for Rafe. Did Rafe still care for Summer Wind?

She went to the window and watched her husband and the Indian girl cross the compound. She'd been living in a fantasy world, Caitlyn thought dully, foolishly assuming that Rafe loved her just because he enjoyed sharing her bed. Would he leave her now that his first love had come back to him? Would she be able to let him go?

CHAPTER
SIXTEEN

THEY HAD BEEN ON THE TRAIL FOR TWO days, a long two days.

Caitlyn rode in silence, her thoughts turned inward. Rafe had left what little money he had with Scott and Nate. It wasn't much, but it was enough to tide them over until they were well enough to return to the Circle C. The state of hers and Rafe's finances preyed on Caitlyn's mind. She had been counting on the money from the sale of the herd and now, instead of returning home with over nine thousand dollars, they were broke. She had made several scathing remarks about the Indians who had stolen over eight hundred head of prime cattle and killed four men, but Rafe did not share her feelings. He lamented the loss of the men, but he was philosophical about the loss of the herd.

"They're hungry, Caitlyn," he had said, referring to the Indians as if that justified everything.

"We're liable to go hungry, too," Caitlyn had retorted unsympathetically.

Rafe had looked at her for a long time, his eyes sad. "I lived with the Lakota, Caty," he reminded her. "The buffalo are disappearing. The People are hungry. What would *you* do if your children were crying, your parents were starving? Dying?"

"I'd get a job," Caitlyn had retorted, but she had known her answer was unfair, and that Rafe's point had been well made. Nevertheless, the fact remained that the money she had been counting on was gone. The Circle C needed repairs, the bank loan had to be paid off, and the payroll had to be met.

But those were not the thoughts that haunted her now. For the tenth time in an hour she gazed surreptitiously at the Indian girl. Summer Wind was beautiful. Her freshly washed hair was thick, black, and glossy, making Caitlyn feel that her own blond hair was washed out and lifeless in comparison. Summer Wind's skin was a smooth reddish brown, her eyes large and dark, fringed by sooty lashes. And her figure was faultless. She stayed close to Rafe, taking every opportunity to touch him. And because she spoke very little English, they conversed in Lakota, making Caitlyn feel like an outsider.

Resentment swelled in Caitlyn's heart as she saw Summer Wind smile at Rafe. She resented the Indian girl's presence in their lives. But stronger than her resentment was the jealousy that boiled in her veins, deep and hot and ready to explode. She had never experienced anything like it before and it frightened and repelled her.

Rafe was well aware of Caitlyn's turbulent emotions; his own were equally unsettled. He had thought all his feelings for Summer Wind had died with Hump Back Bear, but he discovered he was not immune to her beauty or her smile. She had been the first woman he had ever had affection for, and he was surprised to find he still cared for her, though not in the same way he cared for Caitlyn. But he had no time to try and untangle his feelings now. They were in hostile country, and he needed to keep his wits sharp and his eyes open. He could not afford to relax his vigilance by letting himself ponder the two very different women riding beside him.

Summer Wind took over the preparation

of dinner that night. She was accustomed to skinning game and cooking it over a camp-fire. Caitlyn made no objection when Summer Wind took the rabbit from Rafe's hand, but Rafe saw the flicker of anger in Caty's eyes. He shook his head ruefully, wondering how the Lakota warriors who had more than one wife kept peace in the lodge.

When the rabbit was cooked, Summer Wind offered Stalking Wolf the biggest por-tion, then divided what was left between herself and Caitlyn. She knew the white woman objected to her presence, and the thought made her smile. Stalking Wolf had been Summer Wind's favorite suitor. She knew he had once loved her; he had killed a man because of her. Perhaps, if she were very lucky and very clever, she could win him back again.

Rafe sat between the two women while they ate, aware of the ever-growing tension that hummed between them. Summer Wind was all smiles as she chatted with him about old times, her liquid black eyes warm when she gazed at him.

Caitlyn remained mute, her expression sullen. She did not appear to be paying any attention to Rafe and Summer Wind, but she was acutely aware of every smile that passed between them, of the many excuses Summer Wind found to reach out and touch Rafe's arm, his thigh, his hand.

Caitlyn rose to her feet, unable to watch the two of them any longer. "Excuse me," she said coldly, and turning on her heel, she stalked into the darkness, tears stinging her eyes and burning her throat.

She walked for a long time, unmindful of the distance, heedless of the danger of straying so far from camp. The night was warm and dark, comforting, somehow. Here, alone, she could let her tears flow unchecked. She was losing Rafe to the Indian girl and she didn't know how to fight it. Perhaps there was no way to fight it. Rafe had said he liked living with the Indians; perhaps he would take Summer Wind and return to the Black Hills. She knew he could not return to the Lakota, but another tribe might take him in.

She heard muffled footsteps and then Rafe was standing behind her, his arms folding around her waist.

"Come back to camp, Caty," he said, his voice low, his breath warm when it whispered against her ear.

"Why should I?"

"Because I want you to."

"You don't need me. You've got Summer Wind to keep you company."

"You're my wife," he reminded her.

"Does *she* know that?"

"Of course she knows."

"But she doesn't care."

"What do you mean?" It was a stupid question; he knew exactly what she meant.

"She's always flirting with you, touching you, talking to you in her language so I can't understand. She's still in love with you," Caitlyn said bitterly. "A blind man could see that."

"She's just grateful because I got her away from Beech, that's all."

Caitlyn made a very unladylike sound of disgust.

"Caty . . ."

"Send her away, Rafe. I don't want her here."

"I can't, Caty."

"I understand." She turned to face him. "You're still in love with her."

"No." Rafe shook his head. "I don't love her, not the way you mean. But I feel responsible for her. I can't just abandon her."

"Fine." She placed her hands on his chest and pushed him away.

"Caty."

"I'm going back to camp," she said curtly. "I'm tired."

"Dammit, Caitlyn, why can't you understand?"

"I understand only too well," she retorted, and all the while a little voice told her to keep still, that she was only making things worse. Behaving like a shrew would only send Rafe into Summer Wind's arms.

With her head high, she started toward camp, but Rafe would not let her go. Reaching out, he grabbed a handful of her hair and yanked her against him. She uttered a little shriek of pain, certain he had jerked out a handful of her hair. But before she could lash out at him, he was kissing her, his mouth hard, brutal, his arms holding her captive. He kissed her as if he wanted to hurt her, and he did hurt her, the force of his kiss grinding her lips against her teeth. And then his tongue plunged into her mouth like a dancing flame of fire, searing all else from her mind, draining all the strength from her limbs, leaving her limp and pliant in his arms.

She was dazed and breathless when he took his mouth from hers. His eyes were dark, ablaze with passion and some mysterious expression she could not fathom.

"Rafe." Her eyes searched his. "Tell me you love me, only me."

"Stalking Wolf? Are you there?"

Rafe cursed under his breath as Summer Wind's voice broke the stillness. He kissed Caitlyn one more time, a short quick kiss of promise, and then he let her go.

"We're here," he called.

Summer Wind moved through the trees until she found him. As she had suspected, he had not gone to check on the horses, but on his woman. She glanced from Stalking Wolf to Caitlyn and felt a sense of victory. Whatever had been about to happen between them had been thwarted by her approach.

"I was afraid," Summer Wind said, slipping her arm through Rafe's and smiling up at him. "Beech found me at night."

Rafe nodded. "Let's go back to camp and get some sleep. Caty?"

She nodded. Ignoring the hand he offered her, she started toward camp, her back rigid, her palms fairly itching with the desire to slap Summer Wind's face. Afraid indeed! The girl wouldn't be afraid of a two-headed snake.

Caitlyn slept little that night, and in the morning there were dark shadows under her eyes. Summer Wind looked lovely and well-rested. There was a glow in the Indian girl's eyes, a smile on her lips, as she made breakfast and carried it to Rafe.

Caitlyn refused to speak to him all day, even though she knew that she was being childish, and that such behavior would only drive him farther away. But she was afraid. So afraid.

Fear at losing Rafe to Summer Wind

turned to terror for her own life as they topped a low rise later that day and rode into the midst of a dozen warriors.

Caitlyn stared in horror at the hideous paint that streaked their faces, the scalps that fluttered from their lance tips, and the feathers entwined in their long black hair.

She turned frightened eyes on Rafe, her heart hammering a wild tattoo. These were the people who had killed her brothers and her father. Would she now meet the same horrible fate? Her gaze settled on a long blond scalp, so similar to her own, and she felt her own scalp prickle as she imagined one of the warriors hacking off her hair and attaching it to a scalp pole.

Rafe felt the hair on the back of his neck raise as the warriors boxed them in. They were Cheyenne, allies of the Lakota, but he recognized none of them. He felt a quick stab of fear as the warriors gazed admiringly at Caitlyn and Summer Wind. The braves were armed and painted for war. It would be a great coup to kill him and capture the women.

He raised his right hand in the traditional sign of peace, but before he could speak, Summer Wind rode toward one of the warriors.

"*Hou, sic'esi*," she said, smiling. "Hello, cousin."

Shinte Galeska frowned and then smiled. *"Hou, hankasi,"* he replied. "You are far from home."

"I have come for a visit," Summer Wind said cheerfully. "This is my husband, Stalking Wolf."

Shinte Galeska kneed his horse forward and the two men grasped forearms in greeting.

"Who is the white woman?" Shinte Galeska asked.

"A slave," Summer Wind answered with a wave of her hand. "Pay her no mind."

Rafe threw Summer Wind a warning glance, but she only smiled archly and asked her cousin how his wife and family were.

Caitlyn stared at the Indians uneasily as Summer Wind conversed with them. Her palms were coated with sweat and her mouth was suddenly dry as Summer Wind waved a negligent hand in her direction. The smile on the Indian girl's face made Caitlyn decidedly uneasy. What was going on?

Summer Wind reined her horse alongside that of the warrior she had been talking to and they started back the way the Indians had come. The other warriors raced ahead, leaving Caitlyn and Rafe to follow in the rear.

"What's going on?" Caitlyn asked nervously. "Where are we going?"

"To their village."

"Their village!" Caitlyn exclaimed. "Why?"

"It seems one of the warriors is Summer Wind's cousin. She told him that I was her husband and that we had come for a visit."

"What did she say about me?"

Rafe chewed the inside of his lip a moment before answering. "She told him you were our slave."

Caitlyn glared at Rafe, unable to believe her ears. "How could you let her tell such a lie?"

"What did you want me to do, call her a liar in front of her cousin?

"I guess not," Caitlyn muttered. No wonder Summer Wind had looked so smug. A slave, indeed!

The Cheyenne camp was laid out in a large circle with tipis of various sizes. Most were painted with moons or suns and stick figures representing horses or people, deer or buffalo.

Caitlyn's anger at Rafe quickly dissipated as she was surrounded by Indians and she stayed close to his side, needing to be near him, to feel his strength. Surely he would not let these savages harm her.

"Relax, Caty," Rafe murmured, giving her shoulder a comforting squeeze. "We'll only be here a day or two."

A day or two, Caitlyn thought. She could stand anything for a day or two.

The Indians stared at her, fascinated by her long blond hair and bright green eyes. They pointed at her as though she were some rare species of animal, talking rapidly in a harsh guttural tongue, occasionally reaching out to touch her fair skin, or stroke her hair. She cringed at their touch, was humiliated by their laughter.

Shinte Galeska took them to his lodge and introduced Rafe to his wife, Rainbow Woman, a tall, slender woman with enormous black eyes, a wide forehead, and a generous mouth.

Summer Wind and Rainbow Woman hugged each other, then sat down on a pile of furs and began the pleasant task of bringing each other up to date on what had happened since they had last seen each other.

Shinte Galeska invited Rafe to sit down, then offered him his pipe, leaving Caitlyn standing alone near the door.

"Sit down, Caty," Rafe called softly. "Over here, behind me. Don't talk."

Caitlyn sent him a mutinous glance, but she did as she was bidden. She had no robe to sit on, so she sat on the hard ground, her legs tucked beneath her, and tried to make some sense of the conversation between

Rafe and Shinte Galeska, but the language was unlike anything she had ever heard before and she was amazed that anyone could understand it.

After a few minutes, Rainbow Woman offered Rafe and her husband bowls of venison stew. Then she handed one to Summer Wind and prepared to sit down again.

Just then, Caitlyn's stomach growled loudly. Rainbow Woman frowned, then glanced at Summer Wind. "Do you want me to feed her?"

Summer Wind was about to say no when Rafe spoke up, "I would appreciate it if you would feed the white woman," he said, smiling. "She is a good worker and I would not see her strength depleted by a lack of food."

Rainbow Woman nodded, then grudgingly offered Caitlyn a bowl of stew. She had no love for the whites and it annoyed her to share her food with a paleface woman.

After dinner, the women sat in the back of the lodge, talking softly, while Shinte Galeska complained of the increasing number of white eyes crossing the plains, of the small Arapaho village that had been massacred several days earlier. He spoke of the Sun Dance, just passed, and lamented the fact that Stalking Wolf had missed it.

Shinte Galeska offered Rafe his pipe again, and then the two men went outside. Rainbow Woman and Summer Wind rinsed out the bowls, and then they, too, stepped outside.

Caitlyn sat there for a moment, angry at the way Rafe was ignoring her. Frowning, she rose to her feet, intending to find him and tell him so, but as soon as she stepped outside, Summer Wind ordered her back into the lodge.

"You slave," the Indian girl said haughtily. "Stay inside."

"I will not," Caitlyn retorted.

"Stay inside or you will cause much trouble," Summer Wind hissed. "Here, I am wife to Stalking Wolf, not you."

Stalking Wolf. Caitlyn repeated the name in her mind as she glared at the Indian girl, too angry to notice that Summer Wind's English had improved drastically in Rafe's absence.

She felt her spirits rise when she saw Rafe returning to the lodge.

"What's going on?" he asked.

"She won't let me outside," Caitlyn said petulantly. "She said it would cause trouble."

Rafe let out a long breath. "I'm afraid she's right, Caty. An Arapaho village was wiped out by the Army last week, and tempers are high. It might be wise for you to stay out of sight."

314

"What are you going to do?"

"One of the warriors is celebrating the birth of his first son. He's giving a feast in his child's name. As a guest of Shinte Galeska, I was invited to attend."

"What am I supposed to do?"

"Stay inside and sit tight. I'll be back as soon as I can get away."

Caitlyn glanced at Summer Wind. "And what will she be doing?"

"Sitting with the women."

Caitlyn's shoulders drooped disconsolately. She did not like it here, and she wanted to go home. Without another word, she turned on her heel and went back into the lodge and sat down on a thick buffalo robe. She hated to admit it, but she was lonely and scared. The lodge was filled with alien smells and furnishings. The ground was hard beneath the robe. From outside came the sound of laughter and singing and the rhythmic beat of a drum. She heard voices she could not understand.

Bored, she rose to her feet and peered outside, curious to see what an Indian celebration was all about.

She quickly spotted Rafe. He was sitting next to Shinte Galeska, nodding as the warrior spoke to him.

There was a change in the beat of the drum and one of the men stood up and walked to the center of the circle. Dropping his robe, he began to dance around the fire. She could not understand his words, but she had the impression that he was telling a story about a battle he had fought, and how he had killed three enemy warriors.

She was surprised when, a few minutes later, Rafe stood up. He did not speak, but she had no trouble understanding what he was doing. In steps and movements that were easy to follow, he told of hunting the buffalo with the Lakota, how his horse had stepped into a prairie dog hole and been crushed to death when it fell beneath the hooves of the herd. He had barely escaped with his life, and then, on foot, he had brought down a big buffalo cow with a single well-placed arrow.

He was magnificent to watch. Clad only in breechclout and moccasins, he was a sight to take her breath away. The orange flames cast shadows on his swarthy skin and ebony hair, making him seem like something out of a dream. Or a nightmare. There was an eagle feather in his hair, a streak of paint across the bridge of his nose, and a copper band around his right bicep. She did not stop to wonder where he had gotten such things; she only knew that he looked as if he belonged there.

She watched the other men as they danced, each man's steps unique, stirring up the dust as the drums beat faster and faster. There were shouts and war cries from the dancers, answering cries from the spectators.

The women danced next, their steps more subdued. She saw Summer Wind among the women, and her heart grew heavy with despair. The Indian girl had borrowed a doeskin dress from one of the women and the garment fit as though it had been made for her. She wore her long black hair loose, parted in the middle. Huge earrings dangled from her ears, a shell necklace lay against her throat. The part in her hair had been painted with vermillion. She looked primitive and sultry and quite, quite beautiful.

There was a pause in the drumming, and when it began again, the women had formed a large circle. They shuffled slowly to the right and then to the left and when the drumming stopped, each woman went to the man of her choice and tapped his arm. Summer Wind went straight to Rafe and when she tapped his arm, he rose to his feet and followed her to the circle. Now the men and women stood facing each other. The drumming resumed and the dancing began. The couples never touched as they moved right and left, forward and back, but there was a undercurrent of sexuality in the moves, a sense of waiting, of expectation.

Caitlyn stood up so she could see better and at that moment, Summer Wind smiled at Rafe, her eyes aglow, her expression radiant.

She couldn't watch anymore. Closing the lodge flap, she curled up on the buffalo robe, her heart aching.

She was still awake when Rafe and Summer Wind entered the lodge an hour later, followed by Shinte Galeska and his wife.

She listened as Summer Wind and Rainbow Woman exchanged a few words, and then Summer Wind crawled under a pile of furs on the left side of the lodge. Caitlyn nearly choked when Rafe crawled in beside her.

This was carrying their little charade too far, Caitlyn thought, stricken by the idea of her husband sharing a bed with another woman.

She stared at Rafe, saw him shake his head, warning her not to make a scene. Feeling wretched, Caitlyn buried her face in her arms, trying to block out the whispers of Shinte Galeska and his wife as they settled down for the night. She heard Summer Wind whisper to Rafe in Lakota, heard his hushed reply, and then there was only silence.

It was a long time before she fell asleep.

* * *

Someone was shaking her arm, and she groaned softly as she opened her eyes, her whole body feeling stiff and sore after a mostly sleepless night.

"Wake up," Rafe said.

"What's wrong?" Caitlyn asked anxiously.

"Nothing. Shinte Galeska has asked me to go hunting with him."

"You're not going!" Caitlyn cried, frightened at the thought of being left alone with the Indians.

"I've got to go, Caty. It's an honor to be asked, and I've no reason to refuse."

"Aren't I a reason?"

"You're supposed to be a slave. Don't worry, Summer Wind will look after you."

"Oh, sure," Caitlyn muttered sarcastically.

"Caty . . ." He placed a finger over her mouth when he saw she was about to argue with him. "Listen to me," he said urgently, his voice low. "I don't want to do anything to arouse Shinte Galeska's suspicion. I've been banished from the Lakota. It's like a death sentence, Caty. The only reason I'm still alive is because I killed Hump Back Bear in a fair fight, but the fact remains that I killed one of the People. If Shinte Galeska finds out what I've done, there's no telling what might happen. He has a quick temper. I know all this is hard on you, but I'll only be gone for a

319

day, two at the most. Trust me, Caty, please.''

"I do, but if we're in danger here, doesn't it make more sense to leave right away?''

Rafe let out a long breath. "I promised Summer Wind we'd spend a few days with the Cheyenne if she'd behave herself.''

"You mean she's blackmailing you?''

"In a way. She had a bad time of it with Beech and she wanted to spend some time with the People again. Who knows, maybe she'll decide to stay here.''

"How can she stay? You two are supposed to be married.''

"We'll get a divorce.''

"I didn't know Indians believed in divorce.''

"They do, and they're a lot less complicated than in the white world.''

"Really?''

"Yes. When a woman wants a divorce from her husband, she simply returns to her parents. In this case, Summer Wind would stay with Shinte Galeska and declare our marriage is over.''

"Could you do the same thing?''

"It's a little different for a man. If he tires of his wife, or decides she's unfit, he waits until the next dance and then he announces that he's throwing his wife away and whoever wants her can have her.''

"How embarrassing,'' Caitlyn remarked,

thinking she had never heard of anything so uncivilized. Marriage was a sacred covenant and as such should not be taken so lightly.

"Maybe, but you have to remember that a lot of Indian marriages are arranged by the parents. They don't always work out, and I imagine a little embarrassment is better than living with a man who doesn't want you."

"I suppose."

Rafe took Caitlyn's hands in his. "Will you be all right while I'm gone?"

Caitlyn shrugged. "I guess so." Ordinarily, she would have begged him not to leave her, but the thought that Summer Wind might decide to stay with the Cheyenne was too tempting to pass up.

"I've got to go," Rafe said reluctantly. "They're waiting for me."

Rising, he reached for Caitlyn's hand and pulled her to her feet. "I'll miss you," he murmured. His hand stroked her back and lingered in her hair, and then he lowered his head and kissed her fervently.

"Hurry back," Caitlyn said, forcing a smile.

Rafe nodded. "You can count on it."

Caitlyn followed him out of the lodge. He had discarded his buckskin shirt and the early-morning sun caressed his broad shoulders. There were moccasins on his feet, a knife sheathed on his belt, and a red headband kept his hair from his face. His skin was as dark as that of Shinte Galeska.

Summer Wind led Rafe's horse forward, and he swung into the saddle. Shinte Galeska handed Rafe a bow and a quiver of arrows, and Caitlyn felt a twinge of unease. Rafe looked as Indian now as he had the first time she had seen him.

In moments, a half-dozen warriors had gathered near the lodge of Shinte Galeska.

Rafe sent Caitlyn a long look, silently assuring her that everything would be all right in his absence.

Summer Wind tugged on Rafe's ankle and he looked down at her.

"Good hunting, my husband," she said, smiling up at him.

"Take care of Caitlyn," Rafe said.

Summer Wind nodded, her expression sullen. If only the white woman would disappear, then she and Stalking Wolf could stay here with the Cheyenne forever. They could have a good life together, and she would give him sons, many sons. If only the white woman would disappear.

Rafe gave Summer Wind's shoulder a quick squeeze, but he had eyes only for Caitlyn. He sent her a warm smile of farewell and then followed the other warriors out of the village.

Rainbow Woman waved to her husband

and then went to stand beside Summer Wind. "Come along," she said. "I must go gather wood and water."

"Let the white woman do it," Summer Wind said, and Rainbow Woman smiled in agreement. Going into the lodge, Rainbow Woman returned with a large gourd, which she thrust into Caitlyn's hand.

"Go to the river and fetch water," Summer Wind said imperiously. "And wood."

"I will not."

"You will do it if you wish to eat," Summer Wind snapped. "Hurry now."

Muttering a very unladylike expletive, Caitlyn headed for the river, her mind busily contemplating the many ways she would like to dispose of Summer Wind.

Kneeling beside the river, she filled the gourd, then placed it on the ground beside her and gazed into the distance. She could see a group of young boys shooting arrows at a bear skin pegged to a tree, and further down river she could see a trio of young girls splashing in the water.

Twenty minutes later, she left the river and walked toward a grove of trees. For a moment, she considered running away. Probably no one would look for her. Certainly Summer Wind would be glad to see the last of her. But the thought of wandering alone across the plains was less than inviting. She would be alone, prey to wild animals and Indians and whatever other dangers lurked in the wilderness. Better to face the devil she knew, she mused, than to go out to meet a new one.

It took only a few minutes to gather an armful of wood and then, with a heavy sigh, she returned to Rainbow Woman's lodge.

It was just after noon when the women began to play a game. Each woman had four sticks that were blackened with charcoal on one side and white on the other. Caitlyn stood behind the players, trying to discover the object of the game. After several rounds, she realized that when all four sticks were thrown and came up black, the player won two points, all white was one point, and mixed colors were zero. She was surprised to find that the Indian women were avid gamblers, wagering robes, moccasins, and household goods on a single throw.

As the betting grew heavier, a couple of warriors joined the group and the game grew louder and more intense.

As time passed, Caitlyn noticed that one of the warriors often looked her way. She saw him whisper to Summer Wind, who nodded. The warrior looked up at Caitlyn and smiled and Caitlyn felt a sudden chill.

Her uneasiness increased when the warrior left the circle, then returned leading a fine bay mare. He pointed at Caitlyn and then at the horse, and though Caitlyn could not understand what he said to Summer Wind, she knew that he was wagering his horse on the next throw. If he lost, Summer Wind would have a new horse; if he won, he would have a new slave.

Summer Wind glanced over her shoulder at the white woman. Dare she accept Tonkalla's wager? She quickly weighed Stalking Wolf's anger against the prospect of ridding herself of the white woman. The fact that Caitlyn did not belong to her was of no consequence. She was white, the enemy.

Summer Wind turned back to Tonkalla. "It is a bet," she said, and tossed the sticks on the ground.

Caitlyn murmured, "Oh, no," as all four sticks came up white.

A muscle worked in Tonkalla's jaw as he took his turn. It seemed to Caitlyn that the sticks fell in slow motion. The warrior loosed a loud cry of victory as all four of his sticks showed black. He had won.

Caitlyn shook her head as he walked toward her. "No," she said, backing away from him. "I don't belong to you."

Panic rose within her, shattering her outward calm, as the warrior laid his hand on her arm. "No!" she screamed. "Leave me alone!"

Summer Wind jumped to her feet and handed the warrior a strip of rawhide.

"No," Caitlyn sobbed as the warrior bound her hands behind her back. "No, you don't understand. I'm Rafe's wife."

But her protests were in vain. The warrior did not understand English so her words meant nothing. She struggled in vain as he dragged her through the camp toward his lodge and pushed her inside.

Caitlyn fell to the floor, unable to break her fall with her hands bound behind her back. Scrambling to her knees, she scooted to the rear of the lodge, her heart pounding with fear, but the warrior did not approach her. Instead, gesturing for her to stay there, he returned to the game.

The hours passed slowly. Each time she heard footsteps nearing the lodge, her heart lurched in dreadful anticipation, but no one entered the lodge. She could hear the Indians as they went about their business— women laughing, calling to their children, the high-pitched shrieks of young girls at play, the shouts of the boys, the soft cry of a baby. Dogs seemed to be barking constantly.

Frightened, she closed her eyes and prayed that Rafe would come back soon.

The hunt was a success. Shinte Galeska had found a small herd of buffalo grazing in a meadow not far from the village and the warriors chased the herd, each man bringing down one or more of the huge shaggy beasts.

Rafe had loved every minute of it, the thrill of the hunt, the exhilaration of the chase. It had been exciting, following *pte* again, feeling the surging power of the horse beneath him, hearing the sibilant hiss of the bowstring as he let an arrow fly, and lifting his voice in the age-old cry of victory as he brought down a prime cow.

The warriors had feasted on the choice parts of the buffalo, smacking their lips at the taste of fresh liver and tongue. Because they had not brought any women along, the men skinned the carcasses and quartered the meat, which they then packed in the hides. There would be a big feast when they returned to the village, with singing and dancing and food for all.

Rafe was feeling jubilant as they rode into camp two days later. His eyes quickly scanned the lodges, looking for Caitlyn. But it was Summer Wind who came running to meet him, a smile of welcome on her face as she reached for the reins of his horse.

"The hunt was successful," she remarked.

"Very. Where's Caitlyn?"

Summer Wind lowered her gaze. "I have done a terrible thing," she murmured.

"What are you talking about? What terrible thing?"

"I let Rainbow Woman talk me into playing the stick game," she said, still not meeting his eyes. "One of the warriors offered a fine bay mare against the white woman. I was sure I would win and the horse would be mine. She was such a lovely mare. But . . ." Her voice died away. She could feel Stalking Wolf's tension as he began to realize what she was saying, and suddenly the thought of facing his anger was more than she could bear.

"Go on," Rafe said, dismounting.

"I lost."

"Where is she?"

"Tonkalla has her in his lodge."

"Damn!"

Rafe turned on his heel and started off across the camp.

"Where are you going?" Summer Wind called.

"To see if I can buy her back," Rafe replied.

With an effort, he fought down his anger as he made his way to Tonkalla's lodge. Taking a deep, calming breath, he scratched on the lodge cover.

"Enter," Tonkalla invited, and Rafe ducked inside. He saw Caitlyn immediately. She was sitting in the back of the lodge, her hair mussed, her face drawn and pale, her eyes filled with apprehension. He shook his head slightly, warning her to keep still.

Tonkalla smiled at Rafe as he invited him to sit down.

"Are you hungry, my friend?" the warrior asked.

"Yes, a little," Rafe replied, knowing it would be considered a breech of etiquette to refuse his host's hospitality.

Tonkalla's wife offered Rafe a slice of smoked buffalo meat and then left the lodge. Rafe ate without really tasting it, trying to decide how best to approach the reason for his visit.

Tonkalla offered Rafe his pipe next, and the two men smoked and then spoke of the hunt. There followed a lull in the conversation, and Tonkalla looked at Rafe expectantly.

Rafe cleared his throat. "I wish to buy back the white woman you won from Summer Wind," he said, deciding the direct approach would be the best. "Summer Wind is jealous of the yellow-haired woman and she gambled her away without my permission."

Tonkalla shook his head. "I do not wish to part with her. My woman, Little Deer, will give birth soon. Her mother has gone to the place of spirits, and I have no female relatives to help her. She will need a woman to help with the work after the child comes."

Rafe nodded sympathetically. "I understand. But I have become very fond of the white woman. She is good beneath the buffalo robes."

Tonkalla smiled, and Rafe cursed his choice of words. Telling the warrior that Caitlyn was good in bed was not the way to get her back. Most Indian men did not have intercourse with their wives until after a baby was weaned.

"That is another reason I desired to have the white woman," Tonkalla admitted, sending Caitlyn a lust-filled glance. "A slave is less worrisome than a second wife, and more easily disposed of if she causes trouble."

Rafe nodded, suddenly glad that Caitlyn did not understand the Cheyenne tongue. "I will give you my horse and rifle for the woman."

Tonkalla frowned thoughtfully. A new rifle was tempting indeed, but not so tempting as the woman with pale skin and yellow hair.

"I will keep the woman," the warrior decided, a note of finality in his voice.

Rafe swore under his breath. Rising, he glanced at Caitlyn, and then at Tonkalla. "May I speak to her?"

"Of course," Tonkalla said generously. "I will leave you alone to say good-bye."

"*Le pila mita,*" Rafe murmured. "My thanks."

When they were alone, Rafe knelt in front of Caitlyn, his hands cupping her shoulders. "Are you all right, Caty?"

She nodded, too close to tears to speak.

"Caty, I'm sorry." He drew her into his arms and held her close, his hand lightly stroking her back. He could feel her trembling in his arms and he cursed Summer Wind for her treachery. "I tried to buy you back," he said, "but Tonkalla refused."

"You can't mean to leave me here!" Caitlyn exclaimed.

"Of course not." He held her tighter. "I'll think of something, don't worry. In the meantime, do whatever Tonkalla tells you."

"Do you want me to sleep with him, too?" Caitlyn asked, pushing him away.

"Don't be silly."

"I'm not being silly. I'm scared. I want to go home, and I want to go now!"

"Caty, please be patient. I can't just walk out of here and take you with me. Not now, not in broad daylight."

"When?"

"Tonight if I can arrange it."

Caitlyn nodded, her eyes filling with tears.

"I'll get you out of here as soon as I can," Rafe said quietly. "I promise."

She didn't say anything, only stood there

331

gazing at him through eyes damp with tears.

"Caty, Caty." He took her in his arms and held her close. He could only imagine how frightened she had been in his absence. Guilt rose in his heart as he realized that while he had been out having a good time, she had been sitting in Tonkalla's lodge, frightened and alone.

"I'd better go," he said reluctantly. "Don't be afraid. Tonkalla won't hurt you."

Caitlyn sniffed back her tears. "Tonight," she reminded him. "I'll be waiting."

"I'll come for you." He kissed her then, savoring the sweet taste of her lips, knowing he would kill Tonkalla or any other man who dared touch her.

Stepping outside, Rafe saw Shinte Galeska striding toward him, a huge grin on his face.

"My woman told me of your loss," the warrior said, chuckling. "Two women in one lodge can be trouble sometimes, but Summer Wind seems to have solved it for you."

"Yes," Rafe agreed, forcing a grin.

Shinte Galeska slapped Rafe on the shoulder. "I know you were planning to leave us tomorrow, but you must stay for the feast. The women are preparing the food even now."

Rafe nodded. He had no intention of leaving the Cheyenne camp without Caitlyn.

CHAPTER
SEVENTEEN

CAITLYN SAT OUTSIDE HER CAPTOR'S LODGE, the remains of a meal in a shallow bowl on the ground beside her. The Indian food was palatable, if different, but her mind was not on food. The women had been cooking all day and now, with the feasting over, the Indians were dancing and singing and generally having a good time. The babies and toddlers had all been put to bed; the older children could be seen playing on the outskirts of the adult circle. Several men were engaged in a boisterous dice game off to one side, while a number of young maidens strolled around the camp, showing off in their new finery.

But Caitlyn had eyes only for Rafe. She was seeing him through new eyes as he made himself at home in the Indian village. He seemed to belong here, among these dusky-toned people. Time and again she wondered what she would do if he decided to stay. And time and again she reassured herself that such a thing would never happen. Rafe loved her. She knew it, even though he had never said the words. He would not leave her at the mercy of another man.

Summer Wind hovered near Rafe, smiling at him, touching him, openly admiring him, and Caitlyn felt her jealousy flare. Rafe was only a man, after all. How long could he gaze into Summer Wind's adoring eyes and not be moved? How many times could Summer Wind smile at him, caress him, before he took what she was so boldly offering?

Caitlyn closed her eyes, unable to watch the two of them any longer. She gave a strangled sob as images of Summer Wind and Rafe sharing the same bed within a dark lodge played across her mind.

In desperation, she tugged against the rope that bound her hands, but it only caused her pain as the rawhide bit into her wrists. Tears flooded her eyes and she bowed her head so no one could see her weeping.

Lost in misery, she uttered a sharp cry when she felt a hand on her shoulder.

"Caty."

Joy filled her whole being at the sound of his voice.

Rafe swore under his breath when he saw the tears glistening in Caitlyn's eyes. Cupping her face in his hands, he kissed her lightly and then, very gently, he wiped the tears from her cheeks with his fingertips.

"Don't cry, Caty," he murmured. "Please don't cry."

"I want to go home," she pleaded. "You promised to come for me last night. Where were you?"

"I couldn't get away. I waited until I thought everyone was asleep, but Summer Wind followed me out of the lodge."

"Summer Wind! Summer Wind! I'm sick of that name, of her and your promises!"

"Dammit, Caty, be reasonable. I'm doing the best I can to get us both out of here with a whole skin. I don't like this any more than you do, but Summer Wind is Shinte Galeska's cousin and if she tells him the truth, I could be killed for being here, and then where would you be?"

Caitlyn was instantly contrite. He was right, of course, only it was so hard to be patient. So hard to bide her time when she was so frightened all the time.

"I'll come for you tonight if I can, Caty. Please believe me."

"I do. I'm sorry for what I said. You must think me an awful coward."

"No, you're doing fine. Just hang on."

"I will."

"Be still," he said sharply, and stood up.

Caitlyn frowned, and then scowled blackly as she saw Summer Wind hurrying toward them.

"Oh, there you are," Summer Wind said, smiling archly. She went to Rafe's side and placed her hand on his arm. "I'm tired," she said, speaking English for Caitlyn's benefit. "Shall we go to bed?"

Rafe sent a pleading glance in Caitlyn's direction, his dark eyes begging her to trust him.

"Come along, husband," Summer Wind said, tugging on his arm. "It grows late."

Rafe started to disengage her hand from his arm but then Tonkalla appeared out of the shadows. He nodded at Rafe, then grabbed Caitlyn by the arm and hauled her to her feet.

Caitlyn sent Rafe a look that tore at his heart before the warrior dragged her into the lodge.

"Shall we go, husband?" Summer Wind said sweetly.

"Shut up," Rafe hissed. And at that moment, he didn't know who he hated more, the man who now owned Caty, or the woman who had made it possible.

Caitlyn scrambled to the rear of the lodge as Tonkalla pulled the flap closed. Thus far, he had not touched her, but she feared that was about to change.

Murmuring to her in his own tongue, the warrior walked toward her and when she tried to avoid him, he reached out and grabbed a handful of her hair. Dropping to his knees, he jerked her down beside him. His hands were rough as he ripped her shirt, his eyes hot as he admired her fine white skin and full breasts.

Caitlyn uttered a small cry as he yanked her skirt down and then dispensed with her underthings. She cringed as his hand slid down her thigh, then moved toward her breast.

Help came from an unexpected source. Shrieking like a banshee, Little Deer charged into the lodge, a stick in her hand. Screaming in Cheyenne, she pounded her husband's back with the stick, berating him at the top of her lungs for trying to bed the white woman.

Covering his head, Tonkalla ran out of the lodge. Sweet relief washed through Caitlyn, and then she gasped with pain as the stick came down across her bare shoulders.

Little Deer was shouting at her, obviously reviling her, warning her to stay away from her husband.

Caitlyn nodded, her shoulders stinging with pain where the woman had struck her.

When Little Deer's anger subsided, she pushed Caitlyn to the ground and tossed a buffalo robe over her nakedness. Then, muttering to herself, Little Deer crawled under her own covers and closed her eyes.

Caitlyn smiled in the darkness. Thank goodness, Indian women were jealous, too!

Summer Wind pulled Stalking Wolf into the shadows. They never had a chance to be alone in Shinte Galeska's lodge, but here, in the darkness, it was peaceful and quiet. And private.

"What are you doing?" Rafe asked as Summer Wind drew him deeper into the forest.

"Finding a place where we can be alone."

"Why?"

"Do you not want to be alone with me?"

"Not now. I've got to find a way to get Caitlyn away from Tonkalla."

"You do not need her," Summer Wind said urgently, placing her hands on his chest. "I will be your woman. We can stay here with our brothers, the Cheyenne. We could have a good life together."

His eyes burning with rage, Rafe thrust Summer Wind from him. "Caitlyn is my wife," he hissed. "I cannot abandon her."

"She is not your wife any longer," Summer Wind retorted. "She is Tonkalla's slave now and nothing you can do will change it."

"Is that so? Well, my conniving little vixen, I can always tell Shinte Galeska the truth, which is what I should have done in the first place."

"Hah! He will be insulted if he learns that you have lied to him. Perhaps he will kill you. Perhaps he will kill us all."

"I could easily kill you myself," Rafe muttered irritably.

Summer Wind's expression softened. "Let me be your wife, Stalking Wolf. I will do anything you ask." She put her arms around him and kissed him, pressing herself against him so he could feel her breasts.

But all Rafe felt was disgust. His hands closed over her arms and he pushed her away. "That won't work this time, Summer Wind. I've tasted your lying lips before, remember?"

"You will not change your mind? You will not stay here with me?"

"No."

"Very well. I hope you do not regret it."

"What the hell's that supposed to mean?"

Summer Wind shook her head. She had

asked him to stay with her, had practically begged him not to leave her for that pale-skinned woman. She would not ask again. Wordlessly, she left him standing there, her mind racing as she plotted her revenge.

Rafe gazed after her for a long moment, a sudden chill replacing the warmth of the night.

When he returned to Shinte Galeska's lodge some twenty minutes later, he found Summer Wind, Shinte Galeska, and seven warriors waiting for him.

Rafe let out a long breath. Judging by the smug expression on Summer Wind's face, and the grave look in the eyes of Shinte Galeska, he knew he was in trouble.

Shinte Galeska stepped forward and then Rafe noticed all the men were armed.

For a fleeting moment, he considered making a run for it, but there was no way he could outrun an arrow; no way he could leave Caitlyn when there was still a chance, however slight, that he could get her away from Tonkalla.

He did not resist when one of the warriors tied his hands behind his back, then relieved him of the knife he carried on his belt.

"Come," Shinte Galeska said curtly, and led the way toward the chief's lodge.

All the high-ranking warriors of the tribe were present in the lodge of Two Moons when Rafe and his escort arrived. The low murmur of voices subsided as Shinte Galeska and the other Cheyenne sat down, leaving Rafe standing in the center of the lodge, alone.

He stood straight, his head high and proud, as his gaze slowly swept the lodge.

The council listened attentively as Shinte Galeska stood up, and in a voice laced with conviction, accused the warrior known as Stalking Wolf of having willfully violated the laws of the People. He explained the reason why Stalking Wolf had been banished from the Lakota, then went on to say that not only was Stalking Wolf guilty of killing one of the People, but that he had lied to the Cheyenne, as well, by claiming the woman Summer Wind was his wife, when, in truth, he had kidnapped her and the white woman from Fort Laramie.

Rafe swore under his breath, quietly damning Summer Wind for having concocted such an outrageous lie.

He thought briefly of calling her a liar, of demanding that they summon her to the lodge and make her tell her lies to his face, but such a move would gain him nothing. The council would not be inclined to take his word over Summer Wind's.

His jaw tightened as the council deliberated his fate. There were three choices available to them: they could kill him, punish him physically, or let him go.

He knew, by the stern expressions on the faces of the assembled warriors, that they would not let him go.

He held his breath as the chief of the tribe stood up.

"Stalking Wolf, you have heard the accusations against you. Have you anything to say?"

Rafe shook his head. What *could* he say? He *had* been banished from the People; he could not deny the most serious of the charges.

"Tomorrow, at dawn, you will be stripped naked and whipped out of camp."

"Damn." The single word, softly spoken, carried a wealth of frustration.

Whipped out of camp. Not only would it be painful, but humiliating as well. It was a severe punishment, one he had escaped at the hands of the Lakota only because he had not killed Hump Back Bear in cold blood. He had not expected the Cheyenne to impose it upon him now. He would have to run the gauntlet and survive so that, somehow, he could come back for Caitlyn.

Summer Wind was standing outside when Rafe followed Shinte Galeska out of the chief's lodge. Their eyes met briefly, and Rafe could almost hear the sound of her vindictive laughter. "I hope you do not regret it," she had said. Well, he was regretting it now, he thought ruefully. Regretting the fact that he hadn't left her back at Fort Laramie.

Dawn came much too quickly.

Stripped naked, his hands tightly bound behind his back, Rafe was led to one end of the village. Ahead of him, forming two parallel lines, stood the men and women of the tribe. All were armed either with sticks, clubs, or lances.

A heavy stillness hung over the village. Even the dogs were quiet.

He saw Summer Wind standing at the far end of the line, a sharp stick in her hand. He threw her his best devil-may-care grin and then, amid a thunder of drums, he hunched over and began to run. The earlier stillness of the village was broken by the steady beat of a drum and the shouts of the crowd as they rained blows on his head, back, shoulders, and legs.

Sticks and clubs fell on him like angry fists, raising long red welts, while lance tips pierced his skin, drawing crimson drops of blood. He ran steadily onward, the rhythm of the drums echoing inside his head. Knowing it would be death to fall, he struggled to keep his legs under him.

And then, miraculously, he reached the end. The blows stopped. The drumming ceased. The crowd fell silent.

With an effort, Rafe stood erect. Turning, he raked the crowd with one long disdainful glance. Then he saw Caitlyn standing near Tonkalla's lodge, her eyes revealing her horror at what she had seen. She took a hesitant step toward him, and he shook his head, warning her away.

Then he headed away from the village, his head high, until he knew he was out of sight. Only then did he surrender to the pain. Slowly, he dropped to his knees, his head hanging, his breathing ragged. Closing his eyes, he fell heavily to his side, waiting for the worst of the pain to pass. He could feel blood dribbling down his side, mingling with the sweat that bathed his body.

He lay there for a long time. The grass was cool beneath him, the sun dried the sweat from his skin, and a gentle breeze helped revive him.

Rising, he searched for a sharp rock and laboriously rubbed the rawhide over the edge until, at last, the rope frayed and broke, freeing his hands. He began to walk, putting distance between himself and the Indians. At a shallow waterhole, he took a long drink, then washed the blood from his body. Already, dark bruises were forming on his arms and legs, intertwining with the long red welts the clubs had raised. Miraculously, he had received no broken bones but he was sore all over. Lord, he'd never ached like this in his life.

Weary and hungry, he found a sheltered glen and crawled inside. He had to find some clothes, a weapon, and a horse. He also had to get Caitlyn away from Tonkalla but first he had to sleep.

Summer Wind stared after Stalking Wolf for a long time. She had expected to feel a sense of satisfaction when she saw him being struck down, had thought she would feel exhilaration when she brought her own stick down across his back. But now, watching him walk away, his body oozing blood and sweat, his head unbowed, she felt only remorse. He was a good man, a proud man, and she had wronged him. He had saved her from a life of degradation with Beech, had surrendered to her wishes to spend time with the Cheyenne, and she had repaid him with treachery.

Burdened with guilt, she turned to find the white woman staring at her.

"What happened?" Caitlyn asked. "Why did they beat Rafe and send him away?"

Summer Wind looked away, unable to face the white woman, unable to admit she had been the cause of what had just happened. Mute, she turned and hastened toward her cousin's lodge. She needed time alone, time to think.

Caitlyn stared after Summer Wind, a vast emptiness opening within her heart. Rafe was gone and she was alone, at the mercy of a jealous Cheyenne woman and her husband whose every look promised that, sooner or later, he would have her.

But her fears for her own safety seemed unimportant now. Rafe had been hurt, how badly she did not know. He was naked, without food or weapons in a hostile land. He dared not show his face in the village again, and she wondered how far they were from civilization. How far would he have to go to find food, clothing, and shelter? A doctor if he needed one? And why had the Indians sent him away?

She glanced in the direction Summer Wind had gone. Was it possible the Indian girl had said or done something to cause trouble? But that was ridiculous. Summer Wind loved Rafe. Why would she want to see him hurt?

It didn't make sense, but she worried over it all day. Little Deer was a hard taskmaster, demanding that Caitlyn be kept constantly busy. During the morning, Caitlyn fetched wood and water, helped Little Deer skin a deer, and prepare a thick wild-smelling soup of venison, onions, and sage. She shook out the buffalo robes that were used for bedding, swept the lodge floor, and fetched more water. And all the while Caitlyn thought of Rafe.

But even as she worked, she was learning how the Indians lived. Caitlyn had often thought that Indian women did all the work while the men took their ease, gambling and lounging about with their cronies. She realized now, after only a few days in the camp, that the warriors spent long days and nights on guard duty, keeping watch for an enemy attack. They also spent long hours, sometimes days, away from home in search of game.

She developed a grudging admiration for the Cheyennes' ability to create a life in the wilderness, but it was not a life she wanted to share.

Slowly, the hours passed, and Rafe was never far from her thoughts. Neither was the desire to escape. Rafe could not help her now. Somehow, she must find a way to escape before it was too late, before Tonkalla had his way with her. Somehow . . .

CHAPTER EIGHTEEN

It was dark when he awoke, and he groaned softly as he sat up. His entire body ached and it hurt to move. In the moonlight, he could see the dark bruises that marred his skin.

He gazed up at the black sky, judging it to be about ten o'clock. Lord, he'd slept over twelve hours.

Rising, he hobbled toward the water hole. A long drink quenched his thirst and eased his hunger. Returning to the glen, he sat down, cussing softly as each movement awoke new areas of pain.

He had to think, to plan, but the ache in his body made it hard to concentrate. Rest, he thought, that was what he needed. And with that in mind, he curled up on the ground and slept.

Summer Wind tossed and turned all through the night. Waking or sleeping, she saw only Stalking Wolf, his long bronze body hunched over as he ran for his life. Her dreams were filled with the angry beat of a drum, with the sharp smack of sticks and clubs striking human flesh, of blood oozing down his flanks as a lance tip cut into his skin. No matter what he had done, he did not deserve such cruelty.

In the hour before dawn, she left Shinte Galeska's lodge and made her way toward the river. Anyone seeing her would think she was answering a call of nature. Hidden in the folds of her skirt she carried a breechclout she had stolen from Shinte Galeska, a knife, a roll of pemmican, and a small pot of salve.

The cheerful chatter of a blue jay penetrated Rafe's dreams and he woke suddenly, staring at the green canopy overhead, wondering where he was.

Sitting up, he uttered a mild oath as pain and memory returned hand in hand.

Rising, he reached out to steady himself against a tree. Then, moving as stiff and slow as an old man, he went to the waterhole. It did not ease his hunger this morning.

"Stalking Wolf."

He whirled around at the sound of her voice, his eyes burning with a clear and bitter rage.

"What the hell are you doing here?" he demanded gruffly. "Haven't you caused enough trouble?"

"I came to help."

"Now why don't I believe that?"

"It is true." She held out the pemmican, knife, and wolfskin clout. "These are for you."

"Why? Less than two days ago you were out for blood."

"I behaved badly. I let anger rule my heart."

He eyed her suspiciously, unwilling to trust her.

"Take this," she said, thrusting the pemmican into his hand. "You must be hungry."

"Probably poisoned," he muttered, but he ate it anyway.

Summer Wind watched him, her conscience hurting. There was hardly a place on his arms, back, shoulders, and legs that wasn't discolored or swollen.

"I brought salve for your wounds," she offered when he had finished eating.

Stalking Wolf nodded. Lying on his stomach, he closed his eyes as Summer Wind applied a thick greenish-yellow salve to his back. The ointment was cool against his skin, quickly drawing the fire from his bruised flesh. Her hands were gentle as she worked the salve into his skin, massaging his arms and shoulders and thighs. Her touch was soothing, unintentionally provocative.

Drawing a deep breath, Rafe sat up. "Thanks," he muttered, wondering what the hell he had to thank her for. It was her fault he'd been hurt in the first place.

Summer Wind wiped the salve from her hands. "Are you sure we cannot have a life together?" she asked, her voice softly imploring.

"We've been through all that before," Rafe replied wearily. *And look where it got me*, he thought bitterly.

"I know." Rising nimbly to her feet, Summer Wind tossed the breechclout into his lap. "Good-bye, Stalking Wolf."

He stood up, the clout falling, unnoticed, to the ground. "Summer Wind, wait."

She looked at him, her dark eyes filling with hope, and he cursed under his breath. How did a man ask a woman he had rejected to bring him the woman he loved?

Summer Wind tilted her head to one side, a nasty suspicion growing in the back of her mind.

"Summer Wind, I . . . could you . . ."

"It's her!" Summer Wind exclaimed angrily. "You want me to bring her here!"

"I know it's asking a lot, but—"

"No, I will not!"

"Dammit, you've got to help me. I can't leave her."

"No."

Rafe swore under his breath. Damn stubborn woman. Apparently if she couldn't have him, neither would Caitlyn.

"Would it help if I got down on my knees and begged?"

A flicker of amusement danced in Summer Wind's eyes and then was gone. "Would you?"

"Do I have to?"

"You ask much of me," she remarked with a slight shake of her head.

Rafe quirked an eyebrow at her as he gestured at the numerous wounds on his body. "I think I have that right."

A wave of guilt assailed Summer Wind. Perhaps she was being unfair. Stalking Wolf had saved her from the man, Beech, after all, and she had known Caitlyn was his woman all along. Stalking Wolf had never lied to her, never made her any promises. Now that he was leaving, it would serve no purpose to keep Caitlyn from him, and yet . . .

"Would you really get down on your knees and beg?" she asked.

"What do you think?"

"I think I would enjoy it."

"I'm sure you would."

Summer Wind stared at him. He was a magnificent man. Even bruised, his skin discolored and swollen, he was wonderful to look at.

"I must go," she said abruptly. "I make no promises about your woman."

"I understand."

He watched her out of sight, wondering if he would ever see Summer Wind or Caitlyn again.

Caitlyn spent a sleepless night. Her fears for Rafe kept her awake long after Tonkalla and his wife were sleeping soundly. She wondered how badly Rafe was hurt, if he had found shelter for the night, if he was in much pain.

But it was fear for her own future that drove her out of the lodge and into the predawn darkness. Rafe would not be able to help her escape now. She was on her own, and determined not to spend one more day in Tonkalla's lodge.

Earlier, Tonkalla had insisted she dress as a Cheyenne woman. At the time, she had objected, but now she was grateful. Clad in a doeskin tunic and moccasins, with a blanket draped over her head to hide her blond hair, she left the village and made her way toward the river. She moved cautiously, expecting at any moment to feel Tonkalla's hand on her arm, to hear one of the night guards challenge her, but nothing happened.

When she reached the river, she turned south, walking in the direction Rafe had taken when he left the village. He had a good head start on her, but he was hurt. Surely, if she walked very fast, she could overtake him.

The sky grew light as the hours passed. She ran until her sides ached, and then she walked. And then she ran again, constantly checking over her shoulder to see if she was being followed.

Later that morning, Tonkalla questioned his wife about the white woman's whereabouts.

"She has gone for food," Little Deer replied, knowing it was a lie.

Tonkalla grunted softly, the white woman's whereabouts temporarily forgotten as Little Deer served the morning meal. Later, when her husband had gone to visit his uncle, Little Deer went to the river and carefully obliterated the white woman's tracks.

"Run fast," Little Deer murmured. "Run fast and far and hide well. One woman is enough for my husband."

* * *

Rafe spent most of the morning sleeping. Just after noon, he went to the water hole, where his unexpected presence spooked a couple of horses that had strayed from the Cheyenne herd.

His eyes thoughtful, Rafe sat near the water's edge and began plaiting a lariat from some vines growing nearby.

The horses, drawn by their thirst as much as by their curiosity, returned a short while later. Heads lowered, ears twitching, they stared at the man sitting beside the water hole.

Cautiously, their nostrils flared to breathe in his scent more readily, and they stepped closer. Wild horses would not have returned, but these horses were not wild. They snorted and pawed the ground when he slowly stood up, but they did not run. Speaking softly in the Cheyenne tongue, Rafe approached the closest horse and slid the lariat around the horse's neck. The gelding tossed its head, as if objecting to being caught, and then allowed Rafe to scratch its ears.

"Things are looking up," Rafe murmured. The gelding, a large bald-faced bay, docilely followed him back to the glen. The second horse, a short-barreled buckskin mare, followed along behind.

* * *

For the first time in her life, Caitlyn wished she were an Indian. Perhaps then she'd be able to find Rafe. Certainly only an Indian would be able to trail someone across the trackless prairie. She looked about and saw only a sea of grass and scattered stands of timber. She would never find him, she thought, discouraged. She'd never find Rafe, and she'd never find her way back to civilization, either.

She was tired, hot, and thirsty when she heard a horse snort behind her. Resigned, she turned around, expecting to find an angry Tonkalla riding toward her. Instead, she saw Summer Wind.

The two women stared at each other for a moment—Caitlyn's expression wary, Summer Wind's filled with annoyance.

"You stupid woman," Summer Wind said abruptly. "What are you doing way out here?"

"I fail to see how that's any of your business," Caitlyn replied defensively.

"We have no time to argue," Summer Wind said. "Little Deer is running out of excuses for your absence. Hurry now, we must go."

"Go where?"

"To Stalking Wolf."

"Rafe! You know where he is?"

357

"Yes." Summer Wind extended her hand. "Come."

With trepidation, Caitlyn took Summer Wind's hand and swung up behind her. She had no reason to trust this woman, but even going back to Tonkalla would be better than perishing in the wilderness.

But Summer Wind did not take her back to the village. Instead, she rode toward a stand of trees that enclosed a shaded glen and there, sheltered from view, they found Rafe.

Caitlyn slid off the back of the horse and flew into his arms. "Rafe, oh, Rafe," she murmured.

"Caty." He hugged her close, grimacing a little as she hugged his back. He was still sore, but this was an ache he could stand.

Rafe looked at Summer Wind and smiled. *"Le pila mita."*

Summer Wind nodded. "You had better go. Little Deer has been making excuses for the white woman's absence all day. I think Tonkalla will get suspicious soon."

"What will you do?"

"I think I will stay with the Cheyenne."

"Be happy, Summer Wind."

"Safe journey, Stalking Wolf." She gazed at him a moment more, wishing things had turned out differently between them, and then she wheeled her horse around and rode away toward the village.

"We'd better go," Rafe said, giving Caitlyn a squeeze. "Can you ride bareback?"

"If I have to."

"You have to."

He took the blanket from Caitlyn and tore off several long strips which he fashioned into bridles and reins.

"Ready?" he asked.

"Yes."

He pulled her close for a moment, his lips moving in her hair, and then he lifted her onto the back of the buckskin mare and handed her the makeshift reins. Then, vaulting onto the back of the bay gelding, he led the way through the trees and out onto the prairie.

He threw Caitlyn a broad smile of encouragement and then urged his mount into a lope, knowing their only hope was to put a good distance between themselves and the Cheyenne.

They rode for hours beneath a blinding sun and a cloudless sky, pausing now and then to breathe the horses. They had no food and no water, but Caitlyn did not complain. They were free and that was all that mattered.

It was well after dusk when Rafe drew rein for the night. Caitlyn slid to the ground, her whole body weary. Rafe's arms were a welcome support and she rested her head on his shoulder, feeling as though she had come home at last.

"Do you think they'll follow us?" she asked.

Rafe shrugged. "I don't know." He placed his hand under her chin and lifted her head, his dark eyes gazing intently into her own. "Did Tonkalla touch you?"

"No." Caitlyn smiled. "He tried once, but Little Deer hit him with a stick."

Rafe chuckled. "Thank God for jealous wives," he muttered, and then he hugged Caitlyn hard, knowing he would never have forgiven himself if she had come to harm. His right hand played over her back and shoulders while his left hand held her close. They stood that way for a long time, with Caitlyn's head tucked under Rafe's chin. Slowly, she became aware of the heat spreading between them, of the sudden heaviness of her breasts where they pressed against his chest, of the rising thrust of Rafe's manhood.

"Caty." His voice was low, imploring.

"Mmmmm?"

"Are you tired?"

She nodded, a smile turning up the corners of her mouth.

"How tired?"

"Very," she teased.

His lips moved in her hair as his hand

stroked her back, the curve of her hip. His other hand dropped lower and pressed her hips against his, letting her feel the power of his need.

"*Too* tired?" His breath was hot against her ear, his tongue moist as he nibbled at her earlobe.

"What did you have in mind?" she asked innocently.

"What do you think?" he growled, grinding his hips against hers.

"Oh, that." She was laughing now, her eyes bright as she tilted her head back to better see his face.

"Yes, that," Rafe replied, and before she could blink, his mouth closed over hers. His kiss was ardent, insistent, and completely wonderful, and Caitlyn leaned against him, her arms reaching up to twine about his neck, her body molding itself to his. She felt the heat of his desire through the folds of her skirt and it quickened her own, leaving her breathless and pliant and, oh, so willing.

Rafe loosened the ties at her shoulders and the dress slid to the ground. He removed his clout, then dropped to his knees and removed her moccasins, his hand caressing her foot.

He lifted one hand and she placed hers in it, and he drew her down beside him. Caitlyn's hands slid over his biceps, across his shoulders, down his chest, reacquainting herself with the strength and power of the man who was her husband. She gloried in the taut muscles that rippled beneath her fingertips, in the sharp intake of his breath as her hand stroked the inside of his thigh, teasingly, tantalizing, until he groaned with pleasure and pain. Bending over him, she kissed his face, the tips of her breasts brushing against his chest, like velvet stroking steel.

Rafe let her touch and tease and explore until he was ready to explode, and then he rolled her onto her back and returned touch for touch and kiss for kiss until they were both breathless, caught up in a dizzying inferno.

And then, at last, they surged together, reaching for that blissful paradise where, for one brief, magical moment two people became one.

Later, Caitlyn wept softly as she studied the horrible bruises and welts that marred his back and shoulders. A long red welt ran across his buttocks, the backs of his legs were bruised and swollen and she wondered how he had managed to ride bareback all day without complaint.

"I'm all right, Caty," Rafe assured her. "Don't cry."

"What happened, Rafe? Why did they beat you?"

"Summer Wind got mad because I wouldn't divorce you and marry her. She told Shinte Galeska that I had been banished from the Lakota for killing a man, and that I had kidnapped the two of you from Fort Laramie. The Cheyenne did the only thing they could do."

Rafe grinned. "I guess Summer Wind's conscience started to bother her and she came looking for me. I asked her to bring you to me."

Caitlyn snuggled against him, thankful that Summer Wind had found her, thankful to be back in her husband's arms.

With a sigh, she gazed up at the moon, shining full and bright overhead. "Pretty, isn't it?"

"Yeah. You see the dark spots on the moon? The Cherokee have a legend about the sun and the moon that explains those spots."

"Really? Tell me."

"Well, it seems that when the Sun was a young woman, she had a brother, the Moon, who lived in the West. The Sun had a lover who used to come every month in the dark of the moon to court her. He would come only at night and leave before daylight, and although she talked to him, she could never see his face in the dark and he would not tell her his name. The Sun was always wondering who her mysterious lover was.

"Finally, she came up with an idea to discover her lover's identity. The next time he came, as they were sitting together in the dark, she dipped her hand into the cinders and ashes of the fireplace and rubbed her fingers over his face, saying, 'Your face is cold; you must have suffered from the wind.' After a while, he left and went away again. The next night when the Moon came up, his face was covered with spots, and then his sister knew he was the one who had been coming to see her.

"He was so ashamed that she knew that he kept as far away as he could at the other end of the sky. Ever since he has tried to keep a long way behind the Sun and when he does sometimes have to appear near her in the West, he makes himself as thin as a ribbon so he can hardly be seen."

"That's marvelous," Caitlyn remarked. "Do you know any more stories like that?"

"Yeah. The Indians love to tell stories. At night, during the winter, they spend hours relating stories and legends."

"Tell me another."

"I'd rather start a legend of my own," Rafe murmured as he traced the outline of her jaw with his fingers, "about Stalking Wolf, a mighty warrior, who made love to his woman all night long."

"Far be it from me to stand in the way of a legend in the making," Caitlyn replied with a seductive smile as Rafe covered her body with his own.

Caitlyn breathed a sigh of relief as familiar landmarks came into view. At last, after three weeks on the trail they were home!

The journey from the Cheyenne village had been long but virtually trouble-free. They had spent some nights going to bed hungry, but for the most part Rafe had managed to find enough food and water to sustain them. Twice, they had seen Indians, but always from a distance. Each sighting filled Caitlyn with dread, so certain was she that Tonkalla would find her and take her back to the village. She had seen the Indians through different eyes during the few days they had spent in the Cheyenne camp. She knew now that they were not complete savages, that they were capable of love and laughter, of joy and pain, but she had no desire to live among them again.

The cattle drive that was to put the ranch in the black had been a disaster, she mused ruefully. Four men had been killed, eight hundred head of cattle had been run off by

Indians. Instead of making a profit of almost nine thousand dollars, they had come up empty. How would they rebuild the herd now, she wondered bleakly. Where would they get the money to pay off the bank loan, to pay the hands' wages, to buy seed, and other necessities?

And yet, despite everything, Caitlyn felt her heart lift when the ranch house came into view.

"Home at last," she murmured. She glanced at Rafe, riding beside her. "Sometimes I didn't think we'd make it.

Rafe nodded. The ranch *was* a sight for sore eyes, he thought, especially after all they'd been through.

Paulie and Rusty came out to meet them, the welcome in their eyes turning to confusion when they saw Rafe and Caitlyn dressed in buckskins. Paulie glanced down the road, frowning, when he saw that Rafe and Caitlyn were alone.

"Where's Scott?" Paulie asked. "And Web and the others?" Paulie glanced at the brief wolfskin clout Rafe was wearing. "What are you doing in that get-up?"

"It's a long story," Rafe answered. Dismounting, he helped Caitlyn to the ground and handed Paulie the horses' reins. "You go on up to the house, Caty," he said, "I'll fill Paulie and Rusty in on what happened."

Caitlyn nodded. There were many things that needed to be discussed, but right now all she could think of was a hot bath and a glass of cold milk.

Rafe waited until Caitlyn was out of sight before he asked Paulie the questions that had been preying on his mind since they left the Cheyenne.

"Anything strange happen here while we were gone?"

Paulie shook his head. "No. Why?"

"Did you go into town for anything?"

"Yeah, a couple of times."

"Did you see Wylie?"

"No, but then, I wasn't looking for him."

"What's this all about?" Rusty asked.

Succinctly, Rafe told the two men about the cattle drive, about the Indian attack on the herd, about Web's statement that he had seen Wylie with the Indians.

"And you think Wylie was behind the attack," Rusty remarked. "But why? What would he have to gain by helping a bunch of Indians steal our cattle?"

Rafe shrugged. "I don't know. Revenge, maybe."

"Against who?" Paulie asked.

"I'd say I was the most likely candidate," Rafe suggested wryly. "I embarrassed him at the Fourth of July dance, and as far as he's concerned, I took his job away from him."

"And his girl," Rusty added. "He was always certain Miss Caitlyn would marry him."

"I don't know," Paulie said, shaking his head, "I can't picture Abner dressing up like an Indian and stealing the herd."

"I can," Rusty said with conviction. "So, what are we gonna do?"

"For now, nothing," Rafe said. "We've got no proof other than the word of a dead man." He ran a hand through his hair and over the growth sprouting on his chin. "Scott and Nate should be turning up any day now. I kinda thought they'd be here by now."

"You look beat, boss," Paulie remarked. "Why don't you go up to the house and get cleaned up?"

"Yeah, that's a good idea. You two keep your eyes open. I'm afraid we may be in for more trouble before this is over."

CHAPTER NINETEEN

Scott and Nate returned to the ranch two days later. Both men looked a little pale and a trifle thin, but both had fully recovered from their wounds and seemed to be in good spirits. They'd had to hole up several times to avoid being spotted by Indians, Scott said, but other than that, their journey had been uneventful.

Rafe and the men got together in the tack room that night after dinner, and Scott repeated what Web had said about seeing Abner Wylie riding with the Indians.

Rafe rubbed a hand over his jaw. "Maybe they weren't Indians at all," he mused aloud. "All the pony tracks I saw were made with shod hooves."

"Not Injuns," Paulie exclaimed. "You don't mean to tell me you think white men attacked the herd and scalped Wishful and the others?"

Rafe shrugged. "If the price is right, you can find men who are willing to do just about anything."

"I can't believe it," Paulie insisted, shaking his head. "I rode with Abner for almost five years."

Rafe glanced out the door, his expression thoughtful. The two Crow warriors who had attacked Caitlyn had been Indians, sure enough, but what about the ones who had stolen the herd? He hadn't seen any of them up close. During the attack it hadn't occurred to him that the raiders might be white men dressed up like Indians. He recalled the bodies of Wishful Potter and the others. All had been crudely scalped. Looking back, he remembered thinking that the warrior who had taken Potter's scalp didn't have much experience judging by the sloppy job he'd done.

"Listen, Paulie," Rafe said, "I want you and Nate to stay close to the house from now on. Scott, you and Rusty go out and round up whatever cattle you can find. I think we'll keep what's left of the herd close to home for the time being. And keep your guns handy."

The men nodded. If Abner Wylie was looking for a fight, he'd get one.

"What about you?" Paulie asked. "Maybe you'd better start wearing a sidearm. It's a lot easier than packing a rifle everywhere you go."

Rafe grunted thoughtfully. "Maybe you're right. I'll take care of it tomorrow. I'm going into town to see if I can buy a couple of draft horses to replace those we lost in the fire." His jaw went hard. "I'll see if I can find a couple of men, too. We might need the extra help."

"I'll go along with you," Rusty offered.

"No, I want you to stay here." He let his gaze light on each man's face. "I don't want to worry Caitlyn with any of this until I know for sure there's something to worry about."

Rafe insisted on going into town alone, telling Caitlyn she needed to stay home and rest. Mounted on the bald-faced bay he had stolen from the Cheyenne, he rode into Cedar Creek. He knew Caitlyn was broke, but he had enough money to meet the payroll for the next few months. The money, won playing poker at Frenchy's, made a comfortable bulge in his hip pocket. Paying off the loan at the bank was another matter. Apparently the Circle C had fallen on some hard times four years earlier and Carmichael had borrowed six thousand dollars from the bank. That loan was due October 1. He figured there were about a hundred head of cattle left on the ranch. Carmichael had never run a big herd; most of his business had been tied up in mustangs, catching them, breaking them, and selling them to the Army. Only they hadn't had any luck with horses in the last year, either, thanks to the Indians.

The town was quiet when he rode in. He turned his horse toward the blacksmith shop, knowing if there were any draft horses for sale, the smith would likely know about it.

As it turned out, Clyde Hooper wasn't aware of any animals for sale at the moment, but he said he'd keep his ears open and let Rafe know if he heard of any.

Rafe's next stop was the gun shop. He had never worn a six-gun, preferring a knife or a good Winchester rifle, but he could see the wisdom of wearing one, especially now. After a few minutes of deliberation, he selected a .44 Colt, a black leather holster, and gunbelt. The .44 felt heavy on his hip and he drew it a few times, getting used to the feel of it in his hand. He bought enough ammunition to supply a small army and stuffed it into his saddlebags, then rode to the saloon, knowing any unemployed cowhands would likely be there this time of day. But it was not really cowhands he was looking for. He wanted a couple of gunmen.

It took a moment for his eyes to adjust to the saloon's dim interior after being out in the bright sunlight. Glancing around, he saw that the room was empty save for the ruddy-faced bartender and two men sitting at a table in the far corner. One of the men was Abner Wylie.

Abner was looking prosperous, all decked out in a red silk shirt, whipcord britches, and a pair of hundred-dollar snakeskin boots. A new cream-colored Stetson was pushed back on his head.

Unconsciously, Rafe's hand rested on the butt of his Colt as Wylie glanced up and met his gaze. A long silence passed between the two men, and Rafe knew without asking that Wylie was the man behind the attack on the Circle C cattle.

Rafe's hand caressed the smooth walnut butt of the Colt. It would be madness to draw against Wylie. The man was fast, too fast, and yet he deserved to die.

Wylie stood up slowly, his hand hovering near his holster, a challenge in his eyes as he waited for the half-breed to make the first move.

The saloon doors swung open and a tall, stoop-shouldered man stepped inside. He glanced at the two men who stood staring at each other at the far end of the room, and then addressed the bartender.

"What the hell's going on here?" he demanded.

"Nothing, Sheriff," the bartender answered. "Yet."

Abner grinned as he sat down, but his pale blue eyes never left the half-breed's face.

"Stay away from the Circle C," Rafe said quietly. "We know who stampeded the herd."

"What herd?" Abner asked. "I don't know what you're talking about."

"Don't you?"

Abner shook his head. "Why don't you tell me?"

"Old man Web recognized one of the rustlers. He lived just long enough to identify the man. If I ever see the murderin' bastard near the Circle C, I'll kill him without a call."

"Hey!" the sheriff called. "That's pretty strong talk."

"Yes," Rafe agreed, his gaze on Wylie's face. "It is." He backed toward the door, his hand still resting on his gun butt. "Good day to you, Sheriff."

Abner let out a sigh, releasing the tension that had been building inside ever since Gallegher entered the saloon. So, he mused,

Web had identified him. Well, it didn't matter. The old man was dead but Gallegher knew, and that was dangerous.

Frowning, Abner emptied his glass and poured himself another drink. The idea of stealing the Circle C herd had come to him months ago in this very chair. He had been quietly cursing Rafe Gallegher, wondering how he could get even with the man who had stolen his job at the Circle C and his woman, when he had overheard Frank Weiss, one of the bankers at Cedar Creek Bank and Trust, telling the bartender that the Circle C was driving a herd to Laramie to raise money to pay off their bank loan.

Just like that, Abner had known what he was going to do. In one fell swoop, he would get back at Gallegher for stealing his job and at Caitlyn for marrying a dirty half-breed. He'd steal the herd, sell the cattle, and buy the Circle C when it was put at auction to pay off the loan.

Or maybe, he mused now, he'd go to Caitlyn and offer to give her the money to pay off the loan if she'd divorce Gallegher and marry him.

Abner grinned as he tossed off his drink. He couldn't lose, he thought smugly. Even if Caitlyn refused to marry him, he'd still be a winner because he'd have the Circle C. He chuckled as he recalled how easy it had been to steal the herd. He'd hired ten drifters to dress up like Indians, and paid them a hundred bucks apiece to run off the herd. The killing and scalping hadn't been his idea, but he'd had to admit it added just the right touch of reality. After paying off the men, he'd pocketed seven thousand dollars, more than enough to pay off the loan.

Congratulating himself on a job well done, he poured himself another drink. The whiskey was the best the house had to offer, but he could afford it.

Caitlyn was standing on the porch when Rafe rode into the yard. She looked at him askance when he dismounted and she saw the gun riding his right hip.

Rafe shrugged. "Paulie suggested it," he said, answering her unspoken question.

"Why?"

"What's for supper, Caitlyn?"

"Don't change the subject."

"He mentioned that wearing a gun was easier than toting a rifle around all the time, and he's right. A cowboy needs two free hands. That's all. What's for supper?"

"You're worried, aren't you?"

"About what?"

"I don't know, Rafe. You tell me."

"There's nothing to worry about, Caitlyn. Nothing but a hungry husband who spent a long day in town."

"Don't lie to me. Something's wrong. I can feel it. I can see it in your eyes."

Maybe she had a right to know. It was her ranch, after all, her men who had been killed, her cattle that had been stolen. "Let's go inside," he said.

Caitlyn listened with growing disbelief as Rafe repeated what Scott had told him at the fort and what had been discussed in the tack room.

"Abner?" Caitlyn shook her head. "Why would Abner attack us? He used to ride for the Circle C. He—he wanted to marry me."

"You refused him."

"But that's no reason to kill men he'd ridden with, no reason to steal our cattle." She shook her head again. "No. I won't believe it. Web must have been mistaken."

"I saw Wylie in town this morning," Rafe said quietly. "He did it. I'd stake my life on it."

"He told you he'd done it?"

"No."

"Then how can you be so sure?"

"I know, Caty. I just know."

"What are we going to do?"

"*We* are not going to do anything. I'll take care of whatever has to be done."

"That's why you bought the gun."

"Yeah."

She went to him then, needing to feel his arms around her. She had never liked Abner Wylie, but she would never have suspected him of being the kind of man who would turn on his friends for no better reason than a rejected marriage proposal. Surely there was more to it than the fact that she had married someone else.

Frowning, she recalled the hatred that had blazed in his eyes the night of the Fourth of July dance when Rafe had knocked him down. Before that, Abner had accused Rafe of stealing his job as head wrangler. And to top it off, Rafe had married her.

She drew away from Rafe and gazed up at him. "He's doing all this because of you, isn't he?"

She had not meant to speak the words aloud, and she regretted them instantly. Rafe had felt guilty because there were those in town who shunned her because she had married him, and now there was trouble with Abner. Men had been killed. She'd come close to being raped. And he felt responsible.

"I didn't mean that the way it sounded," Caitlyn said quickly. "I'm not blaming you."

"Why not? If you'd married Wylie, none of this would have happened."

"Rafe—"

"Let it be, Caty," he said heavily. "Just let it be."

She felt her heart turn to stone as he left the room.

Outside, Rafe swung atop the bay gelding and rode down the valley, his thoughts turned inward. He never should have married Caitlyn, he mused ruefully. He had caused her nothing but trouble from the start. The fact that he was a half-breed had estranged her from some of her friends in town. And now Wylie was apparently seeking revenge for all the wrongs, real or imagined, that he blamed on Caitlyn's husband. No doubt Wylie figured that, with Rafe out of the way, he would somehow win Caitlyn's hand and the ranch, too.

Perhaps she would be better off with Wylie . . . He mouthed a foul oath at the mere idea. She was his. She would always be his. But she would probably be better off without him.

He drew the bay to a halt near the pool, remembering the day he had made love to Caitlyn in the soft grass beneath a canopy of green leaves and bright blue sky. How could he even think of leaving her?

He stared at the calm pool, its depths as green as Caitlyn's eyes. Perhaps he was worrying too much about Wylie. The man would be a fool to try anything else now, knowing that Rafe was wise to him. Surely even Wylie wouldn't be that stupid.

He tapped his heels against the bay's flanks, and the gelding broke into a fast-paced walk. Rafe gave the horse its head, content to do nothing but enjoy the feel of the horse beneath him and the slight breeze that fanned his face. He emptied his mind of all thought, his senses filling with the scent of the earth, the trees, the scattered wildflowers, the sheer beauty of the vast blue sky. His eyes swept the land, lingering on the flight of a red-tailed hawk as it rode the air currents, then plummeted to earth, talons outstretched, as it attacked some unwary rodent. He saw an elk in the distance, and, farther on, a white-tailed deer.

It was dark when he turned for home.

Caitlyn was in the kitchen, peeling potatoes. She did not hear him come in, and he stood in the doorway, his hip resting against the door jamb, watching her. Her hair hung in a single braid down her back. His gaze moved over her slender shoulders, the narrow span of her waist, her straight back and softly rounded hips. She was wearing a simple green dress that was one of his favorites.

Just looking at her filled him with a sense of contentment, of belonging. Walking into the house earlier, he had experienced a sense of homecoming. It was a feeling he had not known before and Caitlyn was responsible for it. She had made her home his, and he was determined to see that she didn't lose it because she loved him. She had spoken the words before, but he had been reluctant to accept them, reluctant to believe.

Caitlyn became aware of Rafe's presence in the room and she turned around, her eyes brimming with joy at seeing him standing hipshot in the doorway, and then her expression grew wary as she recalled how he had walked out on her earlier.

"Dinner will be ready soon," she said. His steady gaze unsettled her. Her tongue licked her lower lip as she braced herself for bad news.

"Caitlyn."

"Wh—what's wrong?"

"Nothing." He grinned sheepishly. "I just like saying your name."

She cocked her head to the side, bemused. He didn't sound like he was getting ready to leave her, and that had been her greatest fear.

He held up his hand and beckoned to her and she went to him without hesitation. His arms were a welcome haven and she laid her head against his shoulder, baffled by his odd behavior. He held her close for a long time, saying nothing while his fingertips caressed her cheek, then slid around the back of her neck to massage her nape. His touch was hypnotic, stirring her blood, making her heart begin to dance.

Gently, he placed his hand beneath her chin and lifted her head. His eyes smiled into hers, capturing her gaze. He had beautiful eyes, she thought, deep and dark, filled with fire. His straight brows and short, thick lashes were a perfect frame for those beautiful eyes.

She was drowning in his gaze when he lowered his head and kissed her. His mouth was warm and soft as it moved over hers, his tongue a silken flame as it slid across her lips. Her head fell back over his arm, her lips parted to receive him. She felt his hand move to her buttocks, and then he drew her close, grinding their hips together so that she could feel his need for her.

"Caty, Caty," he murmured, his breath warm and intimate against her ear. His tongue wove its spell along the side of her neck, and she shivered with delight.

Effortlessly, he lifted her into his arms, his eyes on her face, a question in their glowing depths.

He wanted her, now, but he was asking her permission. She knew it, even though no words had been said. Feeling suddenly shy, she nodded, her arms wrapping around his neck.

"Caty!" He kissed her hard, and then he was carrying her out of the kitchen, down the hallway toward their bedroom. Gently, he placed her on the bed, then moved to draw the curtains.

She followed his every move, her heart pounding like a drum as he came to stand beside the bed. Slowly, deliberately, provocatively, he began to undress, making her heart beat faster and faster as he slid out of his shirt, pulled off his boots, stockings, and trousers. He wore no underwear and now stood naked before her, tall and strong and handsome. And very male. She smiled at the evidence of his desire.

Rafe cocked one black brow at her. "You find me amusing?" he asked, grinning wickedly. "Or are you merely feeling superior because you can hide your lustful thoughts while mine are blatantly obvious?"

"Neither," Caitlyn replied, her smile as radiant as the summer sun. "I'm smiling because you're beautiful, and because you're here with me."

"There's no place I'd rather be," Rafe said softly.

He dropped one knee on the bed and began to undress her, the heat from his gaze bringing a flush to her cheeks, making her skin tingle with yearning. His hands made short work of undressing her and then he sank down on the bed beside her, his arms drawing her close. His hands stroked her hips and thighs, stirring the embers of desire into a raging inferno that culminated in wonder and fulfillment such as Caitlyn had never known. Later, lying in his arms, she was surprised to find the sheets unscorched, the pillows not in flames.

"I love you, Caty."

The words, so unexpected, were spoken softly. So softly, she almost missed them. Tears filled her eyes as he said the words she had so longed to hear.

"I love you," he said again, and the words came stronger this time, as if, having said them once, they were easier to say a second time.

"Oh, Rafe," she murmured. "Please forgive me when I say stupid things. I don't mean to hurt you."

"Caty, don't."

"I love you so much."

"I know," he whispered. "I know." His hands cupped her breasts, then slid down to her belly. Frowning, he raised himself on one elbow and looked into her face.

Caitlyn slid her gaze from his, then, her cheeks blossoming with color, she let her eyes meet his. "It's true," she said, her voice a whisper. "I'm pregnant."

"Caty!"

"Do you mind?"

"Of course not." He sat up and pulled her into his lap. "When? How?"

"The usual way," she said, joy bubbling up inside her like a spring. "It should be born in February, I think."

A baby, Rafe thought, dazed. The idea took some getting used to. *A baby . . . a little girl with Caty's golden hair and emerald eyes. February*. He counted back and realized the child had been conceived on the trail.

"Caty." He crushed her close, too elated to utter more than her name.

Caitlyn sighed with happiness. She had suspected she might be pregnant since they left the Indian village, but she had put off telling Rafe. He had so much on his mind, what with the men's deaths and the loss of the herd. And daily the bank loan loomed darker over their heads. Mostly, she had been afraid to mention it for fear he might not want children. It was a subject they had never discussed.

He held her for a long time, and then he drew away, his eyes filled with reverent wonder as he placed his hand on her belly. "Are you all right?"

"Fine. A little queasy in the morning sometimes."

"It'll pass," Rafe said confidently.

Caitlyn looked at him askance. "How would *you* know?"

Rafe chuckled, amused by her wide-eyed expression. "One of Corrine's girls got pregnant, quite by accident. She was sick in the morning for a couple of months." Rafe shrugged. "Corrine said it was pretty common."

"I suppose the madam of a whorehouse would know such things," Caitlyn muttered. She looked at Rafe, a terrible thought forming in her mind. "You weren't the . . . Never mind."

"No, I wasn't the father," Rafe said with a smile. He fluffed the pillows, then pulled Caitlyn down beside him. "Get some rest. I want you to take it easy from now on."

"I'm fine," Caitlyn protested.

"You heard me. No more heavy lifting, nothing strenuous. And no more horseback riding."

"Rafe, I'm not sick, I'm pregnant. And hungry. Wouldn't you like some dinner?"

Rafe nodded. He was hungry, now that she mentioned it.

Rising, he took her hand and helped her to her feet, his eyes moving over her figure as he tried to imagine how she'd look when her belly was swollen with his child and her breasts were heavy with milk.

A baby, he mused. *His child*. It was an awesome thought.

Watching her move about the kitchen as she prepared their dinner, he pictured Caitlyn with a baby in her arms. He had no trouble imagining Caty as a mother, but he could not visualize himself as a father. He had never spent much time thinking about kids, his own or anyone else's. *A child of his own* . . . he pondered the thought and found it pleasing.

A baby. Perhaps their luck was changing.

CHAPTER TWENTY

THERE FOLLOWED A PERIOD OF PEACE ON THE Circle C. Rafe and the men worked hard six days a week. Sundays, everyone rested.

It was on one such quiet Sunday that Caitlyn persuaded Rafe to go to church with her.

The members of the congregation did a double take as Rafe and Caitlyn entered the chapel. Rafe's expression was impassive, his eyes cold. Caitlyn kept her head up, her hand on Rafe's arm, as they walked down the narrow aisle. Rafe stopped at the first empty pew and allowed Caitlyn to pass in ahead of him. He was aware of the long curious looks the townspeople sent his way, of the low, murmuring voices that rose around him.

"Indian."

". . . breed doing here?"

"The nerve . . ."

Caitlyn squeezed Rafe's hand. *It doesn't matter*, her smile assured him. *I love you.*

Rafe didn't hear much of the Reverend Wilson's sermon, nor did he know that the minister changed his text when he saw Rafe enter the chapel. His original sermon, which was intended to urge his parishioners to be more generous in their tithing, was put aside in favor of the topic of tolerance and love.

Rafe grunted softly as the reverend admonished the congregation to be tolerant of those who were different, to be careful of whom they judged, and to remember that they, too, would one day be judged.

They were leaving the church when Caitlyn saw Abner Wylie riding down the street toward them. She heard Rafe mutter an oath and knew that he, too, had seen Abner.

Abner's gaze rested on Caitlyn, his expression insolent. So, she had the breed going to church now, he thought derisively. Maybe she'd make a good Christian out of the bastard, he mused. Then, when the time came, she could give him a good Christian burial.

Caitlyn felt Rafe's arm grow rigid beneath her hand as Abner continued to stare at her, his pale blue eyes insultingly bold.

"Rafe." Her voice reflected her anxiety as he placed his hand on the butt of his Colt.

"Stay out of this, Caitlyn. This is between Abner and me."

"You promised to leave him alone, remember?"

"I remember."

Abner grinned at Caitlyn's worried countenance. Soon, he thought, pleased, soon she'd be a widow.

Rafe was quiet on the way back to the ranch. Abner Wylie needed killing, the sooner the better.

Caitlyn didn't like the hard look in Rafe's eyes, but she wisely kept quiet, knowing anything she said would only make matters worse.

After lunch, she went down to the corral with a handful of carrots. Red whickered softly at her approach and she smiled, pleased, as he trotted toward her. His leg had healed beautifully and she could hardly wait to ride him again. Unfortunately, that would not be for some time, since Rafe had forbidden her to ride the bay until after the baby was born. Until then, Paulie had been put in charge of exercising Red.

She gave the stallion a couple of carrots,

and then went to see Black Wind. Rafe had bred Red to the mare soon after their return to the ranch. The foal would be born the following May.

Black Wind pranced up to the fence, the filly at her heels. They were very much alike, the foal being a smaller version of the mare.

Rafe came to stand beside Caitlyn as she offered Black Wind a carrot.

"We haven't named the filly yet," he remarked. "Have you got any ideas?"

Caitlyn frowned thoughtfully as she scratched the filly between her ears. "I've been calling her Windy."

"Windy," Rafe repeated as he patted the filly's neck. "I like that."

Caitlyn gave the mare the last carrot and a final pat on the neck, and then took Rafe's hand in hers. "What are we going to do about the loan?" she asked, hating to bring up such a depressing topic.

"I'm not sure."

"It's due in another two months. Where are we going to get six thousand dollars in such a short time?"

"I thought I'd try my luck at Frenchy's," Rafe said, knowing she wouldn't like that idea.

"Gambling?"

"I won't be gambling," Rafe pointed out dryly.

Caitlyn shook her head vigorously. "No, Rafe, that would be like stealing and you'd be taking it from our neighbors." She shook her head again. "There has to be another way."

"How about if I just play the cards I'm dealt?"

"Do you think you could win six thousand dollars in time to pay off the loan?"

"Not in a town this size. But I might be able to win enough to pay the interest and persuade the bank to extend the loan for another year."

"All right, Rafe, if you think that's best."

"Don't frown, Caty. I won't cheat, I promise."

The wagon was black, covered by a dusty white canvas. Bold red letters proclaimed to one and all that if Heath Sharkey didn't have it, it hadn't been invented yet.

Caitlyn listened as Mr. Sharkey listed his goods and extolled the merits of his merchandise, but her attention was focused on the long-legged chestnut mare tethered to the back of the wagon rather than the cutlery he was trying to sell her.

"Tell me, Mr. Sharkey," Caitlyn said when he finally reached the end of his sales pitch, "is the chestnut mare for sale?"

"The mare?" Sharkey said, frowning. "Oh,

the chestnut. You have a good eye for horse-flesh, ma'am. She's prime."

"Yes. Is she for sale?"

"Well, now, ma'am, it's been my experience that everything's for sale, if the price is right."

"How much do you want for her?"

"One hundred dollars," Sharkey said without hesitation. "She's a fine Thoroughbred. Bought her in Kentucky, I did."

"A hundred dollars," Caitlyn murmured.

"And worth every cent."

Caitlyn tapped her foot. A hundred dollars was a high price. Horses were plentiful in the West and usually sold for much less. "Would you take twenty dollars and another horse in trade?"

Heath Sharkey shook his head. "I don't know . . ." He bit back a smile. The chestnut was beautiful, but she'd never been ridden. It was Sharkey's opinion that she *couldn't* be ridden, for she had a wild streak a mile wide. He'd been trying to unload the mare since he left Kentucky, only no one would buy the beast once they tried to ride her.

"I can't afford more than twenty dollars," Caitlyn remarked.

Sharkey grinned. "Well, you caught me in a weak moment, ma'am. Throw in a cup of coffee, and it's a deal."

When Rafe rode in from the range that

evening, he found Caitlyn standing outside the north corral, her arms folded on the top rail, her eyes bright as she watched a leggy chestnut mare prance back and forth.

"Where the hell did that come from?" Rafe asked.

"I bought her."

"Bought her? From whom?"

"A traveling salesman. Isn't she beautiful? Her name's Delight."

"How much?"

"Twenty dollars," Caitlyn admitted. "And one of our horses."

"Twenty dollars, huh?" Rafe remarked. "Well, let's see if she's worth it."

Caitlyn wasn't smiling a half an hour later. Rafe's expression was one of frustration as he tried again and again to saddle the mare, but she fought wildly, her eyes white with terror. She calmed the minute he put the saddle down, but as soon as he picked it up again, she began to buck and strike, her ears laid flat, her teeth bared.

"She's been abused," he said later that night at dinner. "We might be able to break her with a lot of time and patience."

"I guess I shouldn't have bought her without asking you first," Caitlyn said.

Rafe shrugged. "If Red likes her, it'll be worth it. She's a beautiful animal. We'll put her in with Red next week. That'll give her a chance to settle in and get used to her new surroundings."

As it turned out, Red and the mare took to each other right off. Paulie, Caitlyn, and Rafe watched from a discreet distance while the stallion courted the mare, marveling at the beauty of the mating ritual.

Each night after dinner, Rafe spent a few minutes with the chestnut, talking to her, getting to know her. He left a brightly colored saddle blanket over the top rail of the corral, and a worn saddle near her feed bin.

After several days, he began to carry the blanket into the corral with him until the mare no longer shied away from it.

Next, he placed the blanket on the mare's back. He didn't scold her when she shook it off, only picked it up and put it on her back again. And again. And again, until she realized it wasn't going to hurt her.

The saddle came next. He let the mare sniff it, then he placed it on her back and cinched it lightly. He talked to her all the while, until he could saddle and unsaddle her without any trouble. Only then did he try to ride the mare. The chestnut bucked a couple of times, for pride's sake, Rafe said, and then she settled down and walked quietly around the corral.

Caitlyn clapped her hands, glad that no

one else had taken the time to gentle the chestnut mare, that no one but Rafe had realized that patience and perseverance were better than force and harsh words.

Hand in hand, Rafe and Caitlyn walked back to the house. Life was good, Caitlyn thought as she rested one hand over her belly. They had a fine stallion, two good mares, and the filly. Next year, they would have two more foals. Rafe had won enough money playing poker—honest poker, he had assured her—to pay the interest on their loan. The bank manager, Mr. Walden, had agreed to extend the loan for another year. He had frowned when he signed the extension, remarking that someone had been making inquiries about the state of the Circle C loan. He hadn't recognized the man interested in buying up the loan, Mr. Walden had said, but he'd be sure to get the man's name if he showed up again.

Yes, she thought, life was good, and only promised to get better.

CHAPTER
TWENTY-ONE

ABNER WYLIE CURLED A LEG AROUND THE saddle horn as he rolled a cigarette. He had spent the last several days lurking around the outer edges of the Circle C, hoping to catch Caitlyn alone, certain she would accept his offer once she heard it. Night after night he sat in his room, imagining how pleased she would be when he offered her the money to pay off the bank loan. He could see it all so clearly. He would find her, offer her the money she needed, and she would be so grateful for his help, she would divorce Gallegher and marry him. Each time he visualized the scene, it became more real.

And now, after two weeks of waiting and

watching, his perseverance was about to pay off. Earlier, he had seen Gallegher, Scott, and Jackson ride away from the ranch. Now he saw Caitlyn and Paulie riding toward the pool at the far end of the valley.

Like a drifting shadow, Abner followed them, his eagerness building with each passing moment. Soon, he thought, soon Caitlyn and the ranch would be his, as they were meant to be.

Caitlyn sat beside the pool, her bare feet dangling in the water as she watched Paulie bait a hook.

"Fish tonight," Paulie called confidently as he cast his line into the water.

"You clean 'em, I'll cook 'em," Caitlyn called back.

It was a beautiful day, she mused, all green and gold and warm. She wished Rafe were here beside her, but he had gone with Scott and Nate to check the west fences. They'd be gone all day, she thought regretfully. But then she smiled. She would see Rafe tonight and every night of her life. She had never known love could be so wonderful, so all-consuming. Or that it continued to grow, day by day, doubling and tripling until it filled her whole heart. A touch, a smile, her name on his lips, and joy welled within her breast, its warmth spreading through her like warm sweet honey.

She waved at Paulie as he walked around the pool, disappearing from sight behind a stand of timber. As soon as Paulie was out of sight, her thoughts returned to Rafe. Again and again she had thanked her lucky stars for a man like Rafe Gallegher. He was all she had ever hoped for and more.

That she had once thought of Rafe as a savage made her smile. She wished she could speed time forward so that she could see their child, hold it to her breast. In her mind's eye, she imagined Rafe cradling their baby, and she hoped for a son with coal-black hair and dark eyes and smooth tawny skin.

Leaning back on her elbows, her eyes closed, she thought of names: John, David, Joshua, Jacob, Robert . . . But no, none of them would do. If her child was a boy, maybe she would name him Raiford Carmichael Gallegher.

She was happily picturing Rafe teaching their son to walk when she heard hoofbeats. Sitting up, she looked over her shoulder, hoping to see Rafe riding toward her.

Instead, she saw Abner Wylie. Caitlyn's mouth dropped open in surprise as he cantered toward her. What on earth was he doing here? A niggling fear rose in her throat as she recalled that Rafe had accused Abner of stealing the herd. She stood up as Abner drew his horse to a halt and dismounted.

"Afternoon, Caitlyn," Abner said, smiling affably.

"How are you, Abner?" she replied.

"Fine, just fine." His eyes raked her boldly from head to foot, and his smile broadened, as if he had a wonderful secret. "You're looking well."

"What are you doing here?"

"I came to solve all your problems."

"My problems?" Caitlyn said, frowning. "I don't understand."

"I know you're having trouble meeting your loan at the bank. It's due in October, isn't it? And you don't have the money to pay it."

"It's been taken care of."

"How?"

"That's none of your business," Caitlyn said sharply.

"I don't believe you."

"Well, it's true nonetheless."

Abner frowned. Things were not going as he had planned.

"You'd better go, Abner."

"So you don't need my help," Abner mused aloud. "And I don't suppose you'll marry me, either, now that you don't need my money."

"Marry you!" Caitlyn exclaimed. "I'm already married."

"You could divorce him," Abner suggested. "No one would think the less of you for divorcing a half-breed. Hell, you never should have married the bastard in the first place."

"I'll thank you to keep a civil tongue in your head, Abner Wylie!" Caitlyn snapped.

"Sorry," he muttered absently. "What if Gallegher was out of the way?"

Fear pricked Caitlyn's heart, and with it came a growing suspicion that Abner was a little crazy.

"I'm sorry, Abner," Caitlyn said gently, "but I don't love you."

Abner's hand's balled into tight fists. It wasn't fair, he thought angrily. Dammit, it wasn't fair for Gallegher to have it all while he, Abner Wylie, had nothing! He had been prepared to kill Gallegher to win Caitlyn, but he realized now that killing the breed would accomplish nothing.

He smiled faintly as a new idea formed in his mind. If he could not have Caitlyn, then, by damn, neither would Rafe Gallegher.

A feral grin twisted his lips as he recalled the man he had met in Frenchy's the night before. The man had said his name was Manuel Ramos and in the course of their conversation the man had let it slip that he worked for Juan Maldonado, a well-known Comanchero who dealt in the buying and selling of human flesh. Abner nodded, pleased with his cleverness. He would sell Caitlyn to Maldonado and in so doing, he would hurt both Caitlyn and Gallegher.

Yes, he thought to himself, he would sell Caitlyn to Maldonado, and he would be her first customer.

He was about to order Caitlyn to get on her horse when Paulie strode into view, a cane fishing pole slung across his shoulder.

For the first time in his life, Abner panicked. Muttering, "Damn you, Paulie," he drew his gun and fired.

Caitlyn screamed as Paulie crumpled to the ground, a splash of crimson staining his left temple.

For a moment, time stood still. The sound of the gunshot died away, the gunsmoke dispersed by the breeze. Paulie lay still and silent as death.

Abruptly, Abner jammed his gun into his holster and grabbed Caitlyn by the arm.

"Come on," he said brusquely. "We've got to get the hell outta here."

"No!" Caitlyn tried to wrest her arm from Abner's grip, but his hold was like iron. He dragged her to her horse, thrust her into the saddle, and tied her hands to the saddle horn with his kerchief. Taking up the reins, he mounted his own horse and, leading Caitlyn's mare, rode hard for town.

Caitlyn pulled against the ropes that bound her hands to the bedpost. Fear and desperation overrode the pain in her wrists as the rope cut into her flesh, leaving bloody smears on the pillowcase.

Abner was mad, she thought, totally mad. He was going to sell her to a Comanchero, who was going to sell her to a brothel. A brothel! At least she wouldn't have to worry about getting pregnant, she thought, and laughed. The high-pitched sound was near hysteria, and she drew in a deep, calming breath. This was no time to panic, she told herself. Abner would be back soon. He had promised to bed her before the Comanchero claimed her, as if that made everything all right.

Hurry, hurry, the words echoed inside her head as she struggled to free herself. She had to get away, had to be gone before Abner returned.

It was dark when Rafe and the others returned to the ranch. Rafe bid Scott and Nate good night after he looked after his horse, then walked briskly toward the house, eager to see Caitlyn.

He frowned, his steps slowing, as he

neared the porch. All the windows were dark, no smoke rose from the chimney.

Opening the front door, he stepped into the entry. "Caitlyn?"

His footsteps were loud as he crossed the parlor to the kitchen. "Caty?"

He checked their room next, thinking she might have fallen asleep early, but the bedroom was dark and empty, as were the other two bedrooms. Where could she be?

Leaving the house, he went to the cookshack. Scott, Nate, and Rusty glanced up from their dinner.

"Something wrong?" Scott asked.

"Caitlyn's gone."

"Gone!" Nate exclaimed. "Gone where?"

"I don't know." Rafe drove his hand through his hair. "Where's Paulie?"

"He went down to the pool with Mrs. Gallegher this morning," Rusty recalled.

"Did you see them come back?"

"No. I rode out to check the north range this afternoon. Didn't get back till near dark."

"Consuelo?"

"I have not seen her, *Senor* Gallegher. I went into town to visit my sister shortly after breakfast. I was gone all day."

"Damn!" Turning on his heel, Rafe stalked out of the cookshack and hurried toward the barn where he threw a saddle over the bay.

"Wait up!" Scott said, coming up behind Rafe. "We'll go along."

But Rafe couldn't wait. "Catch up," he called, and rode out of the barn. Urging the bay into a lope, he headed for the pool at the far end of the valley. Thoughts of Indians tormented his mind. *Just let her be alive.* The unspoken prayer repeated itself in his thoughts as he rode through the starlit night.

The bay whinnied and snorted and Rafe heard an answering whinny from his right. Reining in that direction, he saw a horse silhouetted against the sky. And then he saw the body sprawled in the dirt.

"No!" The whispered word erupted from Rafe's throat as he reined the bay to a halt and vaulted from the saddle.

But it was not Caitlyn. It was Paulie. A dark stain covered the right side of the boy's head, and his breathing was shallow and labored.

"Gallegher?"

"Over here, Scott," Rafe called, and moments later the Circle C hands were there beside him.

Nate dismounted. Then hunkering down on his heels, he examined Paulie's head. "He's hurt bad, boss."

"Yeah."

"That wound needs stitching."

"Let's get him on a horse," Rafe said. "Scott, take him up in front of you."

Paulie groaned, his eyelids fluttering open as Rafe and Nate lifted him. "Wylie," he croaked, and then his body went limp.

"Is he dead?" Scott asked, his voice brittle.

Rafe shook his head. "Unconscious. Scott, you and Nate get him back to the house. Rusty, you go get the doc, and tell him to hurry."

"Where're you going?" Nate asked.

"To look for Caitlyn."

"You can't track her in the dark."

"The hell I can't."

"You go along and look for Caitlyn," Scott said, his sharp glance warning Nate and Rusty to keep quiet. "We'll look after things here, don't worry."

Minutes later, Rafe stood alone in the moonlight. Ground-reining the bay, he studied the ground, checking for sign. Perhaps a white man could not track in the dark, but he was not a white man. He was a half-breed Cherokee, a Lakota warrior, and his woman was in danger. He could not wait for daylight, not when Caitlyn's life might be at stake. He felt his hatred for Abner Wylie rise, twisting like a knife in his vitals. If anything had happened to Caitlyn, Wylie would wish for death a hundred times before it came.

With an effort, he fought down the urge to kill, concentrating instead on the task at hand. His eyes perused the ground in ever-widening circles, and then he saw the tracks, two sets of shod prints heading east. The riders were moving single file, the lead horse carrying a heavier burden than the second.

Mounting the bay, Rafe followed the tracks, his mouth set in a grim line, his eyes glittering like those of a predator on the scent of game, or blood.

CHAPTER TWENTY-TWO

CAITLYN UTTERED A SMALL CRY OF PAIN AS she jerked her left hand free, leaving a long strip of flesh adhering to the rope as she did so.

For a moment, she closed her eyes, trying to cope with the burning pain in her wrist. She was struggling to untie the rope on her right wrist when she heard the key turn in the lock. A moment later, Abner stepped into the room, followed by a tall, dark-skinned man sporting a black eye patch over his left eye.

Abner grinned. "Well, Manuel, looks like we got here just in time."

The stranger nodded, his lips drawing

back in a grin as he let his gaze wander over Caitlyn. She was a prize all right.

"She'll do," he said in a gruff voice. "How much do you want for her?"

"A thousand. In gold."

The stranger nodded again. "On delivery."

"One condition, Ramos" Abner said. "I want one night with her before Maldonado takes her."

The stranger shrugged. "You will have to discuss that with Juan." He glanced over his shoulder as he heard footsteps in the hall. "Let's go."

Abner drew his knife and cut Caitlyn's hand free. "Behave yourself," he warned. "Don't try anything cute. Don't talk to anybody, or do anything to draw any attention our way, understand?"

"Why are you doing this?" Caitlyn wailed as Abner urged her toward the door. "Abner, please let me go."

"No. I offered to help you and you turned me down. Well, Mrs. Gallegher, if I can't have you, neither will that damned breed. And when the Circle C is put on the block, I'll buy it. You think about that while you're flat on your back in some cheap brothel."

"Abner, please don't do this!"

"Be still, woman!"

With Abner on one side and the stranger on the other, Caitlyn left the room and walked down the stairs to the main floor. She glanced left and right as they left the hotel, hoping to see someone she knew, someone who would help, but the street was virtually deserted.

Abner lifted her into the saddle and took the reins of her horse.

Five minutes later they had left Cedar Creek behind.

Abner drew his horse to a halt as soon as they were out of sight of the town. Pulling a length of rope from his saddlebag, he lashed Caitlyn's hands to the saddle horn, and then they were riding again, Manuel Ramos setting a brisk pace.

They rode for hours. Occasionally, Ramos dropped back to be certain they weren't being followed. Once, Caitlyn saw him dismount to cover their tracks, and a sense of hopelessness descended upon her.

Caitlyn began to shiver as night closed around her, but it was not the darkness or the lowering temperature that caused the chill, but rather the knowledge that she was at Abner's mercy, and that mercy was the one thing she was not likely to receive.

On and on they rode, the men seemingly tireless. Caitlyn clung to the saddle horn, her head lolling forward, her eyelids heavy.

It was well after midnight when Ramos called a halt. Looking around, Caitlyn was surprised to find that they were in Greenwater Junction, a small farm town some thirty miles east of Cedar Creek.

"We'll spend the night here," Ramos declared. "Maldonado will meet us across the river tomorrow night."

"Do you think it's wise, staying here, I mean?" Abner asked.

"This is a decent town," Ramos said with a sneer. "They're not expecting trouble, and we're not going to give them any."

"Whatever you say," Abner muttered.

"We'll get two rooms and take turns keeping an eye on the girl."

"You take the first watch," Abner said, leering at Caitlyn. "I want to get some sleep. First."

Ramos nodded agreeably. "Suits me." His hand glided down Caitlyn's arm. He laughed softly as she jerked away.

"You're not to touch her, Manuel," Abner said, his pale blue gaze drilling into the other man. "No one touches her until I do."

"Okay, okay," Ramos muttered irritably. "I can wait." He grinned salaciously. "I think she'll be worth it."

A cold, icy fear clutched Caitlyn's heart, numbing her inside and out so that nothing seemed real. Indeed, this could not be real.

She followed Abner into the hotel, stood beside him while he signed the register as

Mr. and Mrs. Brown from Nebraska. She felt his hand at her waist as he guided her up the stairs, found their room, and ushered her inside. It was a small room, with one window, a double bed, and a four-drawer chest. A roach scuttled across the floor as Abner lit the lamp.

Ramos entered the room a few minutes later. He tossed his room key to Abner, then sat down on the edge of the bed and began pulling off his boots.

"Remember," Abner said sternly. "She's mine first."

"Yeah, yeah. Go get some sleep."

Abner sent a last lingering glance at Caitlyn, then left the room. Soon, he thought, soon she would be his.

Caitlyn stood in the middle of the room, unmoving, her mind refusing to comprehend what was happening. It was all a dream, she thought, a bad dream. Soon she would wake up in Rafe's arms and they would laugh about it together.

"Hey, girlie," Ramos called. "Get those clothes off, and come here and be nice to Manuel."

Caitlyn continued to stand where she was, unmoving. She heard his voice, but the words didn't register. She had withdrawn into herself, into a world where nothing existed but Rafe and their unborn child. It was a beautiful place, quiet and serene.

Ramos tossed his boots under the bed and stood up. "Hey, you deaf?"

Muttering an oath, he walked over to the girl and stared at her. "Hey!" He frowned when she refused to answer. And then, his patience at an end, he hit her, his fist driving against her chin, knocking her backward so that she landed on her back across the bed.

"That's fine," Ramos drawled, and then he was on her.

Reality was hot vile breath, grasping hands that squeezed her breasts, punishing lips, and a slobbering tongue. The rising heat of a man's lust. With a cry of outrage, Caitlyn began to struggle, determined to die before she let this man defile her. Fear for her unborn child gave her strength and she wriggled free only to find Ramos grinning at her.

"I like a woman with spirit," he mused. "Come on, little one, fight me some more." Lazily, he reached out and slapped her, hard, rocking her head from side to side.

Caitlyn recoiled as she saw his hand coming toward her again. Then, in a move born of desperation, she leaned toward him, her hand snaking toward his holster. The gun was heavy in her hand.

Ramos laughed. He was still laughing when she squeezed the trigger.

The gunshot roused Abner who jumped out of bed and ran down the hall. The door to Caitlyn's room was locked and he kicked it in to find Caitlyn kneeling on the bed, a gun in her hand, the barrel still smoking.

Abner swore as he glanced at Ramos sprawled across the bed and Caitlyn turned slowly in his direction. Her face was as pale as new-fallen snow, her eyes unnaturally bright. Her expression did not change as she lifted the gun and aimed it in Abner's direction.

Abner's eyes widened, and then he pushed past the crowd that had gathered in the hallway and ran down the stairs and out of the hotel.

The moon went down and Rafe lost the trail in the dark. Agitated by the delay, he paced the ground. The tracks seemed to be headed toward Cedar Creek, but he couldn't be sure, nor did it seem likely that Wylie would take Caitlyn into town. He puzzled over that as he unsaddled the bay stallion and rubbed him down with a handful of grass.

It seemed the night would never end. Stretched out on the hard ground, he closed his eyes and images of Caitlyn filled his mind—Caty fixing breakfast, smiling at him from across the table, sitting before the fire mending one of his shirts . . . struggling in

Wylie's arms.

He sat up, a muffled oath on his lips. *Caty, Caty, I'm coming*.

Sleep eluded him. Rising, he rummaged in his saddlebags for a strip of jerky, gnawing the stringy beef absently as he stared into the darkness willing the minutes to pass.

He was back on the trail at first light, his eyes intent, his mind set on one thing, to find Caitlyn. Once he had her back, he would deal with Abner Wylie. And Wylie would die.

Cedar Creek had not yet awakened when Rafe rode into town. He went to the hotel because it was the only establishment open.

Will Staley was sweeping the floor when Rafe entered the hotel.

'Mornin','' Will said, his voice betraying his surprise at seeing Rafe.

"Have you seen Caitlyn, Will?"

"As a matter of fact, I have. She was here yesterday. Came in with Abner Wylie. They left, oh, about suppertime."

"She left with Wylie?"

"Yeah." Will Staley nodded, as if to reaffirm his own words. "There was another man, too. A stranger. Dark skin, dark hair. Wore an eye patch over one eye. Never saw him before." Will rubbed a hand over a bewhiskered jaw. "They all rode out of town together."

"Did you speak to Caitlyn?"

"No. She left with the two men, like I said. I don't think she even saw me."

"Thanks, Will. Did you see which way they went?"

"East, I think." Staley nodded. "Yeah, east."

Rafe was out of the hotel before Staley had finished talking. Swinging into the saddle, he reined the bay stallion east. The tracks were harder to follow there, but Wylie's mount had a distinctive way of moving and after an intense twenty minutes, Rafe had picked up the trail.

Tracking was considerably easier in the daylight and he pushed his horse hard, begrudging the minutes he had to stop and rest his horse. At noon, he let the stallion graze for thirty minutes, knowing if he didn't give the animal food and rest, it would soon be worthless.

He stood in the shade of a tree, pounding his fist against the trunk, too tense to relax, too concerned for Caitlyn to rest.

He'd been on the trail for five hours when the tracks disappeared. Cursing, Rafe dismounted, his gaze sweeping the ground, his heart pounding. He had come too far to lose her now.

He began to walk in narrow circles that grew ever wider, and as he did so, a satisfied smile played across his lips. Few white men could erase a trail without leaving another one, and this man was no exception.

Swinging into the saddle, Rafe rode on. He was no longer tired, and unaware of hunger or thirst as he closed in on the man who had taken his woman.

CHAPTER
TWENTY-THREE

THE CELL CAITLYN FOUND HERSELF IN WAS A small, square stone room with a stout oak door and no windows. A single narrow slit cut high in one wall admitted air and light. An iron cot and an enamel slop jar were the room's only furnishings.

Caitlyn sat on the edge of the cot, her elbows resting on her knees, her head in her hands, and her eyes closed.

She had killed a man. Shot him, not once, but four times. Worst of all was the knowledge that she would do it again.

What kind of a person was she? She had always abhorred violence of any kind, had been revolted by bloodshed, and sickened by cruelty. And now she had killed a man. Why wasn't she sorry?

She let out a long sigh, wondering at her lack of emotion. She felt nothing. Not sadness, not grief, not sorrow. It was as if all her feelings had died with Manuel Ramos.

Time passed ever so slowly. The light filtering into her cell gradually grew bright as the sun climbed in the sky, and she wondered if she'd ever walk in the sunlight again.

Shortly after noon, a man brought her a large bowl of vegetable soup, two slices of buttered bread, and a cup of hot black coffee, but she couldn't eat. The food tasted like ashes in her mouth.

Lying down on the cot, she stared at the narrow slit of sky visible through the opening in the wall. She had killed a man. People were hanged for murder. But surely they would not hang her, not now, not when she carried a new life. Surely the law would be merciful and withhold sentence until her child was born. Rafe's child.

Rafe. She felt the tears well in her eyes, felt the ache in her throat, but the overwhelming numbness that overpowered her kept her tears at bay.

Poor Rafe. He would never know what had become of her. Ramos had erased their tracks so that no one could follow them.

She placed her hands over her stomach. Poor little baby. Perhaps it would never know life at all, and if it did, it would never know its mother. She was hanged, people would say, hanged for killing a man, and her child would be ashamed.

Exhaustion spun a web around her and as she drifted to sleep, she wished that she had killed Abner Wylie, too. After all, they could only hang her once.

It was dusk when Rafe rode into Greenwater Junction. He left his lathered bay stallion at the livery barn with orders to rub the animal down and give it a generous helping of hay and grain. And then he walked slowly down the street, his eyes searching for some sign of Caty or Wylie or a dark-haired man with an eye patch.

Greenwater Junction was a small town, one that had little to offer. There was the livery barn, a small hotel, a smaller restaurant, and a mercantile store. No post office. No sheriff's office. No telegraph office.

The hotel seemed his best bet and he went their first. A balding, middle-aged man sat behind the front desk, reading a mail-order catalog. He glanced up as Rafe entered the room.

"Help you, Mister?"

"I'm looking for a woman."

"Sorry, this is a hotel, not a brothel."

"Not that kind of woman," Rafe said.

"Don't matter what kind you're looking for. We don't have any here. Not even a chambermaid."

"I'm looking for my wife," Rafe said irritably. "She might have stopped by here sometime last night or maybe this morning."

"Blond woman?" the desk clerk asked. "Pretty, with green eyes?"

"You've seen her?"

The man snorted. "I'll say. She killed a man last night. Shot him four times."

"Where is she now?"

"Behind the mercantile store. We got a place there where we keep prisoners."

"You got a lawman in this town?"

"Wendell Monroe acts as town marshal."

"Where is he?"

"Gone. He rode off to the county seat to get Judge Hastings. Won't be back until tomorrow sometime."

"I want to see my wife."

The desk clerk lifted his shoulders and let them fall. "Afraid I can't help you there."

Rafe swore under his breath, then muttered, "Thanks for your help" and left the hotel.

He quickly found the small stone building located about twenty yards behind the mercantile store. He felt his gut tighten at the thought of Caitlyn locked inside, like an animal in a cage.

"Caty?" He called her name when he reached the heavy oak door.

There was no answer from inside.

"Caty?" He called her name again, louder this time.

Caitlyn came awake at the sound of her name. Had she been dreaming? She glanced out the window and saw that night had fallen. And then she heard it again, Rafe's voice calling her name. She slid out of bed and walked toward the door. "Rafe?"

"It's me. Are you all right, honey?"

"Yes."

He placed his hands on the door and pressed his forehead against the cool wood.

"Rafe? Are you still there?"

"Yeah. What happened, Caty?"

"I killed a man. Heaven help me, Rafe, I killed a man."

"Take it easy, honey. Everything will be all right, don't worry, I'll—" He broke off as he heard footsteps behind him.

Turning, he saw a huge man coming toward him, a tray balanced on one meaty hand, a gun in the other.

"Who the hell are you?" the giant demanded. "What are you doing here?"

"My name's Gallegher," Rafe replied warily, "and I'm talking to my wife."

"Your wife!" Lem Moody exclaimed. "Well, I'll be damned. I didn't know she was married."

"Who are you?" Rafe asked, his gaze fixed on the gun in the big man's hand.

"I'm the blacksmith, Lem Moody. Monroe left me in charge of the prisoner while he's gone."

"Can I see her?"

Moody's thick black brows bunched together. "I don't know."

"Please."

Moody pursed his lips. It was obvious the half-breed wasn't used to begging. "Take off that gunbelt and knife and I'll let you in," he decided. "How long do you want to stay?"

"As long as she does."

"You sure?"

"I'm sure."

"I don't know about that."

"She's pregnant," Rafe said. "I don't want her to be alone."

Moody's expression changed from doubt to sympathy. "Okay. Shuck that iron."

The huge man took a step back as Rafe removed his gunbelt and knife, then he thrust the tray into Rafe's hands. "Don't try nothing funny," he warned. "I'm a good shot."

Rafe nodded, and Moody stepped toward the door, the gun still aimed at Rafe as he put

426

the key in the lock. For a moment, Rafe was tempted to make a grab for the gun, but he fought the urge. There was no point in doing something rash until he found out just what Caitlyn had gotten into.

The door swung open and Rafe hesitated a moment before he stepped inside. He did not like small spaces and this place was hardly bigger than a closet. But then he saw Caitlyn. Placing the tray on the floor, he pulled her into his arms.

"Say, Moody," he called over his shoulder, "how about bringing me something to eat? I'll pay for it."

"Okay." The big man stared at Rafe and Caitlyn for a moment, then closed the door.

Rafe shuddered when he heard the key turn in the lock. The room was dark, dreary, and small. So damn small.

"Rafe?"

Her voice was filled with anguish and when he looked at her, he saw the despair in her eyes.

"It's all right, Caty. I'm here." He pulled her toward the bed and sat down, drawing her into his lap. "Tell me what happened. Everything."

"I went fishing with Paulie. He walked around the lake and I was sitting there alone when Abner rode up. He said he'd give me the money to pay off the bank loan if I'd divorce you and marry him. I told him I didn't want a divorce, and he got angry. He drew his gun and I thought he was going to kill me, but just then Paulie came back and Abner shot him." Tears welled in her eyes. Poor Paulie, dead because of her.

"He's alive, Caty," Rafe said.

"Are you sure?"

"I'm sure." He did not tell her that Paulie was badly wounded and probably dead by now. There would be time for that later, when she was out of this place. "Go on. What happened next?"

"Abner took me into town. He locked me in a hotel room, tied to the bed, and when he came back, there was a man with him."

"Who?"

"Manuel Ramos. He asked Abner how much he wanted for me, and Abner said a thousand dollars. Ramos agreed and we left the hotel and came here to meet someone named Maldonado."

"Juan Maldonado?"

"I think so."

Rafe swore. "When were they going to meet?"

"Tonight. Across the river."

"Did you kill Ramos, Caty?"

"Yes," she whispered, her voice filled with regret. "He was . . . he was going to . . .

He'd told Abner he wouldn't touch me, but as soon as we were alone, he told me to get undressed. And then he hit me. I guess I grabbed his gun. I don't remember. But I remember pulling the trigger. I shot him again and again and . . ."

Tears flooded her eyes and poured down her cheeks. "There was blood everywhere, and I just kept squeezing the trigger . . ."

"It's all right, Caty," Rafe said. His hands stroked her hair and back, his words calm and soothing even as he felt the anger building inside him. Wylie would die for this, and he would not die easy.

Caitlyn buried her face in Rafe's neck. She had not asked how he found her, and it no longer mattered. He was there and that was enough. She snuggled against him, welcoming his strength, the warmth that turned away the room's chill.

"Rafe, I'm so afraid."

"Don't be. I'm here. I won't let anyone hurt you."

"I killed a man. They hang people for that."

"It was self-defense, Caty."

"No. I wasn't fighting for my life, only to keep Ramos from touching me. Surely he didn't deserve to die for that."

"Like hell. If you hadn't killed him, I

would have.''

"What if a jury decides I'm guilty? They won't hang me until after the baby is born, will they?''

She drew back so she could see his face, her eyes filled with torment. She didn't want to die, but she had killed a man and she would pay the price the law demanded. But how could she leave this life and face the next knowing she had caused the death of her child, too?

"Dammit, Caty, you didn't do anything wrong! You've got every right to defend your honor as much as your life. And if a jury doesn't see it that way, then to hell with the law. I won't let them hang you.''

She sobbed his name as she threw her arms around his neck and began to cry.

Rafe held her tight, knowing she needed to let it all out, all the fear, all the guilt and remorse. He had killed men, and no matter what the cause or provocation, it was not an easy thing to accept. The weight of taking a human life was a difficult cross to bear.

He murmured to her, telling her he loved her, caressing her hair, and then just holding her close. He had planned to stay with her until the judge returned, but not now. He would go when Moody brought his dinner. Wylie was meeting Maldonado tonight, and he intended to be there. Wylie had a lot of explaining to do, and he was going to do it in front of a judge.

Rafe lay beside Caitlyn on the narrow cot, his eyes resting on her face. She was asleep, her lashes like dark fans on her pale cheeks. He had insisted she eat something, and then he had held her until she fell asleep in his arms. His gaze moved to her belly and he placed a gentle hand there, his heart swelling with love for his unborn child, and for its mother.

The minutes passed slowly; the inside of the stone cell grew cold and Rafe drew a blanket over Caitlyn. How could he leave her there alone?

He heard the key in the lock and he slid out of bed.

"Gallegher?" It was Moody's voice. "I've got your dinner. Stay away from the door. I've got a gun, so don't try anything."

"I hear you," Rafe replied.

Slowly, the door swung open, and Rafe saw Lem Moody outlined in the darkness. "I'm coming out," Rafe said.

Moody frowned. "Thought you were staying the night?"

"I changed my mind."

"Rafe!" Caitlyn scrambled from the cot. "Don't go!"

"I've got to, Caty. I'll be back as soon as I can."

"Where are you going?"

He turned to face her, his eyes warning her to be silent. "I'll see you as soon as I get back."

She shook her head, her eyes begging him not to go. He was going after Abner. She knew it and dreaded it. Rafe was no match for Abner's gun. "Please don't go."

"I have to, Caty." He placed his hand behind her head and pressed his lips to hers. "I'll be back."

He gave her a final hug and then he was gone.

CHAPTER
TWENTY-FOUR

Rafe MOVED SILENTLY THROUGH THE DARK-ness, his bare feet making no sound as he picked his way along the riverbank. He had shed his boots, shirt, and hat—and civiliza-tion.

He was Stalking Wolf, the warrior, again. Armed with his Colt and a knife, he drifted noiselessly through the night, pausing every now and then to listen to the sounds of the land and sniff the wind.

Earlier, he had gone to the hotel and picked up Wylie's tracks only to lose them at the outskirts of town where the ground was hard and strewn with gravel. There was always a chance he could pick them up again, but he was betting that Wylie would keep his appointment with Juan Maldonado rather than have Maldonado come looking for him when Ramos failed to show up.

He paused, his fingers tightening around the butt of the Colt, as he smelled smoke. Step by slow step, he followed the acrid smell.

He found Wylie and Maldonado hunkered around a thrifty fire a good two miles from Greenwater Junction.

"Where's Ramos?" Maldonado was saying. "And the girl?"

"Where's the money?" Abner countered.

"You'll get it when I get the girl," Maldonado retorted. "Not before."

"But it's here? You have it with you?"

Suspicion flared in Maldonado's eyes. Too late, he reached for his gun.

The report from Abner's Colt was sharp and loud, shattering the stillness of the night. There was a muffled thud as Maldonado's body struck the dirt.

Abner was going through the dead man's pockets when he felt the jab of a gun barrel in his back. He froze instantly.

"Stand up," Rafe ordered curtly. "Keep your hands where I can see them."

With a nod, Abner raised his hands over his head and stood up. He grimaced as his gun was plucked from his holster.

"Put your hands behind your back."

"Who are you?" Abner demanded. "What do you want?"

"Do it!"

Rafe lashed Wylie's hands together, making sure the knots were good and tight. "Turn around."

"You!" Abner exclaimed. "I should have known."

"You know any prayers, Wylie?" Rafe asked. He slipped the gun into the waistband of his pants and withdrew his knife.

"What're you gonna do?"

Rafe grinned wolfishly. "What do you think?" Rafe slid his thumb over the blade. It was razor sharp.

"Let me go," Abner said, stifling his fear. "I'll make it worth your while."

"How?"

"There's six thousand dollars in my saddlebags, and another thousand in Maldonado's pocket."

"Where'd you get six grand?"

"Don't you know?"

"I want to hear you say it."

"And if I refuse?"

Rafe's expression didn't change as he stepped forward and drew the edge of the blade across Wylie's left cheek.

Abner yelped with pain, his eyes showing white as he felt the blood trickle down his face. "All right, all right!" he hollered as Rafe raised the knife again, "I stole her cattle and sold them. The money's hers. Take it."

"I aim to." The blade sliced into Wylie's other cheek. "What were you going to do with Caitlyn?"

Abner backed away from the rage glittering in the half-breed's eyes, certain the man would kill him if he told him the truth.

"Answer me," Rafe said, and his voice was as cold and quiet as the grave.

"Nothing," Abner said, his mouth dry with fear. "I . . . nothing."

Rafe snorted. "The truth, Wylie, or I'll slit your lying tongue."

"I . . ." Abner swallowed hard, his gaze fixed on the knife in the half-breed's hand, and the blood, *his* blood, dripping from the end. "I was just trying to scare her into leaving you and marrying me."

"The truth, dammit!"

"All right!" Abner shrieked. "I was jealous! Jealous because she loved you. I decided if I couldn't have her, neither would you. I was gonna sell her to Maldonado for a thousand bucks and then leave the territory."

"Caitlyn's in jail," Rafe said, his voice thick with anger. "Locked up like a damn dog, and it's all your fault."

A long shudder ran through Abner, and he knew he was as close to death as he'd ever been. Gallegher's eyes were deep and black, like bottomless pools in the pits of hell.

"We're going back to Greenwater Junction," Rafe said. "We're going to wait for the judge from the county seat, and when he shows up, you're going to confess everything. And you'd better hope they turn Caitlyn loose, because you'll wish you'd never been born if they don't."

Wylie nodded. A cell in the nearest jail looked a hell of a lot safer right now than where he was.

Rafe glared at Wylie. He thought of the Circle C cowhands Wylie had killed, of the cattle he had stolen, and of the terror he had caused Caitlyn. The desire for vengeance ran hot in his veins. This man was the enemy. He had taken cattle that were not his. He had kidnapped Caitlyn. He deserved to die a slow, lingering death.

Rafe grimaced, his expression deadly and filled with the lust for blood, as he contemplated the many ways he could torture Abner Wylie before he let him die. So many ways, and each more painful, more terrible, than the last.

But he needed Wylie alive and that thought filled him with an overwhelming sense of frustration. Muttering a wordless cry, he drove his fist into Wylie's face, experiencing a deep sense of satisfaction as he felt the man's nose break, felt the quick flow of warm blood on his hands.

The sudden violence released the tension within Rafe and he let out a long sigh. It was foolish to waste time and energy on a bastard like Abner Wylie when Caitlyn needed him.

CHAPTER
TWENTY-FIVE

Caitlyn's trial was over in a matter of minutes. The defense stated her case simply: She had been kidnapped by Abner Wylie and Manuel Ramos, and she had killed Manuel Ramos in an effort to defend her honor, and possibly in defense of her life. The jury, comprised of twelve hard-working family men, wasted no time in finding her innocent.

Abner Wylie was tried for cattle rustling and in the end, he confessed he was guilty. There was no proof he had killed any of the Circle C cowhands; in fact, he insisted that any killing had been done by the others without his knowledge or consent. Warrants were issued for the arrest of his accomplices, and Wylie was sentenced to ten years for cattle rustling.

It wasn't enough, Rafe mused, not nearly enough, but it would have to do.

He sat on the edge of the bed while Caitlyn finished dressing. They had spent two nights in the hotel, and now both of them were anxious to be on their way home.

Home, Rafe thought. It had a nice ring to it. He felt his heart expand as he watched Caty. She was his home, his life, his reason for living.

"Well," Caitlyn said, looking around. "I guess I'm ready."

"I've got a surprise for you before we go," Rafe said.

"Really? What is it?"

"This." Rafe tossed his saddlebags to Caitlyn. "Look inside."

Curious, Caitlyn opened the worn leather pouch and peered inside. "Rafe," she murmured, "where'd you get this?"

"It's yours, Caty. From the sale of the cattle."

Caitlyn frowned. "Abner gave this to you?"

"In a manner of speaking. There's six thousand dollars there, Caty. More than enough to pay off the bank loan." He'd almost had seven thousand dollars, Rafe mused, but at the last minute he'd left Maldonado's cash behind. Stalking Wolf would have taken the white man's money without a qualm, for there was honor and glory in stealing from one's enemy, but he was a civilized man now, and civilized men did not rob the dead.

"Oh, Rafe." Caitlyn dropped the saddlebag to the floor and moved into his arms. The hours she had spent in that dreadful cell, the agony of not knowing where Rafe had gone or if he would return, and the nagging fear that the jury would find her guilty of murder, had all been worth it. Rafe was here beside her now and she knew no matter what setbacks the future might hold, they could overcome anything so long as they were together.

She lifted her face for his kiss, and as his mouth touched hers, she felt the first faint flutter of life from the child growing in her womb.

"What is it?" Rafe asked.

"Your son just kicked me," Caitlyn replied, her voice filled with wonder.

Rafe's gaze dropped to her stomach. "Did it hurt?"

"No. A new life, Rafe," she murmured solemnly. "We've created a new life."

"Only the first of many," he promised, and then he kissed her, one hand cradling the back of her head, the other splayed across her belly where his child did somersaults, unaware of the joy shining in his father's eyes, or of the tears of happiness that sparkled on his mother's cheeks.

They paid off the bank loan the day after they returned to the Circle C. Caitlyn felt like jumping up and down as Mr. Walden handed Rafe the loan documents.

"Paid in full!" she exclaimed happily. "Oh, Rafe, let's celebrate!"

"Sure, Caty, anything you want."

"A new hat," she decided as they left the bank and started down the boardwalk. "And a candlelit dinner. And something for Paulie and the others, and . . . What do you want, Rafe?"

"A kiss," he replied, pulling her into his arms.

"Rafe, not here," she protested, conscious of the people on the street.

"A kiss," Rafe insisted. "Now."

"Is that all you want?" she teased. "Just one kiss?"

"For starters," Rafe answered, grinning wickedly. "I'll think up the rest as we go along." His dark eyes smiled at her. "And that could take years."

EPILOGUE

CAITLYN LET OUT A SIGH AS SHE LOWERED herself into a chair on the front porch. She would be glad when this child was born, she thought wearily. Sometimes it seemed as though she had been pregnant forever.

She felt her weariness evaporate when she saw Rafe striding toward her, their youngest son on his shoulder. The twins, Tony and Luke, walked on either side of their father, while Brenden trailed behind leading Black Wind's newest foal.

"Since you didn't feel like coming down to the barn, we decided to bring the foal to you," Rafe said, smiling at her. "What do you think of the colt?"

"He's a beauty," Caitlyn said, "and he's going to be a bay, just like his sire."

With a nod, Rafe lifted Jimmy from his shoulder and handed the wriggling two-year-old to his mother, then sat on the porch step at Caitlyn's feet.

Caitlyn gazed at the ranch. It was thriving now. They had added two bedrooms, enlarged the barn, and hired more help. Circle C cattle grazed in the hills and Circle C horses filled the pasture behind the house. She gazed lovingly at her four sons, each a miniature replica of his father, and offered a silent prayer of thanksgiving for a life that was full and happy.

"My father would have been proud," she said as she settled Jimmy on what was left of her lap. "So proud." She looked at the corrals next to the barn, all filled with beautiful horses sired by Red. The best had been born to Black Wind.

"We've turned out a good crop all right," Rafe agreed, glancing at Caitlyn's swollen belly. "And not just in horses."

Caitlyn smiled at her husband. "And they're all Thoroughbreds," she said proudly. "Just like their father."

They smiled at each other a long time, their love shining in their eyes, as bright as the sun, until Luke and Tony climbed into

Rafe's lap and demanded to hear their favorite story.

"You know the one," Tony said. "The one where Mother saved your life."

"I know the one," Rafe said, for it was a tale he never tired of telling. "It all began with Black Wind," he said. "Yes, the very same black mare we have now . . ."

Caitlyn sat back, a smile on her face, because she knew the story would have a happy ending.

And it did.

A WANTED MAN.
AN INNOCENT WOMAN.
A WANTON LOVE!

Renegade Heart
Madeline Baker

When beautiful Rachel Halloran took Logan Tyree into her home, he was unconscious. A renegade Indian with a bullet wound in his side and a price on his head, he needed her help. But to Rachel he was nothing but trouble, a man whose dark sensuality made her long for forbidden pleasures; to her father he was the answer to a prayer, a gunslinger whose legendary skill could rid the ranch of a powerful enemy.

But Logan Tyree would answer to no man — and to no woman. If John Halloran wanted his services, he would have to pay dearly for them. And if Rachel wanted his loving, she would have to give up her innocence, her reputation, her very heart and soul.

____2744-5 $4.50